Collins, or the writhing mass of tentacles and limbs he'd become, stood only a few feet away, stinking of shit and blood. His teeth spun in circular rows, ready to feed flesh into his maw. Sounds probably meant to be words buzzed through the mass of distorted flesh, but Kevin didn't even try to understand.

Kevin slapped the pistol into his other hand, locking a finger around the trigger.

One bullet left. Enough. You couldn't double-tap yourself.

IMMORTAL CLAY

Michael Warren Lucas

Copyright Information

Immortal Clay
Copyright 2014 by Michael W Lucas. All rights reserved, including the right of reproduction, in whole or in part in any form. Published in 2014 by Tilted Windmill Press.

Cover art copyright 2014 by Ben Baldwin.

Developmental Editor: Dayle Dermatis
Copy Editor: Cyrano Jones
Cover Design: Ben Baldwin
Book design by Tilted Windmill Press.

ISBN-13: 978-0692326800
ISBN-10: 0692326804

This book is a work of fiction. Names, characters, places, and incidents either are products of the author's imagination or used fictionally. Any resemblance to actual events or locales or persons, living or dead, is entirely coincidental. This book is licensed for your personal enjoyment only.

Tilted Windmill Press
https://www.tiltedwindmillpress.com

Acknowledgements

Thanks to all the folks who helped me with this book, whether they know it or not: Glen T Brock, Stanley Brown, Elaine Diamondidis, Richard E. D. Jones, Kate Macleod, Josh Peterson, AJ Powell, Brian Powell, Sharon Kae Reamer, and Rob Rowntree. My gratitude to two Johns, Campbell and Carpenter, for warping me at an impressionable age.

Most of all, extra thanks to my wife Liz.

And a glass raised to Colin Harvey.

Immortal Clay

Michael Warren Lucas

Prologue

THREE DAYS after the world ended, police detective Kevin Holtzmann awoke when his wife shouted his name.

Kevin wrenched himself upright. Heat slammed into his consciousness. His mouth crackled like parchment. He rolled off the sleeping bag to his knees, pulling his eyes open through the sandy scum gumming them shut. He wondered how he'd slept, but then remembered—exhaustion eventually overpowers even the most voracious fear.

Sheila shouted again. "Kevin!" Barely restrained panic shook her voice, reigniting Kevin's dread.

The afternoon sun highlighted the station wagon on the dusty desert. Light bounced off fresh bullet holes in the russet shell. Kevin had lain pinned under the narrow strip of shadow against passenger door, and he blinked to clear his sight as desert sunlight flooded his vision. His hands rasped against the car as he steadied himself.

Sheila stood on the other side of the wagon, her back pressed against the front fender. A smoky patina stained her exposed skin. Their teenage daughter Julie stood beside her, backed hard against the driver's door. Neither moved.

"Dad!" Julie said, her voice flatter than any fourteen-year-old's should be.

"Here." Julie's dispassionate voice, so unlike his daughter, alarmed Kevin more than Sheila's edgy fear. He spun his gaze around them, looking for the threat. The sun had cracked the horizon right before he went to sleep, but now the rusty hardpacked earth shone in the brilliant light. Probably a lizard or a snake out in the scattered scrub, but as little life as they could hope for. Maybe little enough to avoid attention. The only things between them and the horizon were distant striated hills and, further off, jagged Utah mountains.

Kevin trotted around the front of the car. He'd barely cleared the hood before stopping dead.

The man standing thirty short feet away had a neatly trimmed beard and black hair cascading down to the shoulders of an off-the-rack suit half a size too large for him. The translucently pale skin around his chin and over his eyes amplified the rosacea mottling his cheeks and nose.

Kevin froze for half a second. When he'd still worked Detroit PD homicide, a jury had found Collins guilty of five out of six counts of first-degree murder, as well as rape and a dozen lesser charges. The judge had sentenced him to over a hundred years. How could Collins be here, now?

There was really only one way. The man wasn't Collins. The real Jared Collins had died sometime in the last few days.

The Collins standing beneath the soot-hazed sky was unspeakably more dangerous than the original.

Kevin stared at the pleasantly smiling killer and circled the car to stand beside his wife and daughter. Julie braced her back against the front fender and lined up Kevin's service Springfield XD in a trembling grip, ready to put the stranger down if he came any closer.

"Looks like Saturdays at the gun range paid off," Julie said.

Pride made Kevin's heart pound even harder. Most kids would have been screaming or crying right now. The gun held only two rounds, but Julie carried herself like she had a full clip.

Sheila clenched the greasy machine pistol with a steady but too low grip that would kick up and smash her face if she pulled the trigger. Keeping his eyes on Collins, Kevin put his hand on the weapon and gently tugged it from his wife. His shoulder stung as he nestled the collapsible stock into yesterday's bruises, the warm metal somehow sweaty in his grip.

Having Collins in the line of fire didn't reassure him at all. The four bullets still in the clip would put a man in the ground, but even a full clip only distracted those taken by the alien. The human race had beaten cancer and broken global warming, but the alien shrugged off anything less than incineration.

"Feel better, Kevin?" Collins' voice sounded a little more hoarse than in the courthouse, but still had its jocular lilt.

"He oozed out of the ground," Sheila whispered, standing as close to Kevin as she could get without touching him.

"What do you want, Collins?" Kevin asked.

"Nice ride." Collins nodded at the station wagon. "You modified a hybrid to take diesel? Wasn't that illegal? Official vehicles only? Oh, *that's* right. You're a cop. The rules don't apply to you."

Kevin focused the machine pistol on Collins' chest.

"What's the matter, Detective?" Collins spread his empty hands. "No black humor today? No quips? Not even insulting my parents?"

"What do you *want*, Collins?"

"It's not what I want. It's what Absolute wants."

"Who?" Cold sank into Kevin's gut. He would have happily traded both kidneys for working flamethrower, but they'd left it empty in a parking lot in North Platte.

"He's winning, you know. You nuked Australia and South America into glowing glass, so he tried Africa. You burned that, so he waited. Three years he waited while you built up defenses, and now he's come up every coastline in the world. All at the same time. He *owns* the ocean. He's winning. Smashed through your years of work in two days. You'll be free. Whether you like it or not."

"We'll fight you all the way," Kevin said.

Collins threw out his hands. "Every city is burning right now! You think nuclear winter was bad? Wait 'til you get ash summer on top of it."

Kevin licked his parched lips. The desert heat immediately sucked away the moisture. "Why you?"

The smile split Collins' face impossibly wide, or just humanly fiendish? "I'm *motivated*. That's what they talked about in Marquette, you know. How to get *motivated*, to make your life better, to achieve your goals. Of all the people Absolute claimed, I was the most motivated." The smile vanished. "To find you."

Kevin's hand shifted on the machine pistol. "Go. Before I put a bullet in you."

"Bullets can't stop us." The smile returned. "It's the Second Coming, Homicide Detective Holtzmann. I've dumped the old mortal clay and put on incorruptible flesh."

"You're a copy. A copy of a worthless asshole."

"I have all my memories, all my feelings." Collins' eyes narrowed. "I remember every second I spent in Marquette. Every second I spent hating you. Sixteen years, five months, twenty-two days. And they're all on you."

"You killed—no, *Collins* killed nine women. Even if the DA could only bring charges on six." *Don't treat it like a human.*

"Twenty-eight. But that's Detroit. Who keeps count?"

"It's killed millions."

"Humans killed millions. And I'm pretty sure Absolute has taken *billions*, now. We've had hours."

"And of those billions, you're the one who showed up here. Why? How did you find us?"

"I've kept an eye on you, *Detective*. Checked that pissant town you moved to, but you'd left before we got there. So I thought *what would I do if I was a coward cop*, and it hit me. I'd grab my women and my weapons and run like a scared kid for the most lifeless place I could find."

Kevin flinched. When the final warning went out, the Department had issued every officer a machine pistol and a flamethrower. He'd used his badge to pass the roadblocks and get through the barricades when every other Frayville police officer had stayed, fought, and died. Anger sharpened his voice. "So the alien made you just to take me?"

"Oh, that hit home, did it?" Collins chuckled. "Absolute doesn't understand us. Yet." His fingers wiggled. "He tried. He finds it easier to make us understand him."

Kevin shifted the machine pistol, broadening his stance to better absorb recoil. "For the last time. Why are you here?"

"Because I know you," Collins snarled. "I'm here to give you a choice."

"What choice?"

"Absolute doesn't want to hurt you."

Kevin snorted.

"Really. He doesn't want to hurt anyone. Being forcibly taken messes you up. Trauma. Post-traumatic stress disorder. Like the prison doc talked about. But if you come willingly, or in your sleep, it's easier. *Absolute*," Collins said, "doesn't want to hurt you."

The cold in Kevin's stomach turned into a frozen pit in the afternoon desert heat. "Not a chance. If you move near us, I'll see how much bullets really hurt one of you."

"By all means, I'll stay right here. But if you try to get away..." Collins' fists tightened. "If you try to get away, I get to take you. I'm really hoping you try to run. "

Sheila grabbed Kevin's elbow, looking past him with a taut face. "Honey. Look."

Kevin's hand tightened around the trigger and he followed her gaze, keeping the MAC-10 centered on Collins' torso.

The scattered scrub brush was waving, thrashing, stretching like pulled taffy.

What had been a few cactuses had become spiny branches lashing out towards one another, in the space of two breaths becoming tentacles that reached towards other plants. Where two tentacles touched, they coalesced, becoming a single strand of flexing tissue.

Kevin spun.

The shrubs had formed an irregular circle around them.

"Julie!" he said. "Watch our back!" They should have gotten in the car. They should have shot Collins. They should have done anything except be here, now.

Julie whirled. Her breath caught, then she forcibly steadied herself.

Kevin jerked back to Collins. "So you're the messenger for this thing?"

"I'm more of a disciple," Collins said. "Bringing Absolute's good word, any way I see fit. They tell you all about the good word. In prison." He spread his hands. "You know. Prison. Where you're locked in a small room. They don't let you go. No matter what. *You're* lucky. *You* can get free any time you want. All *you* have to do is touch a plant and wait. You won't feel anything. You won't even lose consciousness. Absolute promises. He's made this offer billions of times, and always keeps his word. You will be you, no doubt. It's proof."

Bile filled the back of Kevin's mouth.

Collins dropped his hands to his sides. The fingers had become impossibly long, reaching almost to his knees. "If you don't go quietly, if you take one step towards getting in that car...then I get to make things happen. However I see fit."

His fingers flailed around each other, still stretching.

"I hope you turn it down," Collins said. "I really do. I could spend all day with you. You and your lovely family."

Tremors ran down Kevin's spine. His mouth clenched so hard that he felt a filling crack. Once the Taken stopped hiding, once they rearranged themselves, they could move impossibly fast.

The family couldn't escape the circle on foot.

They'd never get in the car before tentacles stabbed through the missing windows.

"Do tell me to fuck off," Collins said. The crotch of his pants swelled. "Oh, please."

"Kevin," Sheila said, stepping closer to him.

Kevin's shoulders shook with impotent fury. He welcomed the fury. It drowned out the terror.

"Kevin," Sheila said, more softly.

Sheila face's was open and relaxed. Her hand rested on Kevin's bare elbow. "I love you." She took a deep breath. "It's time."

Kevin felt like a bullet had punched through his chest and blown his heart out through shattered ribs. "There's a way," he hissed. "There has to be a way."

"It's over," she whispered. "The only question is, how."

He spun his head around. The plant tentacles had grown thinner, but more numerous, spreading out. What had been a thin circle had become a ringed hedge of fine mesh. They'd have to jump ten feet high and five across to clear them. His mind whirled faster than his body.

Fear bubbled up over the anger. Maybe a gasoline fire? How could he get the fuel out, cover Collins and the shrubs, and ignite them before they got him?

"I love you," she repeated.

Trapped. Walls clanged shut inside Kevin's mind.

Sheila smiled at him. Her eyes teared up, but she smiled.

Kevin had no idea how much that cost her. His soul seemed to drain away.

"Mom?" Julie said. "*Dad?*" The pistol wove back and forth as his daughter, his amazing daughter, tried to cover the half-circle behind them.

"It's okay, love" Sheila said. "We've talked. We've got a plan, we know what we're doing."

"I love you," Kevin said softly. "Both of you. Remember that."

"See you on the other side," Sheila whispered. Her voice shook. "I'll always love you."

Immortal Clay

Kevin looked back to Collins, or what had been Collins. Tentacles flexed at the end of his arms, long enough to go twice around Kevin's thigh. Collins' pants bulged obscenely, as if he'd grown an extra forearm between his legs. His face remained human, despite the height he'd added as Sheila talked.

Kevin's heart felt like lead, burning lead, but he held his voice steady. "Tell me, Collins." Somewhere, he found the strength to take a step away from his family. "What was it like?"

"Prison sucked."

"No, not that." He needed an extra second to save Sheila and Julie. "When the alien came for you." He shuffled his feet again, gaining a few extra inches.

Collins' face froze.

"I can see you there, in your cell. All of you hard-case convicts. Did it send tentacles in after you? Or did it just ooze between the bars like it oozed out of Antarctica?"

The once-human monster's tentacles stilled. Its face grew even redder.

"Did you scream? Or cry?" Kevin took another step away from his family. "I bet you cried. I bet you bawled your eyes out." He fought to sound cocky, but he felt a balled fist in his throat and his guts quivered like water.

"I can see you pressed up against the corner, crying."

"Yes?" snarled Collins. "Or no."

"You probably shoved your cellmate in front of you. Or did he push your soft, sweet ass in front?"

"Shut up," Collins said. "Tell me no, you asshole."

"You're kind of a pansy. I bet they threw you to the alien. Threw you and watched it rape you."

Collins' face spasmed, then split at the mouth. Rows of sharklike teeth punctured the top and bottom of his distended mouth in a torrent of blood and mucus. "You can't distract me." His voice buzzed and quavered, barely comprehensible. "I see them."

"I'm not distracting *you*," Kevin said. He took one more step and spun towards his wife and daughter.

He couldn't meet Sheila's eyes. They'd talked this through. They'd planned it, talking quietly while Julie slept. And he still couldn't meet her eyes.

Sheila had told him to take care of Julie first. But he couldn't. Julie's back was turned, and Sheila's eyes were fixed on him, a comforting hand on their daughter's shoulder.

He couldn't let Sheila see what had to happen.

He'd promised. But he couldn't.

The first round from the MAC-10 took Sheila at the tip of her nose, just below the eyes. Her eyes tipped back, and the second round took off the top of her skull.

Kevin's eyes were wide. His breathing had stopped.

Four bullets. Three people. But Kevin had seen enough death to know it wasn't a simple on or off state. Death was a grey scale, a spectrum. If enough of Sheila's brain survived, the alien would take her.

They'd agreed that the alien couldn't take them. No matter what.

Two bullets for Sheila. Two left.

Julie screamed, a high shriek like tearing metal. The pistol bucked in her hand as she pulled the trigger.

Collins hissed in sharp pain.

Kevin couldn't think. Horror overwhelmed his brain.

He couldn't do this.

He had to do this.

The third shot went in the side of Julie's head, just above the ear. Fresh blood spattered the windshield.

Somewhere, Collins let out an impossible alien cry.

Julie crumpled. As her knees folded, Kevin put the last bullet into the bottom of her skull. Bone dissolved into a mush of brain and blood.

Kevin's own blood hammered in his ears. He still couldn't breathe.

He didn't think he'd ever breathe again.

Kevin's service automatic flew from Julie's hand, clattering across the station wagon's hood and rattling to the ground. Kevin lunged toward it, throwing himself across the dirt, anything to stop looking at what he'd done, the devastated ruins of his life now heaped on the desert floor.

I'll always love you, Sheila had said.

If he hadn't pulled the trigger, her last words would have been screams.

He fell flat on his stomach, one hand sizzling as it bounced off the sunscorched chrome bumper, the other slapping the dirt. The

Springfield XD gouged his chest, and he scrabbled backwards to try to get his hands on it.

Julie had fired one shot. It should have one more bullet.

Something seized Kevin's ankle and yanked him skyward.

His feet left the ground so hard his back popped. He clawed at the ground, dirt flying as his chest came up. His right hand caught hot metal, and he grabbed the pistol as he flew upwards, suspended by one ankle.

Collins, or the writhing mass of tentacles and limbs he'd become, stood only a few feet away, stinking of shit and blood. His teeth spun in circular rows, ready to feed flesh into his maw. Sounds probably meant to be words buzzed through the mass of distorted flesh, but Kevin didn't even try to understand.

Kevin slapped the pistol into his other hand, locking a finger around the trigger.

One bullet left. Enough. You couldn't double-tap yourself.

Tentacles flailed and thrashed, spiraling up his leg, clamping his torso.

Kevin still hadn't inhaled. He didn't see the point. He couldn't find it in him to care.

Blood rushed to his head.

Collins snapped him from side to side, like a dog with a toy.

Kevin's free leg bounced, wrenching him from side to side. He wrenched his hand to his head. Hot gun metal jammed into the bottom of his chin.

He pulled the trigger.

It didn't move.

He yanked it again, forgetting technique, desperate simply for a bullet to punch through his chin and take the top of his head off, scatter his brains across the desert floor.

The muffled choking noise from Collins was probably meant as laughter.

Kevin looked at the pistol.

A thick, woody tentacle filled the space behind the trigger.

Nausea filled his gut. Kevin's heart felt too heavy, as if it would tear its way through his throat and crash into the ground.

A fleshy tentacle wrapped around his wrist and *squeezed*.

Kevin gasped as his hand involuntarily opened. The automatic, with its one precious bullet, fell to the dirt.

At least he'd saved Sheila and Julie from this.
I will always love you.
Then the tentacles stabbed into his ears, twined into his nose, plunged up his throat, punctured his gut and his chest. Kevin didn't have the air to scream and suddenly he cared very much about breathing.

When I first woke up, I had a blister under my chin. From the hot gun barrel.

Chapter 1

MY STRINGS cut, I collapsed. Rough carpet scratched my face as I hit the ground. The knuckles of my left hand cracked against hard tile. Dust and vanilla filled my nose. Air huffed out of my lungs. I choked, then involuntarily sucked in another breath.

I didn't want to breathe. I didn't want anything.

White carpet a fraction of an inch from my open eye. Tight knobs of fabric in a rippled pattern.

I knew this carpet.

My living room.

I coughed. My lungs burned with dust. Sheila never let the carpet get dusty. She'd badger Julie into vacuuming. One of her chores.

But Sheila was dead.

I'd killed her.

And Julie.

No, not me. *Kevin* had killed her.

Except...I *was* Kevin.

Kevin's appendix had burst a few years ago. I remembered the surgical recovery room. Anesthesia-darkened vision, turning overhead fluorescents dim. A looming shadow of a face said "Yes, you lived," and I—*he*—said "Aw, shit." Occasional glimpses of a light. A ceiling tile. Sheila's face, worried, lips moving too slowly for the words rattling from her. Awakening the next morning, with tubes in veins and cold sterile metal rails along each side of the bed.

Looking back, the surgeon hadn't taken an appendix. He'd sliced out a chunk of a life, and stitched together the severed ends of time as neatly as he did the healthy chunks of intestine around excised necrotic tissue.

Escaping Absolute's grip felt like coming out of anesthesia.

The gun bucking in my hand. Sheila's skull scattering like a thrown puzzle. Julie crumpling halfway through a scream. Those were *my* memories. Mine.

My sight blurred. I clutched at the carpet. Sheila loved vanilla, and breathing that smell filled me with her absence even as I coughed in the dust. Tears drowned my vision.

If Kevin hadn't killed Sheila and Julie, they would be here now. Except they wouldn't be them. They'd be copies. Like me.

I curled around my gut, trying to hold myself together as a sob ripped free of my chest.

The house echoed around me. No sound of television. No radio. Julie always had music going, electronic stuff that made me grit my teeth. The absence hurt like a missing tooth.

Eventually, the tears passed. My mouth burned, my eyes ached. Every beat of my heart felt like a violation. The blister beneath my chin throbbed. I didn't want to be here. I didn't want to be anywhere. But you can't cry forever. Once the shudders stopped, once my breath stopped hitching and became almost normal, I grudgingly rolled to my knees and lifted my head.

Our living room. Pale green walls, with the crown molding a darker green accent. A jar of vanilla essential oils on the mantle. A sound system the size of a shoebox, silent. I heard nothing except my own heartbeat and breath. The electronic picture frame, brightly displaying a small section of upper Michigan's thick pine forest.

The picture changed. Julie holding my hand on that same trip, five years younger than she should be now.

I wrenched my vision away even as my spine quivered, turning to face the row of plants beneath the picture window. Sheila had tended her plants for years, growing herbs in a box and orchids and African violets in luridly glazed pots.

The pots stood intact but lifeless. Empty dirt filled them. A few crumbs of black soil lay on the surrounding carpet.

Everywhere I looked, family stared back. Framed photos of marriage, birthdays, and weekends on the wall, Julie's algebra book dropped carelessly beside her favorite chair, Kevin's weekend shoes piled with Sheila's beside the front door, laces intimately intertwined.

I forced a deep breath. The window. The window wouldn't accuse me. I staggered to the gauze curtains and flung them aside. Streetlights illuminated the asphalt. The silhouettes of neighboring houses stood out against the cloudy sky and trees. A few lit rectangles showed where other houses had lights.

Something shrieked in the darkness, the sound muffled by glass.

A distant gunshot. A scream.

Staring into the night, I tried to think. What had happened?

I remembered the gun in my hand, the blistering hot barrel jammed into my chin. Tentacles stabbed into me. A moment of diffuse pain, a billion billion cold needles searing my nerves.

Then—nothing. Only flickers of memories. Yellow dashes on asphalt. A handful of algae-filled water lifted towards my mouth. Boneless hands wrapped like tentacles around a steering wheel. I remembered a sense of purpose, rules I had to obey.

Had Collins been like that, I wondered? My brain seized on the question, grateful for any thoughts that didn't splash acid on my heart. Collins had announced that if I—if *Kevin*—and his family had accepted the alien eating and copying them, he had to let them, that he could only attack if denied.

Had I given someone the same choice?

My hollow gut burned.

I dropped the curtain. My hands smudged the rough white linen.

My hands were filthy. Arms, too. Dirt saturated my denim pants and crusted the graying hair on my bare chest. I suddenly felt dirty, not just outside but inside. My restless body seized on it.

To my surprise, the blue-tiled stall shower had hot water. The house had solar shingles, so the electricity hadn't surprised me, but I hadn't expected the gas water heater to still work. I tried to concentrate on cleaning the stains from my flesh, feeling the water's warmth grow incrementally closer as dirt swirled around the drain. Knots and snarls in my uncombed hair.

Maybe I should try some of Julie's conditioner to clear it up. The bright purple bottle sat where it always did, promising the smell of apples amidst Sheila's half-dozen shampoos. My vision blurred. My knees sagged.

No. I was not going to buckle again. I grabbed the petrified washcloth, soaked it until it could take a load of soap, and attacked the dirt again.

I needed a moment to realize that something was still on my hand. A ring. Kevin's white and yellow gold wedding ring.

I sagged against the cold wet tile, hot water blasting down, and sobbed until the water ran cold.

Chapter 2

A MORNING in Julie's room, sitting on her unmade neglected bed, clutching the brown teddy bear she swore she didn't need but wouldn't get rid of, faint echoes of her clean baby-powder smell filling my nose, staring at track trophies and posters of boy bands with offensively cute haircuts and folded clothes piled atop her baby-sized dresser, thinking of the new bed set Sheila and Kevin had wanted to buy her and how Julie was going to be a veterinarian or a musician or an engineer. All lost. The teddy bear's single blue crystalline eye held no comfort for the hole in my heart. Afternoons in the family room, leaving the curtains closed, watching photos flicker past on the mantle, wedding album open on my lap. Or the scrapbook, faded Disney park passes from the winter before Julie was born and a yellowed novelty photo of the three of us as Old West characters in a faux saloon and an ultrasound of our miscarried first child.

Over days, the outside tears slowed and stopped. The chasm inside didn't grow any deeper, only more defined.

Kevin had moved through his life with certainty. Growing up wanting to be a police officer. Twelve years in the Detroit PD. Meeting Sheila, a marriage in the city hall, moving out to Frayville, a police detective in a town without much crime to detect, building a future for their daughter. His life now seemed inexorable and unstoppable, as though a tow chain attached to his heart pulled him into a future. Kevin had known what he wanted next, and worked towards it with unhurried certainty.

I didn't have that. I didn't even know if I was Kevin. I only knew the past hurt, and I couldn't stop wallowing in it.

The wedding band burned on my ring finger. Had the alien built a copy of Kevin from raw dust and water before abandoning the carcass? Or had it infiltrated Kevin's body, exchanging living cells for its own like changing a car's tires as it rolled down the freeway? Replacement or suffusion? Did I materialize beneath the ring, or had I pulled it off Kevin's cold carcass? Did it really matter?

I cursed myself for pulling the trigger. And felt obscurely proud of Kevin for having done it.

No television signals, either over the air or cable. The computer said it was late May, only four weeks after we'd fled the town, but the data feed had died with the television.

When I ate, it was leftovers in the fridge. Wrinkled apples, eaten unwashed, and desiccated grapes in the plastic carton. Water straight from the tap. Stray cans of cold beans or fruit cocktail. I heard shouts and screeches and the occasional car from outside the house, and occasionally smelled smoke or trees through narrowly open windows.

Once or twice a day, alien thoughts rumbled up somewhere from the back of my brain. I remembered riding in the back of a truck, ignoring the rain lashing my face at fifty miles an hour. More than once, words rose from the same hollow place. *Legacy. Immanence.* The alien had named itself Absolute for good reason, and I knew that it had let me go because there wasn't anything left to conquer.

The gun-metal blister beneath my chin didn't heal. Maybe it never would.

Days, maybe weeks, I sat in darkened rooms and tried not to feel. I'd probably still be there if the doorbell hadn't rang.

Chapter 3

I SAT hunched on the upholstered and over-padded couch, cradling Sheila's grandmother's beautiful cut crystal vase in my hands, staring into the fractures of light within it and trying to remember everything Sheila had ever told me about it, desperate to remember her every word. It had been a wedding gift. From her new husband's sister. Shipped out from a fancy New York City store with a long name, one that didn't hadn't existed for fifty years or at least wasn't known out here in Michigan.

The doorbell's first deep tone, the only solid noise I'd heard since Absolute freed me, startled me enough that I tossed the vase a couple inches into the air. My guts dropped away as I fumbled at the cool smooth crystal, and I didn't breathe again until the cut edges dug into my palms. I fingered the vase for a moment, reassuring myself that I hadn't broken it, then set it on the glass-topped table.

The doorbell's Westminster chimes echoed through the house, and I stared at the door. Frayville had been good to Kevin and his family. I didn't want to know what it had become. How many people were out there? How many monsters like me?

The door shuddered under frantic pounding. I faintly heard a shout. The voice sounded vaguely like Julie's. I knew better—I completely knew better—but the similarity sufficed to launch me towards the door with sudden hope scrabbling against the walls of my heart. Maybe I hadn't actually killed my daughter. Maybe she'd survived. Or, if I was *really* lucky, some horrible creation of Absolute's had come to destroy me as it had killed Kevin.

I knew I was lying to myself as I wrenched the door open, but I still felt crushed to see a young brunette girl on the small concrete porch. She looked about Julie's age, just in middle school, and wore jeans and a yellow blouse. Tears trailed down alongside her nose and over her cheeks, tracks clearly visible in the morning sunshine.

"What?" My voice sounded rough. I hadn't spoken in days. Maybe weeks. Maybe never.

"Mr. Holtzmann?"

"Yeah." I didn't question the response until the words left my mouth. By then it was too late.

"I'm Alice?" Her voice lilted up at the end of each phrase, making every statement a question. "Alice Tander? Julie's friend?"

My mind froze, nailed in place by memories of joyful mayhem and laughter. Memories from another man's life. Chaotic sleepover parties. A houseful of preadolescent girls. Gleeful pop music sing-alongs until two in the morning, ten girls around the breakfast table, piles of frozen waffles and scrambled eggs and gallons of orange juice.

"You said we could ask you if we were in trouble?"

Always find a police officer if you need help. Knock on my door if you have to, I won't mind. That's what you told kids, even if it wasn't exactly true. You'd mind, but you had to pretend you didn't. Policing wasn't a nine-to-five gig. You did it over dinner and at neighborhood barbeques and even woke up in the night thinking about it.

"That was before." The words came from my gut, without conscious thought. No sweet barbeque smoke in the air today. Nothing but the fresh air of rural northern lower Michigan, cleaner than I'd ever smelled it before, with a faint hint of the girl's too-sweet shampoo. After the end of the world, and teenage girls still had scented hair. "I'm not a cop. Not anymore."

"I don't think there are any," she said. "I tried the police station. But nobody's there and the windows are all busted out. But something's happened to my Dad?"

I blinked at her. My brain sputtered, trying to assemble words out of the dull sludge of my emotions.

"Please? There's other people around, but none of them are police?"

"Were." Was I going to spend the day standing here correcting a fourteen-year-old girl, who already couldn't speak without questioning herself? My heart beat more quickly.

"You've *got* to help me." She brushed one foot unconsciously through the wind-blown dirt scattered on the porch. "Dad said to treat people like I always had."

My grip tightened on the doorframe until the wooden trim dug into my palm and I felt my pulse in my fingers. "Help? You think anybody can help us?"

"You have to," she said. "*We* have to, that's what Dad says, because if we don't nothing will ever get better. And it's got to get better."

My jaw tightened. How had this girl survived? In this moment, I would have been happy to see even a copy of my Julie. I would have set Alice on fire for five minutes with the ones I'd lost. The ones Kevin set free.

Seeing something in my face, she stumbled backwards. Her heel rested half off the edge of the porch. Her eyes watched mine.

"How," I started. I peeled my hand from the doorframe, consciously stretching and relaxing my fingers. "How did you come through?"

She swallowed. "I was asleep," she said.

"And what do you remember? About the time..." I rolled my hand in the air. "The time after."

She stepped back again, wobbling but catching herself. "I—I don't really remember."

"You remember pieces," I said. "I remember pieces."

Her voice quavered. "You said you'd help us."

"That was someone else," I said. *Sorry, kid.* "I've never spoken to you before."

The wooden door closed smoothly, the deadbolt clicking into place. I sagged against the glossy red paint, feeling my heart skip. *You could have been a bigger asshole. Slap her around a bit, maybe hook her on crack.* That sullen anger still burned inside. She'd survived. Julie was dead. Because I'd killed her. If I'd let her sleep through Absolute's incursion, she'd be like me. Here with her friend.

I closed my eyes and took a deep, shuddering breath. Opened my eyes on the living room. The overstuffed blue corduroy couch. Framed photographs of vacations in the national forests, days on the Lake Huron beaches, birthdays on the deck in the backyard. Sheila put the crystal candlesticks on the green-enameled fireplace mantle when she'd packed away the Christmas decorations. A hardwood floor that gleamed of varnish beneath motes of dust.

All that remained of my family.

I'd looked at this same scene many times, on my way out to work in the morning. Memorized each detail, stored them in my heart, always with the niggling worry that I maybe I wouldn't come home again. Frayville was a lot safer than Detroit, but a police detective always ran that risk.

I'd come home, but nobody else had. Like a hermit crab, I lived in an empty shell abandoned by its owner.

"Dammit," I said, turning around to fling the door open. "Hey, kid, wait up!"

Chapter 4

I WALKED in silence, Alice trotting an arm's reach ahead of me. Impatience pulled her forward, fear kept her close. She looked back, seemingly afraid that if she left me behind I'd just go home. Maybe I would have. I didn't want to be on the street. I didn't want to be anywhere.

I didn't want to *be* at all.

The neighborhood looked like we'd had a bad summer storm, or maybe a three-day power outage. Fallen branches lay beneath trees. Too many front doors stood open. Grass—or an alien thing that looked a lot like grass—had grown to a couple inches everywhere, tall enough to have set the Neighborhood Association thugs knocking on doors.

In the years between the destruction of the Southern Hemisphere and Absolute's final attack, Kevin had attended innumerable training sessions about the alien. Supposedly the alien ate every kind of biomass, that every piece of it was a complete living creature. Those lawns were millions of stalks of independent alien life. Was each blade a copy of a specific blade of grass, or had Absolute just made a generic template called "grass" and stamped them out by the billion? Absolute had copied Kevin in detail—as far as he knew. Was each blade of grass replicated? Each sparrow? If not, where was the line?

We'd bought a home in this part of Frayville because each house had its own character. Our ranch sprawled next to a drab gray colonial with spectacularly colorful landscaping and across from a Spanish-style concrete stucco-ish thing. But now the houses, blocky Colonials and towering Tudors and everything, all shared a shroud of emptiness. A front door stood half-open to reveal vacant shadows.

Scattered white clouds scudded through a hazy blue sky, revealing a bright sun tinted orange by lingering fallout and distant smoke. The breeze carried pine and balsam from the cluster of trees at the back corner of our lot.

Robins and sparrows chirped. A dove cooed.

Pebbles and dead leaves crunched underfoot.

The gleaming concrete of Ducasse Street had been replaced only three years ago, right before they glassed the Southern Hemisphere. Nobody did much road work after that, too busy with the whole decentralization thing and the checkpoints and blood tests and all of the rest of the Building the Future programs that hadn't done a damn bit of good. We walked a block west, crossed Horse Stall Street, and kept going.

Alice glanced back at me, lips twitching, face pale, then turned forward again.

I kept walking. I had vague memories of the Tander house, a couple blocks west and a couple blocks north. Julie had wanted a ride there more than once, when it was snowing or raining or foggy or clear and sunny.

Kevin had sworn to defend Frayville. The Defense Department had warned us that Absolute was massing to invade. I—*Kevin*—had taken the flamethrower and the machine pistol, grabbed his family, and ran for the Utah desert. And here was the hometown he'd abandoned, a month or so later, neglected but intact. Strands of relief made my guilt even less comfortable.

Somewhere behind us, a car engine revved. I looked, but the noise came through the trees separating these empty houses from the main drag. *Fuel*, I thought. Governments had limited gasoline production, converting necessary vehicles to more efficient diesel. Nobody would make more gasoline or diesel. How well would these houses work without transportation? Natural gas? Water? Would we all spend next winter in the nearest tenement, huddled together eating tinned bologna while the Arctic wind knifed down?

"How many people have you seen?" I asked. My body didn't want to talk. *I* didn't want to talk. I did anyway. I didn't want to be out on this street, breathing the smells of flowers and trees and old fires. I didn't want to follow Alice. But my inner detective had raised the question when I hadn't been paying attention.

"Not many," Alice said. "A few? I mean, there's Dad and I." The words bubbled out as if under pressure. "My friend Ceren is next door, I've been hanging with her. Her folks haven't shown up yet. Missus

Peterson, the social studies teacher? I saw her. And there were a bunch of people down at the lake a couple days ago. And there's people walking around, some of em I've seen before but a bunch I hadn't. Some of them were kind of whacked out. And there's things that just aren't—" Alice's hands flapped—"just aren't people."

"Aren't people?" Absolute had let copies change form. Could we still do that? I blinked, rummaging through my brain. A fragmented memory of running over concrete, legs stretched to eat more distance, two steps and gone. I couldn't remember *how* I had changed, only that I had *been* repulsively changed. Maybe I couldn't. Memory or fantasy?

The draping greens on the willow tree at the corner of Ducasse and Oak hung too heavy. I squinted against the piercing sunlight, but at this distance I couldn't see anything except thick viridian tendrils drooping under some burden.

I stayed in the middle of the road, away from the grass and the tendrils and everything that might suddenly change form and rip my face off.

The car engine stopped revving. Tires squealed, maybe a few blocks away, making me grit my teeth. I reached for a ticket book, even though I hadn't carried one in years. The gesture, useless. We could race cars now. On the sidewalk. Through the park. Running over toddlers and old ladies as we went.

Toddlers and old ladies. I didn't want to think about them. Would the duplicate of a child grow up? Would someone aged to fragility ever get to die in peace? How long would we copies live?

I wrenched my eyes towards the sky, trying to find something else to think about. No contrails. I couldn't remember the last time I'd seen a sky without lines of white. Frayville sat square in the Selfridge ANG flight path. When sabers rattled, so did our windows.

"Once we saw the eye thing," Alice said, "Dad asked me to stay home. He's been trying to sort out what happened. There's streets you can't walk down because someone's shooting at everyone. He's figuring it out."

The car engine suddenly grew loud enough to make me tighten my spine. I looked over my shoulder. A low-slung blue Corvette rocketed down Horse Stall, crossing my field of view in less than a second. The driver wore dark sunglasses, both hands on the wheel, mouth open in a shout that couldn't overcome the engine's dinosaur shriek. I thought he looked about twelve years old.

Alice's father had gone out to see what he could do to help, while I'd sat at home. He was a better man than I was. Then again, he still had family. A rusty blade of jealousy stabbed my gut.

"Then there's that," Alice said. Her voice had a wistful tone. "It's be pretty stupid to get through the end of the world and run over by Timmy driving like an ass—a jerk. So I've mostly been staying home. I figured out the Blu-Ray player and got into Dad's movies. There's no data, you know? Any idea when they'll get it back on?"

"No idea, kid."

"They've gotta. I'm halfway through *Synners*, can't wait to see the rest of it. I'm going into data, you know? Maybe programming, but I like the protocol security stuff? You know, breaking SCTP?" Her conversation degenerated into a nervous babble that washed over me. I didn't recognize most of the computer terms she used, but I recognized the pattern.

Alice was scared. Like any other teenager, she wouldn't admit it. She'd admit to absolutely anything, except being utterly terrified.

Chapter 5

ALICE AND I traipsed through someone's yard to the back of the Tander residence. The girl had broken my isolation, and annoyance at the disturbance tried to lash me into anger. Instead, I studied her home.

The house was snug and tight, two floors, with a steep solar-shingle roof over battered red brick walls. Glittering suncatchers in the upper windows fractured sunlight into rainbow sprays. Irregular branches sprouting off the round shrubs around the back begged for trimming, but someone had swept the driveway. Thorny roses engulfed a trellis beside the huge, curtain-blocked window overseeing the backyard. If Absolute put eyes in the roses, it could see inside.

Alice touched the handle of the doorwall. Her breath quickened. Her shoulders hunched inward. Her fingers lingered on the handle, trembling.

I instinctively touched my belt, where my service automatic should have hung, and found only the cool leather of my belt. The blister under my chin throbbed. "He's in there?"

Alice jerked her hand back as if she'd dared to pet a rattlesnake. "Yeah." Her voice had lost its questioning tone, and somehow taken her confidence with it. "Upstairs."

"What's his name?"

She knotted her fingers together. "Doug."

"You wait here."

The well-balanced doorwall slid easily open, exposing a darkened family room. I stepped onto the gleaming ochre tile entryway and let my eyes adjust to the gloom.

The room would be comfortable if you lifted the blackout curtains. A sleek leather couch dominated the far wall, flanked by matching bowlegged chairs trimmed with dark wood. Drywall painted a pale color, indeterminate in the dimness. Hardwood floors leading to even darker rooms beyond. Faint hints of leather cleaner and oil soap.

"Doug?" I called.

I suddenly remembered Jared Collins' misshapen changes as he transformed from a human-shaped sociopathic killer to a schizophrenic nightmare. Absolute had freed me. Alice had been freed—at least, she acted like she'd been freed. Maybe she hadn't. Maybe Absolute was just playing games—knock over the world once, then set us up for another go.

I froze for a moment, imagining something like a chitinous octopus sidling across the ceiling at me. My breath caught, and for just a second I convinced myself I smelled saltwater and old fish.

A breeze through the doorwall ruffled my hair.

This was stupid. If Absolute was playing games with us, we were damned no matter what. Alice had seemed freed, and I had to take that at appearances. After all, she couldn't very well copy me again. Could she? At least, *I* hadn't retained any knowledge of how to devour and duplicate someone.

I wondered if I could.

Focus, nitwit. Questions could drown me. I took a deep breath. Dark house. Citizen in distress. "Doug?"

Silence.

The home differed from Kevin's in every way that didn't matter. The dark, heavy furniture seemed selected for appearance and style rather than comfort. Low-voltage outlets for solar direct current were neatly mounted into each wall beside old-fashioned AC three-prong outlets. My feet echoed on hardwood floors polished to a high gloss. Photos hung in stained wood frames rather than plastic. But the photos showed a family, two parents and three children, vacations, graduations, all the holidays they'd celebrated and some celebrations that didn't need holidays. The photos lining the open stairwell watched me as I climbed. Doug was about six feet tall, a little extra meat under the jaw but not enough for jowls, dark hair, pencil-thin moustache over a big grin with irregular teeth.

I found Doug, or what was left of him, in the master bedroom.

Twisted clothes lay scattered across the king-size bed. Shattered glass glittered across the floor, thin splinters still hanging in the broken mirror. A barn musk hung in the still air, so thick I expected it to cloud my vision.

And Doug, naked on the floor.

I tried to calm my hammering heart. I'd expected injury. Imagined tentacled monstrosities. Somehow, this was worse than either. Bile burned my throat.

Doug lay on his back at the foot of the bed, his head shriveled like a deflated soccer ball. His mouth had shrunk, too small to accept a garden hose. His nose retracted almost flat against his face. Eyelids hung slack over evaporated eyes. The thick head of hair hadn't changed, but the skin beneath it was rippled and saggy, as if the skull beneath was a desiccated melon.

I made myself swallow my revulsion. My hand reached for the Department phone on my belt and clenched empty air. Who was I going to report this to, anyway?

His legs had shrunken as well. As had his arms. His limbs curled up towards his torso, like a fetal child or a burned body. The photos had shown Doug carrying a substantial spare tire, but his flesh had evaporated until taut skin showcased his ribs and pelvis. His skin, pink plastic shrink-wrap around gaunt bones and muscle. Every bit of him dry, withered, and shriveled. Every bit but one.

His penis rose more than two feet into the air, as thick around as my forearm, red and swollen. Nothing else on Doug's body moved, but that ridiculous and horrifying monster dick trembled with energy.

Chapter 6

FOR DAYS I'd thought myself dead. In that room, standing at the foot of that bed, watching a still-living penis jut, jerk, and quiver from the withered body of a mostly dead man, I knew I had been wrong. The dead don't feel nausea slowly boil up from their guts, and don't have panic gibbering in the back of the brain. Staring at Doug's body jolted life through me like a defibrillator across the chest.

Doug's penis seemed to turn towards me, although I knew it couldn't. He didn't have any eyes. His ears had shriveled into raisins. Smell? No way my smell could penetrate that appalling, thick animal funk.

The damned thing definitely slanted towards me, though.

I stepped to the side.

The red, swollen head swiveled to follow.

I launched myself out of the room and slammed the door behind me, forcing down bile. It's as if it has a mind of its own. A joke. An excuse. Years in Detroit PD had hardened me. I'd walked in on more bloody aftermath than I could count, pools of blood and flesh and worse soaking into carpet, grass, wood, tile, concrete. Even as a detective in the quiet Frayville PD, I'd been randomly slapped with human wreckage. I'd held people still shivering and shaking after discovering loved ones dead or broken. Somehow, this was worse.

Even if Doug had figured out how to change himself, he wouldn't have done this. Made himself bigger, maybe. Every man wondered at one point in his life what it would be like to hang to the knees. Personally, I figured it would be even more annoying. But wrecking the rest of himself? No. Someone had done this *to* Doug.

I leaned against the cool wall outside the door, pushing out lungfuls of air until my breath slowed and my heart stopped ricocheting against my ribs. I'd thought I was hardened, but recovering my self-control took longer than usual. One too many shocks to my system, I guessed.

I made myself walk back out to the patio, carefully not looking at the photos on the way.

Alice sat on a mesh chair beside the glass-topped patio table. Her eyes were tightly closed, her hands gripping the chair's arms so tightly that her knuckles were white dots. Her lips moved slightly as she talked to herself.

I sat in the chair beside hers.

She didn't seem to notice my presence.

What had it been like for her to walk in and see her father like that? It had assaulted my reason, and I would have barely recognized Doug seeing him on the street. "Alice," I said quietly.

Alice bounced in her seat, eyes blinking open. "Oh!" Her shoulders trembled.

I kept my voice calm and quiet. "I don't want you going back in there. You said you had a friend nearby, Ceren. Can you stay with her for a while?"

Alice nodded. Resigned? Stunned?

The wind carried pine and old smoke. The sun felt warm, but couldn't thaw the chill in my core.

"Can you do anything?" Alice said.

I sucked in a long slow breath through my nose. "I don't know."

She nodded.

I didn't know what could do that to someone. But I knew one thing: it was a crime. A crime in so many ways. And lacking a family, lacking even myself, I desperately needed a crime.

"But you better tell me everything," I said.

Chapter 7

ALICE GAVE me a few places and names before I escorted her next door and handed her to her friend Ceren, another young teen with bright blue hair. Before, kids dressed outlandishly to assert their independence. Ceren was alone now. I couldn't imagine who or what she was declaring independence from. Leaving a traumatized teen with a traumatized friend wasn't the greatest idea, but excluding traumatized people would rule out everyone.

The questions of how Doug had transformed gave me something to aim for, and Kevin's years of experience told me how to reach it. The idea of useful work didn't fill the void within me, but anesthetized a small part of the endless ache.

If I was going to investigate this, I needed a notebook. Writing everything down starts as an annoying chore, but once you spend enough time on enough cases you realize that the notebook is the only thing that saves your sanity. The first time you have to flip through an old notebook to find a name, you're a real police detective. The first morning you have to flip through yesterday's pages to remind you of which particular atrocities you're supposed to look at today, you're a seasoned one. I retraced Alice's path through the hollow neighborhood back to Kevin's house and retrieved a blank notebook and a couple of the black pens Kevin favored from the desk, opened the first page, left a couple blank lines at the top, and wrote down: *Doug Tander.*

I hesitated, gnawed my lips, then added *giant penis*. If I needed to differentiate between people reduced to overblown genitalia, I'd come up with a better label. Or get a flamethrower.

Then the names and places Alice had given me.
Jack's
Winchester Mall—"Legacy"
Edison—substation

Leaning back in the cloth-covered office chair, I rubbed my chin as I studied the list. My thumb jabbed the blister, and I jerked my hand away.

That painful blister on the bottom of my chin had been there ever since—ever. How long had I spent in this house alone? I needed to know the date for my notebook anyway. I booted the computer. The built-in calendar said it was June second, and I scribbled the date on the top of the first page even as my brain churned.

I'd awoken on the carpet on the twenty-second of May. Eleven days later, June second, the blister still hung on my chin, as painful as ever. I didn't mind the pain. I—Kevin—had failed, after all. If he'd been half a second quicker, I wouldn't be here. But shouldn't the blister have healed by now? It seemed larger, more tender than I remembered.

Maybe this was how I belonged. Cain had a scarred forehead, I got a blistered chin. The thought didn't bother me as much as it should. On some level it felt right, like the warmth of the two-tone gold wedding ring I didn't deserve.

My shoulders shuddered. I closed my eyes and sucked in a deep breath, forcing down a seizure of grief. I had all kinds of baggage, sure. More drama than damn near any human being who ever lived. I deserved to be more fucked-up than anyone Kevin had ever arrested. But right now, I had something else to think about. I couldn't spend the rest of my life curled around my pain. You burn out on pain. It leaves you empty, ashen, a husk ready to be filled by the first thing that comes along. In my case, a girl my daughter's age who needed her father.

When Kevin had moved to Frayville, he'd had to learn the streets and people and connections between them, but at least he'd known where electricity and oranges came from and that the state and federal governments both supported and watched him. I didn't know even that much.

In the corner of Kevin's bedroom closet, beneath the suits he never wore, the row of tacks holding down the white knit carpet let free with a quiet ripping sound. They'd done it many times before. Kevin had neatly cut a couple of floorboards to make a hidey-hole about a foot across. I found his backup pistol, not a Springfield XD but an older Beretta fourteen-shot semi-automatic with a shoulder holster. A thousand dollars in cash, painfully gleaned and hoarded over the years. I took the pistol, left the money, pulled on a tweed sport jacket, and headed to Jack's to dredge up what Doug hadn't told his daughter.

Chapter 8

I WALKED down the center of abandoned residential roads to get to Main Street. I didn't see anybody, and tried not to jump nervously at distant clangs and the occasional muffled shout. Others lived, somewhere in town. How far would a shout carry when everything went silent?

Main Street was just as still, lifeless except for trees planted between the sidewalk and the road. I saw very few cars, but that wasn't a surprise—cars had grown increasingly rare with gasoline rationing. I walked down the center of the asphalt, between silent mismatched buildings built one against the next, until I got to Jack's.

Strange yellow-green fruit the size and shape of soccer balls hung from the willow tree outside the bar. I leaned back in distaste, shook my head to dislodge the image, and went inside the red brick single-story building only to get stopped by familiarity.

Jack's is an old bar. The tourists didn't know about it, and the owner didn't advertise. I'd been called here more than once, usually to figure out who swung first. The low ceiling, white walls, and dark brown beams hadn't changed. Neon signs cast reflections on polished wood tabletops and the ceramic tile floor. Stale-beer stench hung heavy in the air, intermingled with old fry fat. You could get a burger here, or, if you wanted fancy, a cheeseburger. But the voices woke me like a bucket of water to the face. I stood in the doorway, warm air blowing past my face into the street, and stared into the room.

Two heavyset women in jeans and loose blouses sat near the silent jukebox, their table so small that their elbows mingled betwixt their half-full glass mugs. A familiar-looking tired man in a stained mechanic's jumpsuit perched alone at the last stool, bottle halfway to his face. Two other men sat in sadly-used leather chairs in front of the cold fireplace, voices raised in civil argument. Two teenagers faced the side wall, the boy with a dart ready to throw, the girl nearby eyeing him impishly, her hip cocked to make his dart fly anywhere except at the battered dartboard. The bartender had a dark bottle in one upraised hand, expostulating at the lady in a dark pantsuit and black lace veil perched on the stool opposite him.

Everyone stopped talking and turned to face me.

I glanced around the room warily. My feet didn't want to walk forward.

Eyes stared at me.

Then I realized I was trying to figure out which of them was human, and which would change shape and eat my face. The answer was: all of them, or none. I forced my lips into a smile and raised my empty hands. "Hello."

The bartender raised his bottle towards me, and tension rippled out of the room. The women turned back to each other. The young man turned back to the dartboard and let fly, as if trying to get the dart in the air before the girl addled his brains again. The dart struck the wooden wall and bounced to the floor, and the girl giggled.

Maybe Absolute freed everyone, but we all carried fear.

I let the door close behind me and walked to the bar. The unfamiliar barman left the older woman and came to meet me. "Welcome to the new Jack's," he said. "The bar's the same, but the people are all different. What can I get you?"

"What have you got?" The vinyl-covered padded stool looked tempting, but I put my foot on the rail and leaned against the scarred wooden bar instead.

"We've gone through all the fancy imports already," the barman said, gesticulating with his bottle. "We've got the usual big-name domestics, plus a few odds and ends of microbrews left."

I might be investigating what happened to Doug Tander, but nobody was going to write me up for a drink on the job. "Strohs."

"Old-fashioned hometown boy." The barman retrieved a can and a glass. "Not enough power to keep it cold proper, but the cooler's got a bit of chill."

The bottle sucked the warmth from my hand. "Cold enough," I said, twisting the top. "Thanks."

"I'm Jack." His face hung from his skull, with pouchy cheeks making lines from his nose and an extra chin draped beneath his jaw. His two front teeth were missing.

"Kevin Holtzmann," I said. Dammit.

"What brings you here?"

I rolled the beer around my mouth, savoring the grassy flavor, then a hint of corn. Swallowed. "Looking for anyone who's talked to Doug Tander lately."

"Doug? Yeah, he's been around. Don't think I've seen him today, though."

I nodded, studying the blue-and-red label on the brown bottle. "Do you have any idea where else he would have spent his time?"

Jack studied me for a moment. "I thought I recognized you," he said slowly, his voice sinking softer. "You're a cop."

"Detective." Another automatic answer my mouth made without consulting my brain.

Jack nodded, keeping his voice low. "You know, I don't know what we need with dee-tectives right now. We got enough trouble. I don't wanna fight, but we don't even know what the law is right now."

"Fair enough." Rather than drain the bottle, I set it gently on the bar. "Tell me, Jack. What are you doing here?"

He shrugged. "What else am I supposed to do? We've got more beer than we can drink, unless a whole bunch more people show up."

I picked up the bottle, swallowed another mouthful. Just because we had enough beer for a small town, didn't mean I had to be the one to drink it all. "You might as well pour drinks, because you've got to do something. I get it." I lowered my own voice. "And Doug's kid knocked on my door a couple hours ago. She's worried about her dad." *In ways I can't even* begin *to explain.* "What else am I supposed to do, but figure out what happened?"

Jack winced.

"I don't really care how late you stay open," I said in a more conversational tone. "I don't care who or what you serve. We all got enough trouble, you'll have to keep your own conscience clean. But a kid's asked me for help, and I'd like to sleep tonight."

"Ah, you don't have ta beat me up with it." Jack chewed his tongue. "Most of the time he talks about getting the main power back on.

Spends a lot of time down at the power station. Talks about time limits. I guess if he don't get the grid back on line in another few weeks, it'll never come back. And solar kind of sucks in the winter. He talks with Teresa and Jesse a bunch, I know." His beer waved vaguely at the women. "Been over at Winchester Mall to see Legacy, of course. And I know he saw Acceptance."

Legacy. That word had bubbled up from my subconscious for days. I wasn't the only one. The whole point of this investigation was to stop digging into myself. "Acceptance?"

Jack nodded. "Over at the church. Saint Michael's. Came back with the shit scared out of him, it took half a dozen shots to get him talking again. But what'd you expect?"

I gave a tight smile. "Appreciate it."

"You haven't seen Acceptance?"

I shook my head. "What is it?"

Jack gazed absently over my shoulder. "He's—damn. He's how screwed we are. Check him out and come back. I'll save half a bottle of vodka for you. The good stuff, if you're back soon." He paused. "If'n you decide to come back at all."

Chapter 9

JACK SEEMED to stare past the dark neon decorations and through bar's dark wood walls, a thousand yard stare that sent disturbing flutters through my stomach. His vagueness annoyed me, but if I didn't want to describe Doug's transformation, how could I blame Jack for not wanting to talk about something? I took a long pull of the beer. "Thank you, sir."

He nodded, his thoughts apparently still in the church down the road. "Hope you come on back. We all gotta hang together." He shook his head, drained his bottle, and moved down the bar to the tired man in overalls.

I took a moment, one foot resting on the brass rail beneath the bar, to scribble in my notebook, then tapped the pen against the pad as if thinking. The taste of the beer lingered in my throat, but a fine taint of scouring powder and bleach crept along at the edges of my nose. At the edge of my vision, near the dart board, a young woman laughed and rested her hand lightly against the guy's bicep for a moment. He replaced the darts in the rack and guided her to a dim wooden booth in the back. But my ears focused on the two women Jack had indicated.

"—do something," one said, her voice a gentle drawl.

"Oh, we'll do something," the other said, cutting each word off at the end. "The whole world's out there. We can be anyone, do anything. I always wanted to see Australia."

I peered in the mirror behind the bar. The blonde said "It's not there anymore," and I turned back to my notebook before she realized I'd looked at her.

"It's there. They burned it to glass, but it's there."

"Why go?"

"Why not?" the brunette said. "We don't have to put up with

anybody's bullshit anymore. We just learn to fly a plane and go. Or forget Australia. Europe. I bet the Eiffel Tower's still there. Haven't you ever wanted to see Paris? Or London? Heck, how about Chicago?"

They both fell silent. I glanced in the mirror in time to see the brunette say "Shit. I forgot."

"S'okay." In the mirror, I caught them both raising glasses.

I picked up my half-empty bottle and walked slowly over to the two women. "Excuse me, ladies." Always start a conversation with strangers by calling them *ladies*, or *ma'am*, or *sir*, or something respectful. It helps set a civil tone for what might be a difficult discussion. "Can I have a minute?"

The brunette looked up. Her hair was cut short enough to almost stand in spikes, with hints of gray scattered among the edges. The battered glasses perched on her nose made her green eyes look overly large. "Who's asking?" She wanted to go to Australia, and still bit the ends off every word as if each had offended her.

"Name's Kevin Holtzmann." I spun a chair from another table around and sat, placing my beer on the table at my elbow.

"Jesse McComas."

"Teresa Umber." Teresa looked in her early twenties, shoulder-length blond hair and narrow shoulders. Her skin was so pale my eyes could trace the underlying veins and tendons.

I nodded. "A pleasure to meet you. I'm checking on Doug Tander. Heard you were friends of his."

Jesse snorted. "Hardly."

"Oh?"

Teresa said "Jesse used to work for Doug, before."

"And you didn't get along?" I said.

"Oh, I did my job all right," Jesse said. "Did all kinds of prep for him, measured, ordered parts. He had the license, but I knew my way around a breaker box better than he did. I wrapped wire with him, swapped out parts, even did a bunch of work without him. But—" She raised her mug and took a drink.

"Does she look like a hooker to you?" Teresa said.

Hookers look like everyone else. "I wouldn't say so."

Jesse set her mug back down. "I'm not one of these types who screams whenever a man's eyes hit her boobs, and I don't mind the boss asking me out. Hell, you can try again if you put some thought into it." She let her gaze roll down my body until they bounced off my wedding ring, and renewed anger infused her voice. "But you don't keep swatting me on the ass or telling me to break out the kneepads and mouthwash every time there's some good news."

"Huh," I said. "And you put up with that?"

"Needed the work," she said. "Had me some trouble when I was a kid, you know? The sort of stuff that gives you a record. Jobs are—*were*—hard to get, and he paid. I made damn sure he paid."

Teresa snorted. "Girl power."

"Girl has-you-over-a-barrel power." Jesse's finger drew a line across a ring of condensation. "He liked having a woman work for him, and nobody else would put up with his bullshit."

"Sounds like a jerk," I said.

"Why do you want to know, anyway?" Teresa said.

"His daughter's worried about him. I told her I'd go looking."

"He has a daughter?" Teresa said.

"His wife died a few years back," Jesse said. "Fallout fever."

I grimaced. Strontium and cesium and the like had almost depopulated the North Pacific coast. Not much had hit Michigan, but people still traveled back then.

"He wasn't so bad when she was alive," Teresa said. "Cut off his supply of woman, though, and he turns into a right asshole."

"So what did he want to talk to you about?" I asked.

Jesse shook her head. "Going back to work for him."

"Like that was going to happen," Teresa said with a chuckle. "What's going on with him?"

"His daughter asked me to find out," I said.

"Isn't he kicking around here?" Jesse said.

Here was where I should pull out my badge and deflect the question. But my badge wasn't my badge and even it was lying in a desert, amidst the bloody tatters of Kevin's clothes. My hand ached where the leather case should be denting my skin. I took a drink, buying time to think. I might not be an officer of the law anymore, but feeling like a cop brought life with it. The trick was making them want to answer my questions. "Not anymore," I finally said.

"What happened?" Jesse said.

"I can't say. I'm a detective with the Frayville PD," I said. "I mean, not anymore. But his daughter asked me to find out what happened. That means I can't go telling everybody everything yet."

"You're a cop?" Jesse said incredulously.

Teresa snorted.

"That's funny?" I said.

Jesse shook her head. "We had trouble with someone right after."

"We ran him off," Teresa said. "But that's when we could have really used a cop."

I shook my head. "I'm sorry about that."

"You weren't there," Jesse said.

"Not your fault," Teresa said. "But what's with Doug? Is he dead?" A strange light shone in her face, an alloy of anticipation and maybe… hunger?

I shook my head. "I—No, he's not dead. But I don't think you'll be seeing him around."

"I don't think we can die," Jesse said. "We've already died."

"You died," Teresa said.

"You surrendered," Jesse said.

"Wasn't much choice."

A tight coil of nausea in my stomach suddenly snapped free, and my nose resurrected the smells of cordite and blood. I clamped my jaw shut to keep my face still.

Jesse caught my expression. "Who gave you the offer?"

I took a deep breath. "A man I put away for murder. Many murders."

"I didn't know the couple that asked me," Jesse said. "They said I could surrender and it would go easier." She stared into her beer. "I fought. I mean, I hit one of them, punched her right in the nose, and my hand just stuck to her head."

"We had guns," I said. "They didn't bother the one that took m—*Kevin*."

"You've got that too?" Jesse said. She reached out and squeezed my hand, her calloused and bony fingers clammy with condensation from her glass. The kind touch sent a disproportionate shudder down my spine. "My name isn't Jesse," she said quietly. "But Jesse's not using her name anymore, and what the hell am I supposed to call myself?"

"We could all go by Bruce," Teresa said brightly.

I tightened my lips.

Jesse squeezed my hand again and let go.

I said "We need acceptance, one way or another."

"Acceptance sucks," Teresa said. "Our way is better."

"Join together," Jesse said. "Fight what makes you mad."

"Support each other, the way people should," Teresa said.

"But Acceptance is right out," Jesse said.

I took a deep breath. "I think I missed part of this conversation."

Teresa furrowed her brow. "I don't think anyone who hooks up with Acceptance comes out right. I haven't heard of anyone who joins and walks away. It's a one-way trip."

"Oh," I said. "The guy in the church." Two months ago, I would have caught that right away. Stress, or change? Maybe I wasn't just a copy of Kevin—maybe I was a *lousy* copy, not as sharp or observant.

"What did you think I was talking about?" Jesse said.

"Acceptance," I said. "Just…accepting what happened. Why would anyone call themselves Acceptance, anyway?"

Jesse studied my face again. "You haven't been out long, have you?"

I felt my face flush. Jesse had just dissolved any hope I had of remaining an authority figure at the moment. "No. I stayed in my house for… a while."

"Don't be embarrassed," Jesse said. "I bet half the houses around here have people in them afraid to come out. We're living in PTSD nation. Hide under the stairs and wear a tinfoil hat."

Teresa said "If Jesse didn't live across the hall, I'd probably still be in my apartment."

I shook my head. Finding out what happened to Tander was a thin film of purpose atop a swirling pool of tarry emotion. I could sink into that morass and never surface again. A deep breath filled my nose with stale beer and fryer grease, with a lingering aroma of flowery perfume from one of the women. "So—Doug. When was the last time you saw him?"

"Yesterday," Teresa said. "He was here yesterday for Terry's dinner."

"Terry?" I said.

Jesse smirked. "*Jack*. Terry always wanted to own a bar named after him. He said it was easier to change his name than change the sign outside. He does dinner every night, cleaning out the deep freeze before everything thaws. He'll throw together breakfast too, if you ask."

I pursed my lips. "The freezer still works?"

"Yeah, I know," Teresa said. "The beer's not cold. He says there's enough solar for the deep freeze or the fridge, not both."

How many freezers were still running out there? And how long would canned food stay good? "Did you talk to Doug last night?"

"He tried to guilt trip me," Jesse said. "Bitched about how hard the work was on his own. He said he needs to get the substation out by Elm Street working. I guess he tried to talk to Acceptance about getting help, but got blown off."

"He was trying to tell you he was desperate," Teresa said.

"He could start by saying he'd keep his hands to himself," Jesse said.

"Should I have told him that for you?" Teresa said.

"No, hon." Jesse patted Teresa's arm. "You did just right. He didn't listen."

"Any other people he might have talked to?" I said.

Jesse shook her head.

Teresa said "Power station... Acceptance... He shot the shit around here, would talk to anyone. But pretty much, he was about electricity and beer. And women."

"Thanks for your time, Miss Umber, McComas." I drained the last of my beer and stood, leaving the empty bottle on the bar as I passed. Doug had been in a few places, but the one that disturbed everyone seemed to be Acceptance. Time to see who—or what—that was.

Chapter 10

SAINT MICHAEL'S Church stood two blocks south of Jack's, looming between a desolate school playground and an abandoned chain drugstore with a rusty pickup truck jammed halfway through the front doors. Centuries ago our ancestors had piled massive stone blocks taller than the trees, mounted real stained glass in the windows, hung a real bell in the belfry, and nailed two-inch-thick oak planks to the floor. Folks back then knew how to build to outlast the end of the world. Their success gave me a grim smile for half a second.

The vast asphalt parking lot on the north side of the building sizzled in the sun and launched a faint oily smell onto the breeze. A shabby greenhouse of knotty lumber and sun-scorched plastic sheeting covered the south parking lot, one of the many built by the whole Building the Future public works and civil defense project after they'd nuked the south. The church's massive dark wood front doors both stood open, propped with antique bricks.

I remembered the bricks. Julie, Sheila, and I had all walked down to Main Street when they had to dig up and rebuild the whole road, and at the bottommost layer they'd found these oversize red bricks. Julie had wanted one—she'd been, what, nine? She could hardly lift the brick, and I—*Kevin*—had spent the whole walk home waiting to swoop in and haul it for her, but she staggered beneath it all the way home. They'd used the brick as a doorstop too, for the deck off the back of the house.

I stopped to steady myself. The memory was so strong, I felt the hazy shadows of Julie and Sheila beside me. I clenched my jaw, focused on the darkened doorway before me, and marched into Saint Michael's.

Inside the church felt at least fifteen degrees cooler than outside, with quiet humid air that sent a shiver up my arms and down my back. My eyes quickly adjusted to the inside, which was only dim in comparison to the brilliant sunshine outside. The vestibule had been swept recently, and the cork bulletin board cleared of all the usual flyers and schedules, the detritus of a vanishing echo. A waft of incense hovered in the air, and the doors into the main hall still showed rows of hard wooden pews and a massive gilt cross mounted on the wall above the pulpit. Someone had cleaned, but not tried to rebuild.

"Hello!" A woman's voice, from further in.

"Hello," I said. I didn't see anyone in the main hall.

"Come on in. Take a load off."

I peered into the hall, looking for some hint on why Jesse and Teresa didn't like Acceptance, why Jack had said he'd save me a bottle. The stained glass windows depicting Bible scenes cast blue and red and green shadows across the pews. The pulpit was enameled a brilliant white, with fine golden trim. A massive wooden wheel chandelier hung from the arched ceiling, and the pipes of an organ loomed on a balcony across from the pulpit. I had never attended service here, but I imagined it would be impressive as anything with the right priest.

A college-age woman popped out of the sacristy. "Come on in."

Maybe Acceptance had moved out. "Thanks." The polished oak floor gently groaned beneath my feet as I passed between the pews.

The woman walked forward to meet me halfway. She carried a few extra pounds, not enough to ruin her figure. Her black hair hung past her shoulders, and shifted with its own static charge. Each finger carried a brightly colored gemstone ring that shattered the light into cheerful sparkles. "Welcome to Saint Michael's."

"So, are you the new pastor?" I said.

She stopped a couple yards short of me. "Call us Acceptance."

"I was told Acceptance was a man."

"We are."

The way she said *we* chilled me. "And female, too," I said slowly.

She nodded. "We welcome anyone. Anyone who needs us."

Standard procedure would have me ask about Doug. Everyone I'd spoken with today had a tendency to flinch, though. Alice had been afraid to talk to me. The people at Jack's had looked at me like I might be a monster. And I'd looked at them the same, because they might have been. This woman sounded like she was discussing next week's church potluck dinner, with no worries beyond whether that goofy parishioner would once again grace the picnic with his infamous cranberry-and-lime gelatin fluff. "What are you, a club?"

"Not at all." She spread her hand over the pew beside me. "Please, sit." She plopped down in the next pew forward and turned to face me, elbows and forearms resting on the polished wooden back.

"*My* name is Veronica Boxer," she said as I settled onto the hard seat. "I was a schoolteacher at Rivertown Elementary a couple of months ago. Third grade. This year I taught thirty-one wonderful children, and two evil ones."

I nodded.

"And you are Kevin Holtzmann, detective with the Frayville police department."

"I'm afraid I don't remember where we met," I said.

"*I* never met you," Veronica said. "But *we* did."

Before, Kevin would have decided that Veronica was intoxicated and treated her as such. After the vague hints at Jack's, though, her disjointed words chilled me rather than annoyed. "Would you care to explain?"

"Absolute took me while I was asleep," she said. "I remember waking up in the dark, knowing that I had a mission. I had to find people, people Absolute hadn't taken yet, and give them the choice. Absolute didn't want people to suffer, but I couldn't turn away. If they fought, I could change to take them. I could command the plants and animals Absolute had already taken. I could take people any way I wanted, any way I thought best, it just had to be done."

I froze. Absolute had taken Jared Collins earlier. Seized him, eaten him, spat out a duplicate. And somehow, Collins had tracked Kevin and Julie and Sheila across a thousand miles of road and desert and empty burning land.

Collins had been "motivated." Absolute had set him free to find and kill my family. Slow anger pooled in my head like molten glass, a translucent red fury that slowly oozed over my bones. Collins had wanted to kill me and torture those I loved—and Absolute had made that possible.

I jerked my attention back to Veronica. She quietly watched me with patient sympathy. "How much do you remember of what you did for Absolute?" she said.

"Not as much as you," I said. Snapshots flashed through my mind. Walking down a road. Peering through a mud-spattered windshield into an empty car. I'd been hunting for something. Had Absolute given me the same instructions? What had I been doing in the days I couldn't remember?

She nodded. "I decided to take my students."

My mouth fell open. Anger still sizzled inside me, but I hadn't expected Veronica to say that, especially not so bluntly.

"I remember the logic," she said quietly. "They trusted me. Absolute would take them anyway. I could make it easier on them. And I—" Her voice caught. "Some of them trusted me. Some of them screamed. Some of them ran. And I…took twenty-two young children for Absolute. I remember every one of them." A hint of a tear glistened in her eye.

I couldn't have told this story. I couldn't even respond to it.

"When Absolute released me, I was in the park. I walked over to a broken window. Grabbed a piece of glass out of the frame. And slashed my wrists. Hard. The long way."

Veronica sat with her arms folded over each other. I couldn't see the inside of her wrists, but her flesh held a healthy richness beneath her weak tan. She saw me looking and uncrossed her arms to reveal perfect pale wrists.

"The cuts closed themselves," she said. I expected her voice to tremble, but from her tone she could have been talking about a nice weekend relaxing at home. "I lost maybe a handful of blood, but I just stopped bleeding. I tried again, and watched the skin crawl shut. It didn't even hurt."

I glanced down at my own wrists. The idea of killing myself had rattled around my mind as I shuffled around Kevin's house, but it had never been more than a momentary impulse. I had the feeling that I *should* want to destroy myself. I should feel the urge to slash my wrists, eat a bullet, jump in front of a train. All I'd really felt was emptiness.

But I'd wondered if I could change my form, as I had vague memories of doing under Absolute's dominion. The answer seemed to be yes, at least part of the time. I couldn't look away from Veronica's face for more than a second, though. Her calm voice and appalling confession transfixed me.

"I heard a gunshot," she said. "Followed the sound. There was an old man lying in the road a couple blocks up. He'd put a pistol in his mouth and pulled the trigger. Blown out the back of his head. I grabbed the gun. Something made me wipe off the barrel—I mean, I was about to kill myself, but I didn't want his spit all over the gun." Tension crept into her voice. "That's when I saw his head closing back. The hole, that terrible pit in the back of his skull, just filled up. He sat up and screamed for God to forgive him."

"I was crying, too." Veronica's voice still quavered. "I told him that we hadn't had a choice. We were compelled to do what we did. I knew it was true—I didn't believe it for myself, but I believed it for him. I remembered too much of what I'd done. I'd never forgive myself. Never accept it."

"He grabbed me—just reaching out for comfort. And that's when it happened."

"What?" I asked. All the moisture had left my mouth. My tongue felt like wood. My breath fell still in my chest.

"We connected," she said. "I knew he understood what I'd done. He knew I had no choice. Just as I knew he had no choice. I felt his understanding, just as he felt mine."

"You read each other's mind?" I said.

Veronica shook her head. "Nothing that fancy. I felt his emotion. His hurt. He needed forgiveness, just as I did. We forgave each other. We've felt each other ever since. Alex is maybe a quarter-mile from here." She raised a hand to point north. "Mike and Mack are over that way. Mack is getting tired, but doesn't want to admit it, even though Mike knows. Danielle Clint—she's the one who met you before—is glad you're still alive. We can get a couple words through, like a name, if we really try. There's eighteen of us now." She raised her chin. "And every one of them is telling me that we didn't have a choice. Every one of them comforted me as I told you my story. They don't know what I'm thinking." The tension drained from her voice. "They only know that I'm hurt, and they want me to know that they accept me as I am. Together, we are Acceptance."

Revulsion knotted my innards. Cold sweat burst from my pores. I pressed myself against the back of the pew. If I'd been standing, I would have backed out of reach. Absolute might have compelled Veronica to do what she had, but flushing away the pain of it felt obscene.

"It's okay," she said. "We wouldn't take anyone by force. Only those who come to us."

I pushed the air out of my lungs, and forced another breath in. *Should have asked about Doug first.* I stilled my face. "Was Doug Tander one of you?"

"None of us are Doug Tander."

"Did you know him?"

"I didn't. We did." Veronica spoke distantly, as if studying print too small to read. "He did electrical work. Did an abduction—an *addition* for us. For Mick. Spare bedroom, a few years ago."

"Did you see him after?"

"He was here, of course. Everyone comes here, either looking for God or looking for us. He left without accepting anything." Her eyes focused on mine. "He was curious. You're here with purpose. You were a police officer." Veronica's tone became incisive. "Something is wrong."

"I'm investigating what happened to Tander."

"Is he dead?"

"You just said we can't die."

"We can die," Veronica said. "We just can't kill ourselves. That's not allowed."

"How do you know that?" I said.

"We haven't killed anyone, if that's what you ask. But we see a lot."

"No—the *allowed* bit."

Veronica shrugged with one shoulder. "Eighteen attempts. Eighteen failures. We don't have any inside knowledge there."

I needed to get back on track. "Did you see anyone with Tander?"

"No." Veronica studied my face. "You're holding onto that investigation like a life line. You're letting it pull you along. I can feel the pain coming off of you. What did you do?"

I didn't do it. Kevin did.

Veronica whispered, "What did you do?"

I jerked to my feet, careful not to touch her. *Keep your hands off my pain.* "Thanks for your time." Backing into the aisle, I said "If you hear anything about Doug, please let me know."

"You need help," Veronica said.

I took a step back, then another, one hand outstretched behind me to feel for obstructions. If she reached for me, I'd hit her—no, that would be a touch. I had shoes. A straight kick into the little woman's gut to knock her back, and I'd turn and run like hell.

"When it's too much," she said, "come back."

Another step backwards.

"We're here for you."

Step. My fingers jammed against a pew. I veered back into the aisle.

"When you can't live with yourself anymore," she said, "we will help you."

Three long backward steps, then I turned and bolted from the church.

Chapter 11

I fled Saint Michael's church, leaping down the stone stairs to the sidewalk. The green grass that had so worried me on the walk with Alice? I dashed right over it, to the concrete strip of Frayville's Main Street without looking for traffic, and didn't slow down through a quarter of a mile of silent storefronts and abandoned cars. Drifting through the house for ten days had killed my cardio, though, and when I couldn't ignore the hard hammering of my heart in my ears or the tightness at the back of my throat, when the bright copper taste of oxygen debt threatened to gag me, I coasted to a halt and rested my hands on my knees as I gulped air.

Acceptance hadn't given me any reason to doubt her. Him? Them? Whichever. I'd seen flesh rearrange itself and plants lashing around like loose fire hoses. I'd berated myself endlessly for killing Sheila and Julie, but how much worse could it be?

Twenty-two children, eaten and duplicated by the shadow of one schoolteacher. Of course she'd tried to kill herself. What had made her connect so deeply with another person, though? Would just touching her cause that connection to form? And what would that connection be like? To always have a pillow of comforting reassurance around you, telling you that everything was okay, you were okay, you'd done only what you had to do? What could, or would, someone do with that kind of support?

Veronica had touched someone and formed a mental bond without trying. Without knowing what she was doing.

What other booby traps had Absolute wired into us? What would happen if I shook a hand? Ate something that looked like an apple? And why had Absolute devoured us all, only to release us as near-perfect duplicates of who we had been?

Immortal Clay

I forced deep breaths until my gut unknotted, then stood straight and looked around. A pizza place with a window of dark neon, a gift shop that looked like the owner had closed for lunch, a sandwich shop with a broken front window. Another willow heavy with melon-like fruits. Frayville had a lot of willows, to suck up the high water table. The air tasted fresh, like unmown prairie. In the last few years I'd learned to ignore the sharp tang of diesel fumes, but their absence made the familiar street feel even more alien.

Veronica—no, Acceptance—hadn't told me anything about Doug, but had told me I needed to be careful. Had I touched anyone today? Not Alice, or Jack. Wait—Jesse had touched me, in the bar. I remembered the cool comfort of her squeezing my arm. My brain hadn't melded into hers. Why had Veronica melted into Acceptance?

I didn't know what triggered that coalescence. Until someone figured that out, I'd have to avoid touching anyone. My hand on someone's sleeve might be okay, but not on their arm.

The sun suddenly glared out from behind a passing cloud. I squinted and raised a hand to protect my eyes. Half the day gone, and I still had to check out the power substation and the Winchester Mall. Someone in either place might know Tander. Both were a few miles down Main Street, in opposite directions. I needed transportation. A few cars sat in angle-in parking spaces, but they all looked like gasoline models. Gasoline had been difficult enough to get, once the Building The Future civil defense project really got going.

A few hundred yards up the road, I saw the back end of a Frayville police cruiser angled across the empty sidewalk. Most of our vehicles had been diesel, and an official vehicle might make people more inclined to talk to me. Or shoot at me. I walked.

The cruiser had hit the brick front of an orthodontist's office, but the bumper didn't even look dented. Maybe the driver had taken his foot off the brake and the car had just coasted into the wall? I circled the dusty car, peering through the tinted windows. Nobody inside. Shotgun clamped in the rack. Computer console neatly closed. Two unused official-issue flamethrowers in the back seat, straps facing the rear doors so the officers could easily slip into them.

I opened the driver's door.

The rags of a shredded uniform jacket, stained with dried blood, filled the seat.

I could imagine what happened. Frayville police worked in pairs. The officers had seen something. The driver had stopped the car. Something attacked him.

The car windows and shell were intact. The attacker had already been inside the vehicle.

Only one set of rags.

Absolute had owned one of the officers before the duo got in the car. At some signal, the copy had attacked his partner. Collins had offered me a choice, but apparently active duty police officers who hadn't abandoned their duties didn't get that choice.

I swallowed my nausea and reached for the tattered clothing. My hands itched to sort through the shreds and find the name stitched above the breast pocket. We only had thirty police officers. I'd know the name. But what good would it do? Instead, I glanced around. No trash can in sight. I dragged the rags out and flung them over the open door, to the sidewalk by the red brick office building.

My fingers found the digital key still plugged into the dashboard. The motor's roar shattered Frayville's silence.

Chapter 12

I EXPECTED more wrecked cars, perhaps even blocked intersections, but instead coasted at a steady ten miles an hour down a desolate Main Street. A gentle breeze came through the cruiser's open windows, and my left elbow automatically found its accustomed place on the top of the door as my right hand gripped the top of the vinyl-covered steering wheel. I could have been on patrol again, and the comfort of routine kept trying to settle into me.

But even my patrols in the earliest part of my career, in the most desolate parts of Detroit, hadn't been this empty. The scene felt alien, as if the world had changed instead of me. I passed the chunky City Hall building, surrounded by lush green park, and didn't see anyone in the playground or on the ball diamond. Someone had broken the glass door of the Smoke Shoppe and pried away the bars behind it. As I rolled past, a gawky man in jeans and a T-shirt ducked out of the door, a carton of Marlboros in each hand.

My hand reached automatically for the siren. Years of practice told me to call it in, roll up on him, flip the siren, and get him in the back of the car. Restraining myself made my teeth ache. I couldn't arrest him. Inside a month, we'd all be looting everything to survive.

And even getting eaten alive and duplicated won't alter some people's nicotine habits.

When the space between the stores grew greater, and greasy family restaurants and grimy plumbing supply houses replaced gift shops and pharmacies, I turned off Main Street and into the industrial district, passing streets named Pine and Oak and Cherry Blossom populated with soulless cinderblock and aluminum "multipurpose" buildings. The Elm Street power substation lurked between two hills across from a meatpacking plant, a compound fifty yards on a side cordoned off with chain link fence topped with concertina wire. The high tension lines marching overhead dropped heavy cables to a tall metal frame filled with cylindrical transformers the size of coffins. The gate in the chain-link fence hung open, the rusty padlock gleaming with a fresh cut, and a corroded pickup truck sat just outside the opening.

I parked the cruiser just outside the gate and walked in. "Hello! Anyone here?"

Metal clattered and clanged against metal behind a truck-sized steel box in the middle of the compound. A man swore. Another clang, then silence for a few seconds before an elderly man pushing a great big paunch lumbered out from behind the box. A few wisps of white hair surrounded his wrinkled face, and his eyes looked freakishly huge through thick glasses.

"Good afternoon, sir," I said.

"What're you doing here?" The man's voice was still deep, but had thinned with age.

"I'm Kevin Holtzmann, with Frayville PD." I gave a little jerk. "Previously with, that is."

"If you're with the police," the man said in a thick Southern drawl, "maybe you could tell me where my flunky is."

"Your flunky? Who would that be?"

"Doug. Doug Tander."

"He won't be coming." Over the years I'd developed rituals and phrases for telling people about a death, but I didn't even know how to describe Doug's condition. "His daughter asked me to check into what happened to him."

He grimaced. "Dammit."

"And who are you, sir?"

"Name's Chad. Chad Brockett." He spoke slowly, as if he individually hand-crafted each word.

"Mind if I ask what you're doing inside the substation?"

"I'm gonna get the main power back on." His parchment-thin transparent skin looked too fragile to protect the veins and sinews beneath. "Doug was helping me."

"Doug was helping you?" Doug had told the folks at Jack's that he was restoring the power.

"Yep. Fifty years at Edison. Lineman. Substation technician. Everything. If it can fry you, I can fix it. Retired up here few years ago."

"Isn't the power generated elsewhere?"

"Used to be Saint Mary's. There's a little coal plant booster here. Few miles west."

"Why were the two of you starting here?"

"Main plant's fine. Nobody fueled it, it'll start right back up." Chad jerked a thumb over his shoulder. "This here feeds the hospital. All them industrial buildings, too. What happened to Doug?"

"He's hurt."

Chad digested that. "Someone did him in." It wasn't a question.

"Why do you say that?"

"Because you're here. Because he was too big on himself. What you think you're gonna do about it?"

I shrugged. "His daughter asked me to figure it out."

"What you gonna do." Chad shook his head. "He was here yesterday. Step-down transformers are blown. Right pain to replace, gotta have the tools and big muscle on top of the know-how. You see anybody wants to get things going again, you send 'em my way."

"I can do that. How late did Doug stay here?"

"Maybe five, six. Said he had to go, he had a hot date."

"Did he say with who?"

"Nope. Said it was a young lady, shaped like this." Chad's hands approximated an hourglass. "Figured he'd show with his nads kicked up to his chin or wouldn't show at all."

I should have checked Doug's bedroom for evidence, damn it. Had Doug transformed during his date? Or had he changed afterwards? Every police officer knew the importance of searching the crime scene, but I'd fled like a frightened kid. I should have interrogated Acceptance further while I was at it. I had to stop panicking about every little weirdness, like a group mind of suicidal people or a heat-seeking three-foot penis. Or melons, or alien grass, or, or, or, or…

I'd learned to look at a bloody murder scene in dank housing projects without puking, usually. I'd learn to take these things as well.

"I don't suppose he said her name?" I said.

"Don't think he right cared about her name. Said he was hooking up after dinner."

Behind me, someone screamed in pain. Someone else shouted obscenities. A clatter and a crash turned my head.

An inhuman screech punched my ears with a voice like several throats in one, bass and high-pitched and glass scraping metal. I'd heard that sound before, in Australian security video footage transmitted just before the North nuked the South. When a normal-looking man changed his shape on a crowded train platform and lashed out at everything in sight with feathery tendrils.

I ran.

Chapter 13

THE PACKING plant was a dismal two-story cinderblock cube, with a jolly sign out front that read "Billy Butcher Meats." The flaking white rolldown garage door looked solidly closed, but a hefty metal pail propped open the conventional door beside it. Someone inside shouted wordlessly in pain. Heart in my throat, I bolted in.

Gleaming, shallow metal buckets dangled chest high from chains that ran up to overhead tracks. The fluorescent lights were off, but scattered solar-driven emergency lights drizzled bright pools and drove away the worst of the shadows. The stench of old blood and guano glazed the air. Near a metal table along one wall, two people jerked and flailed at each other. I barely noticed them before focusing on the severed chicken head crawling across the floor at me.

The beak led, with eyes right behind and above it. Red feathers ringed the eyes and formed a crest around the beak. Fine black and white feathers mottled the rest of the head and the few inches of neck, ending in a ragged red stump. The two red dangling wattles beneath its jaw had stiffened into stumpy limbs that scuttled madly, dragging the head towards me, leaving a smeared trail of blood from the severed neck.

I stepped back into the doorway and, without looking, kicked away the bucket holding the door open. The bucket clattered against the concrete. I stepped back into the building and yanked the door shut seconds before the chicken head reached freedom.

The head stopped short. It hissed, more like a snake than a chicken, but with an unnerving bass note far too deep and strong to come from a severed head. How can something without lungs hiss? Its mad eyes studied me, then it veered right and scuttled for the shadows pooled along the rolldown door.

Another unearthly screech dragged my attention back to the flailing people. A burly flame-haired man struggled to keep hold of a creature about the size of a bowling ball, his arms fully extended and his head turned to the side. An insane array of senseless limbs flailed around his arms and face. An older woman waved a hatchet in one hand, and flapped the other at the man.

"Kill it!" the man shouted.

"Put it down!" she said, with increasing hysteria. "Drop it! Drop it so I can hit it!"

They shuffled around each other, the woman searching for a clear swing, making a tentative hatchet strike and pulling short every time

The man danced to keep the whirling claws and paws and tentacles from lashing his face. A talon at the end of a scaly spaghetti leg slashed across his forehead. He screeched and blinked blood from his eyes. "Just kill the damn thing!"

I glanced around. *There*. I dashed toward a four-foot-tall steel drum near a long metal table. When I leaned into it, the barrel resisted for a moment, then the caster wheels mounted on the bottom squealed into motion. It rolled on rusted-out axles, but it rolled. In the seconds I needed to get the drum over to the struggling pair, the man had suffered another few slashes. Thin, whiplike burns marked the woman's hands and forearms. I grinned when I saw she still held the hatchet.

"In here," I screamed. "Drop it in here."

The man lurched towards the bucket and whipped his arms forward, but the creature stayed with him. That's when I saw the tentacles circling his arms. He wasn't holding the creature, it held him. The woman waved the hatchet at the man's hands, then pulled her swing short, cursing.

I grabbed an empty rectangular meat pan off another bench, turned it upside down, raised it above my head, and brought it down hard on the creature's top side. The impact echoed up my arms, its empty gong almost swallowed by the creature's screech of rage.

The man screamed again, but the tentacles around his arms slipped an inch.

I tightened my grip and swung again.

Again.

Immortal Clay

On my fourth strike, the tentacles slipped from the man's right forearm. He jerked the arm back, blood simmering in the narrow gashes all along his skin. The creature dropped halfway into the darkness of the steel drum.

The tentacle around his left arm slipped another inch, then squeezed more tightly. He shouted, flailing, trying to shake it off.

"Hold still!" the woman said. She reached out with the hatchet, gauged her position for half a second, then chopped.

The hatchet bit tentacle, then the inside of the drum. A metallic hollow boom drowned the creature's screeches and echoed through the room. The hatchet ricocheted off the inside of the drum, and the tentacle snapped.

The creature plunged into the empty drum, hitting with an echoing thud. The metal drum transformed its screech into a chorus of rage. The stench of fresh guano flooded up from the darkness, almost making me cough.

The man grabbed at the tentacle still around his arm. It thrashed blindly, and he clawed it from his arm and flung it into the drum, disgust twisting his features.

We all panted for a moment. Then the man said "So, Becky." He wheezed in another breath. "Any more bright ideas?"

"Oh, you are *not* calling this my idea."

"You said, take it to the packing plant, everything we need's right there."

"You're the one who wanted chicken!"

"I just wanted it, you made me go over to Gulliver's."

"*Made* you?" She jabbed a forefinger into the man's chest. "Once I reminded you about Gulliver's hens, you would'n've stopped if I'd kneecapped you."

Another alien screech drowned out his retort. I peered into the drum.

A joint here. A talon there. I could see, *maybe*, where it had been a chicken. A headless chicken, that is. The legs had grown longer, with extra joints, and the talons thicker. The wings had absorbed their feathers and lengthened into tentacles that lashed against the inside of the cage. White speckles against black feathers intimated at its original coat, but its body seemed too small for its skin. The extra mass for the legs had to come from somewhere, I supposed. The stump of its neck stood upright, a raw red meaty mouth, waving in my general direction. Unnerving as it was, at least it wasn't a giant penis.

"That's an ugly sucker," the man said.

"You said it." I looked up into his angular, bony face, and started to extend a hand, but stopped myself short. Took a step to the side. Held out my hand, not reaching over the open top of the drum. "Name's Kevin. Kevin Holtzmann."

"Mick. This here's Becky." His hard and calloused grip felt reassuring, then my guts fell away. I'd decided not to touch anyone, and here I was shaking hands. Old habits would get me killed. I dropped his hand.

"Thanks for helping him out," Becky said.

"Now don't start that again," Mick said.

"We're all figuring out the rules," I said. "Let me guess. You brought a chicken. Took the hatchet. Chopped off its head. And everything went to hell."

"Pretty much," Becky said.

"Someone had to try a chicken sometime," I said. "Now we know."

"Thank you," Mick said.

"Fried chicken would be good," Becky said.

The thing in the drum screeched again.

"I wanna know why it didn't work," Mick said. "It shoulda."

"The rules have changed," I said, my pulse almost back to normal.

"But Larry killed that deer," Becky said.

"Really?" I said.

"If he can shoot a deer, I ought to be able to chop a chicken," Becky said.

"What did he shoot it with?" I asked.

".30-.30," Mick said, squeezing his shirt over his arms. Blood seeped around his fingers.

"Let's see that," I said. "Have you seen a first-aid kit around here?"

"Back that way," Mick said.

"Becky, would you?" I asked. "Mick, have a seat, let's see what the Headless Chicken from Hell did to you."

Mick's wounds were shallow, long friction burns from finely feathered tentacles. I had him wash in the sink with foaming fruit-scented soap as I took a moment and studied the kit's tube of antibiotic ointment. Did we have to worry about germs? Or would the viruses grow tentacles and tear their way into us? I decided to err on the side of the instructions and dabbed the bandages before wrapping them around each of Mick's forearms, careful to touch only the dressings and not his skin or blood. When I finished, Mick looked like he wore medieval bracers.

"Normally," I said as I tore off a strip of cloth tape, "I'd tell you to get to your doctor or the urgent care."

Becky snorted.

"I don't think they're open right now, though," I said, "so just keep them clean. And if you find a doctor, ask him to check you out."

Mick flexed his fingers. "Thanks, man."

"Serve and protect, that's the rule."

Becky's eyebrows raised. "You a cop?"

"Was," I said.

Mick studied me for a moment. "Yeah," he said. "We all was a lot of things."

I'd always taken pride in being a police officer. Earning the uniform had given me strength and self-assurance I lacked as a kid. Earning my detective's shield had been the proudest moment of my professional life. I knew there were cops who abused their position. That made people distrust all of us. But I couldn't help wondering: until a couple weeks ago, how many people had wanted to give me that distrusting look but didn't dare?

I forced a cheer I didn't feel into my voice. "Still, it's a new start?" My smile felt fake. "We all have to go on from here. No badges, sure, but no records either."

Becky peered into the drum, eliciting another shriek from the monster fowl. The cry echoed through the cinderblock room.

Somewhere further back, I heard the hiss of the ambulatory severed head.

"One interesting thing," I said. "Did you notice the tentacles?"

Mick gave me the "you are an idiot" expression and hefted his hands.

"No, I mean, on the—the chicken," I said. "Right now."

"It's still got them," Becky said. "I ain't goin' in for a closer look."

"But you cut one off," I said. "It's not crawling around loose in there, is it?"

She peered over the edge. "Don't see it."

"So where did it go?" I said.

Mick jumped to his feet and glanced all around the floor.

"I think it's back on the chicken," I said.

"Whoa," Becky said, staring down into the drum. "You know, I think you're right."

I looked back to the darker corners of the room. "I bet if you threw the head in there, it'd reattach. It might even turn back into a chicken."

Mick chuckled. "Now that'd be cool."

Becky said "What good would that do?"

I shrugged. "You cut the head off, it went nuts. But your friend Larry shot a deer, and it died?"

"Yep," Mick said. "We had venison last couple nights. He's trying to eat it before it turns. Never seen a man try to eat a whole deer in three days before."

"Tell him to take it to Jack's downtown," I said. "There's a guy there cooking dinner for everyone, bet he'd love some fresh meat."

Mick nodded. "I'll do that."

"But what about this chicken?" Becky said.

"Shoot something, it dies. Cut off the head, it goes nuts." I shrugged. "If you put the head back in, and it turns back into a chicken...I'd shoot it."

Mick snorted.

I felt pretty good. I'd acted rather than reacted. I'd noticed the reattached tentacle, and thought things through. A police officer wouldn't have suggested a civilian shoot anything, but I felt confident that Mick knew his way around a gun. Whatever he'd been before, he might as well be a chicken rancher now. "Whatever you do, let me know how it comes out," I said. "Fried chicken sounds good to me, too. And I'm not going to cut off a head—"

I stopped, dread filling my bones.

Doug's head wasn't strictly cut off. But shriveled was almost the same thing.

And what, exactly, would a giant heat-seeking penis running on instinct look for?

And who was the closest woman?

"Alice," I whispered.

Chapter 14

PART OF me said that people might be out walking and I should drive slowly through the empty streets, but the cruiser's siren worked. So did the lights. I rocketed back into downtown in about five minutes, palms sweating, only killing the lightshow a couple blocks from Doug's home.

From the front, the Tander home looked like the family had been on vacation for a couple weeks. With the uncut lawn and absence of motion, it only needed flyers stuffed inside the screen door to complete the illusion. I listened carefully, but heard only scattered birdsong and, from a distance, water running. I circled around to the back, but found the doorwall snugly closed.

Check the obvious first. I trotted over to the cheerfully decorated Tudor house next door and pushed the bell. Voices raised in surprise, then feet tromped across a hardwood floor.

Ceren stood about up to my chin, a heavyset girl with hair dyed an impossibly intense, almost metallic navy blue. "Yeah?"

"Is Alice still here?"

"Sure." Alice stepped into view from around the corner. "Mr. Holtzmann? Any news?"

A knot came loose in my chest. "Not yet, but I haven't had much time. Listen, have you gone back into your house?"

"No, not yet. I still need to get some clothes and stuff? We were going to go, a little later."

"Do *not* go back to your house alone. I need to check things out, then I'll come back and escort you to pack a suitcase. Understand?"

"Sure." She peered past me. "Was that your car with the sirens?"

I nodded.

"Is Dad that dangerous?"

I shook my head. "I don't know. I saw some things that made me think he might be. But I still don't know. Not for certain. You stay here until I come back for you."

Ceren crossed her arms and looked effortlessly unimpressed. Teenagers.

"Will you be all right?" Alice said.

"I'm fine. I'm a police officer. This is what I do, remember?"

Alice nodded.

"Stay in there, I'll be back."

As the door shut I caught Ceren saying "What a hardass."

Nothing for it now but to go into Tander's house. I'd screwed up last time, but my brain had started firing again. If Tander's body tried to lash out like the beheaded chicken, I'd shoot it and run. I thought about the flamethrowers in the back of the cruiser, but decided to leave them alone. Frayville didn't have a fire department anymore. I didn't know if any firemen had even survived. One good burst from the flamethrower could spark a blaze that would eat the whole block. Instead, I took a deep breath and walked through the doorwall at the back of the house into the darkened family room.

Closing the doorwall cut off even the soft sounds of wind and water. The sun's journey west brought light through the windows, cutting the gloom from the family room. The faint smells of lemon polish and pine cleaner drifted into my nose. I listened as hard as I could for any sounds of motion as I walked through the photo-laden house up to Doug's bedroom.

I'd slammed the lightweight bedroom door behind me earlier. The flimsy latch had caught, keeping it closed. Fortunately. I half-feared I'd need to search the house for a free range dick. The knob felt cold in my hand. I took a deep breath and pushed in.

Doug now sat on the edge of the bed. He still lay on his back, but it seemed that his arms and legs had both shrunken and shifted. His heels sat on the edge of the mattress, arches and toes hanging over empty space, knees pointed at the lazily turning ceiling fan. He almost looked perched, except for the penis pointed straight at the door, like a tank ready to fire.

I took another deep breath. Doug's animal musk filled my nose and lungs, resurrecting Kevin's memories of drug dens and hourly hotel rooms. The bodies in those places had the decency to stop moving.

The damn thing was staring at me.

I glared at it.

It wobbled.

Enough. You have a job to do. Would it freak you out so much if he'd turned into a giant toe? Or an elbow? An ear? I steeled myself and swept the room with my eyes. A spacious master bedroom, three walls in pale green, the wall opposite the door in a slightly darker green, with a bright white ceiling and enameled white crown molding, the paint perhaps a year or two old. The taller dark wood dresser gleamed, and its top held only a small glass tray with a couple tiny glass bottles atop it. The matching long but short dresser looked both dustier and more cluttered, with sticks of deodorant, folded clothes, and random clutter from emptied pockets piled atop it. A double-width folding closet door filled the wall beside the door. In the far corner, I glimpsed a master bath through a slightly open door.

I walked in, holding half my attention on Doug, the rest on the room. The bottles on the taller dresser were Yves St Laurent perfume, centered on a dust-free glass tray etched in a rose motif. Standing sideways, so as to not turn my back on Doug, I tugged the top drawer open. Women's underwear, socks, and bras, all neatly folded, all with signs of wear.

Doug's wife had died a few years ago. He kept her dresser cleaner than his own, and still kept her clothes. I felt a suddenly flash of sympathy. What would I do with Sheila's belongings? Julie's?

A knot blocked my throat. I slammed the dresser drawer shut.

Thick soft shag carpet covered the floor. Clothes lay scattered across the carpet. A mechanic's uniform shirt, tossed in the corner. A pair of pants with the underwear still compressed inside as if someone had pushed them straight down and stepped out of the whole ensemble. One sock near the dresser, the other near the bed. One man's clothing, hurriedly removed, probably with his enthusiastic cooperation.

The bed was stripped to a fitted sheet. I circled around the other side, keenly aware of Doug's penis turning to follow. It didn't swivel freely, but seemed able to pivot within a little less than a half-circle. It couldn't point straight to the side, but it sure tried. I had to still my guts before I could turn my back on it.

A top sheet and blankets formed a tangled heap on the far side of the bed. Someone had knocked the squat lamp off the dark wood bedside table, sending the shade against the wall and shattering the bulb into a constellation of shards and powder. Some kind of vigorous activity. Maybe a fight, maybe rambunctious sex. No way to tell yet.

I edged towards the bathroom door, a few degrees past the point where Doug's penis could stare at me.

Doug shifted his weight.

I froze.

The shoulder sockets now swiveled backwards, so that when the stubby arms straightened he raised off the bed. His thighs had shrunk, but the shins lengthened, so he could stand on his hands and feet with his belly towards the ceiling. My first thought was of a circus contortionist with broken bones. The deflated head drooped behind, flatter, almost like a beaver's tail with a sketch of a deformed human face on the top. Doug took a careful step, then another, swiveling in place atop the bed to until that ridiculous dick stared straight at me again.

I ducked into the master bathroom and slammed the door, trying to focus on how absurd he looked rather than how horrifying. If anything was left of Doug in that body, if a human being in there was really aware of me, he would have tried to communicate—say, tap on the headboard. With a hand. Did he have much left in the way of hands? I'd seen stubby little things at the ends of his misshapen, asymmetric arms, with tiny toes at the end. Maybe enough finger for balance, but not enough for grasping. Any doubts I had evaporated.

The *person* who was named Doug, the womanizer who couldn't bear to get rid of his wife's belongings or take down the family pictures, a sexist who'd pitched in to try to get the main power on, had died. A badly sketched caricature remained.

The pink-and-white tiled bathroom smelled of strong soap, bleach, and pine tar shampoo. I'd wandered around like a zombie. It seemed that Doug had reacted to his release by making the toilet, sink, and steam shower sparkle. Maybe having his daughter depending on him had made a difference.

The room wasn't perfectly clean, however. A fluffy red towel hung from the rack beside the shower. No—not a towel, a bath sheet maybe, a ridiculously big towel. The outside was dry, but the inner folds were still damp. In this warm but not hot weather, with Michigan's humidity, that towel had probably been used last night. Scattered hard water spots mottled the inside of the cool glass shower stall. Someone had bathed here, not too long ago. Doug? Or someone else?

I stood on the lever to lift the lid of the steel trash can, and caught a flash of black cloth. I smiled, reached in, and pulled out a bra. The metal hooks on the back had been twisted, and one of the straps had snapped. Wearing this would require dedication as well as indifference to metal points poking between the shoulder blades—it was trash now.

Had this been a real murder, we would have brought in a group of crime scene technicians from down in Flint. One of them would have lifted the bra with a pen, put it in a bag, taken it to the lab, told me that it belonged to a left-handed prostitute known for exotic tricks with her earlobes and a rare blood type, then laughed at my face and handed me the real, useless report. I clenched my jaw, lifted the bra distastefully, and sniffed.

Baby powder. A faint floral perfume. And an animal musk similar to what filled the bedroom.

Doug had been here with a woman. They had sex. She'd picked up her clothes, come in here, taken a shower, discarded the unwearable bra, and worn everything else when she left.

And some time during or after the encounter, Doug had changed.

Missus 36D might well have been the last person to see Doug alive. Or the first to see him dead.

A heavy thud from the bedroom broke my thoughts. I whirled and yanked the bedroom door open.

Doug had hopped down off the bed. He still faced the bathroom door, but now lurked only a yard or so away. The four-inch-wide penis head hung maybe a foot from me, bobbing around waist height. The slit at the end hung slightly open, exposing the pink walls of the urethra.

Getting out should be simple. All I had to do was step forward, shove the penis aside, and walk past. I'd checked crumpled bodies for life, even when a dozen bullet holes and the still pool of blood told me it was impossible. I'd held people as they puked their guts out. I'd trod through sewage to pursue a refugee.

But this…no way in hell was I going to handle that—thing. It had no teeth. No blood. I could only imagine what Doug's body would do if it could throw out a few tentacles to catch me like the chicken had caught Mick.

I grabbed the damp red bath towel. Held it before me. Smothered an urge to shout "Toro! Toro! Ole!"

The penis wobbled.

In self-defense training, they tell you to not let the opponent's weapon hypnotize you. You never stare at the gun or the knife, you watch the torso of the person holding it. But I couldn't take my eyes off that round wrinkled crimson dome.

At the very tip, a mass of pearlescent goo swelled from the slit.

"Oh, *hell* no," I said, flinging the towel over the penis.

It swung down, then bounced right back up.

I dashed past.

A cloth-covered limb struck me in the arm.

I quelled a bubble of nausea, then I was past, out the bedroom door. I took two steps into the hall, bounced back, grabbed the door handle, and slammed the door behind me. The door bounced this time, but I caught the handle and pulled it shut. I don't think I've heard a sweeter sound than that latch clicking home.

Hatchets wouldn't work? Maybe I'd get some people to stand by with hoses. Break out the flamethrower.

I made myself walk slowly down the stairs, willing my heart to stop bouncing against my ribs and my breath to slow to a mere pant. What could that thing have done, really? I didn't have an opening big enough for it. Nobody did. It had to be running on reflex, pure mindless instinct, a fractured set of programming from whatever stem of a brain remained.

But I was not letting Alice into this house. Escorted or not.

Then my feet touched the main floor, and I let myself trot down the hall, through the living room, and out the doorwall.

I took two steps across the patio into the afternoon sun, gratefully sucking down a lungful of pine-scented air.

A heavy blunt weight crashed against the back of my head.

I toppled forward onto the paving stones. Brick patio stones scraped skin from my palms as I caught myself.

A bitter voice: "We don't need anyone digging up trouble."
I turned my head.
Someone stood over me. Legs widely spread, braced for heavy work. Arms overhead.
A baseball bat. Swinging down.
Concussion against my temple.
Black-and-white static screeching inside my skull.
Fade to gray.
Nothing.

Chapter 15

MY FOREHEAD and temple had gone numb. The rest of me hurt.

I didn't want to wake up. Nothingness felt better than any part of me.

Steps shuffled nearby.

A damp cloth moved over my forehead.

I lay on something irregularly flat. Hard edges gouged my back.

Blood pounded in my ears, my hands, my feet.

Feet. Something under my feet, raising them. My unsupported knees ached.

My pulse pounded all through me. The pain had a sound, and it crashed cymbals and bass drums along my spine in rhythm with my heartbeat but a fraction of a second behind the beat.

My jaw hung open. My tongue had dried out. I pulled my mouth shut and worked my tongue around. It obeyed instructions, but sluggishly. I didn't blame it.

"Can you hear me?"

A young girl's voice—Julie?

Another young girl's voice. "I think he's done." Was that Julie?

No. Julie was dead. I'd blown her skull apart.

My eyes clanged open and my arms crashed out around me, heedless of the pulsing pain and the sunlight burning my retinas. Something wet and slimy fell off my head.

"Maybe not." The young girl sat above me, looking down. No, not above me, in a lawn chair beside me, her legs curled beneath her. *Ceren.* Her name was Ceren.

I lay on my back, on the Tander's back patio. A couple of jackets lay over me, and a thin rough pad supported and protected my head. I coughed, tasting my own blood and bile.

"Don't move," Alice said. "Hang on a minute." She put the self-cooling chemical compress back against the side of my head. I felt another one beneath my head. "Do you know your name?"

I'm the one who should be checking orientation. "Kevin Holtzmann," I said. My tongue moved thickly, and my voice wavered like it had been out drinking while I lay unconscious. "We're in Frayville, Michigan, the best fishing and hunting tourism town on this side of the state. And Absolute was president until he shoved us all overboard."

Alice paused, looking up at Ceren. "Okay? What do you think? An ambulance should be here by now."

Ambulance? What was she talking about?

They'd done all the rights things for shock. Smart kids.

"The Girl Scout thing quits right before the good stuff," Ceren said.

My hand reached up to explore the new lump astride my temple.

"You're gonna have a nasty lump there," Ceren said. "And there was some blood on the back of your head. Was it Alice's dad?"

"Ceren!" Alice said. "Dad wouldn't do this!"

"No." *You are so right—he'd do something completely different.* "Someone else." *Someone who didn't want me investigating what Doug had become.*

"Do you think you can drink something?" Alice said. "Gatorade?"

I nodded. She brought a straw to my lips. Those electrolyte drinks only taste good when you need them. The flavor lit my mouth like fireworks, and my parched mouth and throat seemed to absorb the icy drink directly without letting any reach my stomach.

I made myself stop after a third gulp, washing the last bit around my mouth before swallowing. No teeth seemed loose, and I didn't taste any fresh blood. "Thanks."

"Sure?" Alice seemed at a loss. "I'm all out of first aid right about now. The class said call 911, wait for help."

"You did good." I shifted my feet to the side, and they fell to the ground. The pounding didn't get worse, so I held the compress to my head with one hand and levered the other beneath me.

"But I *know* you shouldn't be getting up," Alice said.

"No ambulance is coming," I said. "Unless you know something I don't." I shuddered in a deep breath and pushed myself to a sitting position. The back of my neck took a fresh chill, as air hit the damp skin beneath the second cold pack. The throbbing within my skull sloshed around and a faint gray fuzz snuck in around the edges of my vision. Then I was upright—still sitting, one arm locked as a brace, but upright.

Ceren shook her head. "You're crazy. It isn't raining yet, so you can stay right there. Don't get up."

I looked up. The blue sky had turned gray. What had seemed like bright sunlight at first was nothing more than directionless diffusion through thickening clouds. The rain might hold off for hours, but eventually we'd get soaked.

"What time is it?" I said.

"You left a few hours ago," Alice said. "I don't know what time it is, though."

"You told her to stay inside," Ceren said, "so I came out looking for you."

Teenagers. Always looking for a way around the rules.

"What happened?" Alice said.

"You need to both stay out of the house," I said.

"What's going on?" Ceren said.

I drew a deep breath. My chest shook with the effort. The second breath came more steadily. I wished my nerve felt as steady. "Alice. I'm sorry. Your dad isn't going to get better."

The hints of color faded from her face, and her eyes closed. She shook. Tears squeezed through her black eyelashes. Ceren bounced out of her chair and grabbed Alice in a strong hug. Alice completely broke down then, sobbing uncontrollably.

My head throbbed harder and my soul, if I had one, resonated with her grief. It didn't matter that the Alice in front of me was a copy of the original Alice, or that the Doug that had died upstairs was a duplicate of an already dead Doug. Teenagers are all emotion, even alien pod-people teenagers, and the Alice in front of me had all the pain of losing her father. Her sobs rose and fell, an irregular counterpoint to the pulsing pain in my head.

I rolled to my hands and knees, freezing when everything around me went gray. I closed my eyes and focused on my breathing until the lawn stopped swirling. Then I grabbed the back of Ceren's abandoned lawn chair and dragged myself to my feet.

Ceren shot a look of pure malice over Alice's shoulder.

I stepped forward and put a hand on Alice's shoulder, careful to only touch her on the cloth of her blouse. She was distraught, I hurt everywhere, and I certainly didn't need any kind of mental merging with a fourteen year old girl. "I'm sorry."

Ceren's glare sharpened.

Alice's choked down a gasp. "It's okay. I mean—I knew he had to be dead—not dead, but what? Gone? That's not my dad. My dad isn't that. He's—no, he's not. I mean…"

"It's okay," I said. "Losing your dad is hard." Losing a parent is its own unique flavor of hard. *But not as bitter as losing a child.* My teeth creaked against each other.

Alice's breath hitched and stopped. Slow, heavy tears rolled down her cheeks again. I stood helplessly by, holding onto the chair for balance and pressing the cold compress against my forehead. Eventually, Ceren guided her to my chair and helped her sit. Alice huddled in a quiet ball of misery, her breath returning to normal but her cheeks still soaked in tears.

"So," Ceren said, "what now?"

"Don't go in the house," I said. "For any reason. Nobody. Alice, I'll get you some clothes."

"I can take her shopping," Ceren said. "The mall's just a couple miles from here, I have the keys to Mom's car."

"Do you have a driver's license?" I said.

She raised her eyebrows. "Please! Like we need a license to drive now."

My teeth clenched again. "I can't stop you from driving," I said. "But have you ever driven before?"

"I watched Mom drive all the time."

"Not the same. You want to learn to drive, I'll find time to teach you. But for right now, please don't."

She scowled. "I can drive just fine."

"I'm sure you can." I forced another deep breath, to stabilize my mind more than my body. "Look, we're all on our own now. You're going to need transportation. I'm sure you'd be careful, but you've got whoever that idiot is racing that Corvette up and down. He's the one who really scares me."

"Timmy," Alice said.

Ceren looked away. "Whatever."

"Please," I said.

"Fine!" Ceren said. "We'll bike up there. Happy?"

I wanted Alice and Ceren to stay inside Ceren's house, preferably with the door locked and barricaded. I became a cop to help the innocent, and for all Ceren's posing she was still an innocent, naïve kid. A girl in her position might feel that tough-chick posturing was a decent coping strategy, but it would bring her trouble she couldn't yet handle. I'd seen it too many times. "Thank you," I said. "Again—please—don't go into this house."

"We won't go in," Alice said quietly. "Not until you say so."

Another deep breath. "I'll take you in. Eventually. But I have to figure out what happened first."

Alice's face quivered. "What happened to you?"

"Someone jumped me when I came out of your house." I massaged the back of my neck.

"You got mugged?" Ceren said. "Sweet."

"Not sweet," I said. "Baseball bat." I knew exactly what a head blow could do. My brain would bounce against the inside of my skull, causing coup and contracoup injuries. Maybe a subdural hematoma, or even a fractured skull. I probed my head again, but the bone seemed intact. "How long was I out?"

Ceren pulled her phone out of her pocket. "It's right after five now."

I'd come back, when, about one? Two, maybe? I'd lain unconscious for three or four hours.

I gave Alice a thin smile, hoping it showed more confidence than I felt. "We still need to know what happened to your dad. I'm not letting this lie."

Alice closed her eyes. Her chin shook. "Thanks."

I carefully walked to an empty lawn chair, trying to not tip my head and spill out the pressurized fluid that filled my skull. Sitting down eased my aches, but my throat still felt parched. The drink bottle sat a few feet away, but I didn't dare bend over to pick it up. "Ceren, could you grab that drink for me?"

Ceren scowled, but scooted over to lift it to my outstretched hand.

"Thanks." It still tasted cold, almost succulent. "Alice, when was the last time you talked to your dad?"

"Yesterday." She wiped her cheek with the back of her hand. "Before he went out for the day."

"Did he say anything about plans for the day?"

"He was going to work on the power. There's a cranky old guy who's been helping him. He said he'd be home later. Asked if I could hang with Ceren, and he'd knock on the door when he got home."

"But he never came over to get you?"

Alice looked at the ground. "He didn't always come home before."

Definitely not reaching for Parent of the Year. "So you went looking for him this morning?"

She nodded. "He usually comes—*came*—" Alice's voice caught. She drew a shaky breath. "Home in the morning. I crashed with Ceren. Dad doesn't mind. Ceren's folks don't mind either."

In the edge of my vision, Ceren's arms crossed more tightly, and her jaw set. Her whole defense-through-aggression posture grew more thorns. I could see Ceren's parents discussing Alice after her mother's death and deciding to play surrogate mother. We might have turned half the planet to glass, but neighbors still try to help. Once Doug flaked out too, Ceren's parents obviously tried to make Alice feel welcome in their home. They'd tried to step up.

Now Ceren didn't have parents, either.

"Did he say anything to you about having a date?" I asked.

Alice shook her head. "No."

Ceren said "He was always telling Dad about women he'd hooked up with, but only when Alice wasn't around. Or Mom."

"Okay." I closed my aching eyes. "I'm getting somewhere. The person who hit me told me to stop poking into this."

"Did you see who it was?" Ceren said, leaning towards me.

"Yeah. I—I..."

I stopped dead.

I couldn't remember who had hit me. "Ah, dang it."

"What?" Alice said.

I'd turned my head. Looked up.

I clearly remembered the baseball bat, but not the person swinging it at me.

"I saw him," I said.

"Who was it?" Ceren said. "We'll go thump 'em."

I clenched my jaw, making my pulse pound in my face again. The cold-induced numbness on my temple began to seep away, replaced by a bright warmth that hinted at the painful heat to come. My memory held the bat's descent in sharp detail. The face above it? Gone. I remembered seeing someone. I remembered recognizing him. But the face proper wasn't even a blur. I remembered the color black—not brown skin, but actual black.

"I saw him, but—I can't remember him."

"What?" Alice said.

"Short-term memory loss. Head injury." I massaged the crown of my head, as if I could squish my brain into revealing the face.

Ceren snorted, flinging her hands into the air. "Oh, awesome."

I felt like screaming. Instead, I took another sip. The brain has specialized parts for recognizing and remembering faces, and I'd had more than one assault victim with this exact problem. Either the face would come to me, or it wouldn't. My stomach felt simultaneously queasy and empty. What had I eaten today? When Alice knocked this morning, I hadn't eaten yet. I had vague memories of a can of soup yesterday. And today I'd faced down Doug—twice—helped subdue a headless chicken, walked all over the neighborhood.

"So, here's what we'll do," I said.

Alice looked up. Ceren raised an eyebrow at me.

"First, ibuprofen." I set the empty drink bottle down on the table. "Then I'm taking you two to dinner. Ceren, maybe driving has to wait. But how do you feel about going to a bar?"

Chapter 16

CEREN BROUGHT pills out of her house to the patio where I sprawled in the lawn chair, thrusting the brown bottles at me as if daring me to object. In front of the kids, I had to look like I was in charge. I took the bottles one at a time, carefully so my fingers wouldn't shake. Ibuprofen, acetaminophen, and hydrocodone.

"Don't need these yet." I handed the hydrocodone back. "Hang on to them, though. One day you'll be really glad." We'd figure out how to get food, but opiates would be more difficult to acquire. Could you even grow poppies around here? The garden around the patio had flowers, but nothing like poppies. Would we have time and energy for the effort, or seeds? I weighed the other two bottles in my hands, then popped the acetaminophen and dry-swallowed three pills. Would painkillers still work on us? "Thanks."

"No problem." Ceren clenched the bottles in the crook of her arm. "If we're going to dinner, we need to get dressed." Apparently blue jeans and a metaldub concert T-shirt weren't appropriate bar wear. "Come on, Alice, I have some stuff you can wear."

Alice gave me a questioning look.

I shook my hand. "Go on, I'm fine. I need to let this stuff kick in before we walk down to Jack's."

Once they left I sat quietly in the chair, waiting for the pressure and aching to subside. The red brick patio behind the Tander home felt peaceful. A wall of lilacs at the edge of the patio both separated the property from the neighbors and scented the breeze. Two robins chased each other into the oak tree at the back end of the property, leaving me with only outraged chirps and rustling branches as they jockeyed for dominance. For a moment, I studied the moss growing between the patio bricks underfoot. It looked like moss, at least. The giant penis lurking invisibly behind the curtains of the upper floor window seemed part of a different world, but the moss was exactly as alien as the overblown genitalia.

I couldn't remember who had hit me. What else had the blow scrambled? I pulled my notebook from my pocket, found my pen, and took notes. The broken bra, black, size 36D. Doug claiming he'd been fixing the substation, old man Chad Beckett claiming he'd been in charge. I believed Chad, but I'd never hear Doug's perspective. Becky and Mick, fearless chicken killers. By the time I wrote down *baseball bat*, the pounding in my head had receded to a distant throb and it hardly hurt to hold the pen.

After finishing I sat quietly, eyes closed, trying to rest until Alice and Ceren returned.

They came back more quickly than I expected. Alice wore the same jeans she had before, but now had an orange frilly blouse with a neck that cut a little too deeply. Ceren wore pale blue slacks and a sleeveless shirt the same color. Both had too much makeup on and wore a sickly sweet perfume I'd smelled on any number of young ladies trying to act grown up. I think they sell—*sold*—it at those little-girl jewelry shops in the mall. Kevin had bought more than one bottle for Julie, all with names like *Rainbows* or *Unicorns* or *Pop Star of the Season*.

The girls stopped about ten feet in front of me. Alice's mouth was a thin line of defiance under eyes that hoped for approval. Ceren crossed her arms and stared, daring me to criticize.

If Julie had come out dressed like that, I would have sent her back upstairs to wash off half the perfume and add clothes up to the top of her neck. Just how many social mores did I feel like enforcing, and on who? I studied them for a moment, then said, "You ready?"

"Yes," Ceren said. Alice nodded.

"Okay, then." Was I *in loco parentis*? If not me, who? Would Ceren's parents ever show up? No matter what they wore, I'd have to watch them. If a sleazeball sniffed around them I'd interject a sharp pointy elbow into the conversation, with malice aforethought. Absolute had duplicated people like serial killer Jared Collins, so he'd probably brought back the garden-variety scumbags as well. Anyone could show up at Jack's for dinner.

Ceren looked disappointed and Alice nervous as I heaved myself out of my chair. "Let's go."

Walking seemed to help, loosening joints and easing sore muscles. My head cleared further as we paced down the center of the empty street, surrounded by hollow homes. How many of those houses had people inside, too shell-shocked to emerge? I had remained inside until Alice pounded on my door. Maybe we should do a door-to-door survey. Over the next few weeks, hunger would drive people out. Jack's dinners might get pretty crowded.

At least until the food ran out.

The bright sun still hurt my eyes, but thick clouds passed before it more and more. And the day had advanced far enough that the trees cast shade all the way into the road. Frayville had a lot of trees. Absolute had put most of them back.

We passed another willow at the corner of Horse Stall and Holiday. Heavy soccer-ball melons dragged the branches down towards the ground. Maybe we had food. After seeing the chicken, however, I wasn't about to pick one, let alone eat it. Not until I was really, *really* hungry, and maybe not even then.

Ceren trotted ahead of us. "Come on, old man."

I smiled despite myself. "Old man? Come closer, kid, so I can whack you with my cane."

Alice chuckled. Not because it was funny, but because we'd had so much darkness that anything even slightly lighter rated a laugh.

This afternoon, Jack's had seemed like one more facade in a string of empty storefronts lining Main Street. On this second visit, however, the brick front and the backlit sign seemed more welcoming. Four more cars sat around it, civilian models fueled by hoarded gasoline. The difference had to be in my brain. After seeing dozens of empty stores, my soul lifted just from knowing that people gathered here.

Something like people, that is.

The closest thing to people we would ever have.

Chapter 17

"YOU MEANT a real bar," Ceren said as I led them to the narrow door of Jack's.

"What did you think I meant?" I kept my voice light and amused, trying to lie my headache away. The girls both raised my spirits and drove nails into my aching head.

"Dad called Applebee's a bar. It's a restaurant with booze."

"Jack cooks at night." Jesse had said that Jack's real name was Terry—I should have written that down. "I haven't tried it, but why not?"

I opened the door and released a cacophony.

The bar had felt crowded before, but now two dozen people filled the tables and booths, all talking loudly. Dark wood swallowed most of the light, but the polish cast some of it back into the air. The air carried a thick, spicy, meaty aroma that I couldn't quite place—a little too earthy to be Italian, but carrying a lot of the same spice and tomato scent, with a sharpness cutting through it.

I recognized the two men sitting closest to the door. Hulking Eric Hayward drove trucks down at the DPW, salt in the winter and mulch in the summer, and the drain cleaning team in between. He wasn't known for smarts, but he'd always been solid and reliable. Vince diCarlo sat across from him, just as tall as Eric but so skinny I'd always expected his neck to snap under the weight of his head. Vince cleaned the station at night. Not a cop, but the first person Kevin really knew that I'd seen. I—*Kevin* talked with Vince every morning, exchanging jokes, bringing him a fresh donut or cup of coffee every few weeks just to say thanks.

Always thank the janitor, the waiter, and the receptionist. *Always.*

The sight of Vince stopped me. He seemed like a splinter of normality thrust into the flesh of an impossible world. He should be leaning on the locker room doorframe, asking how Julie was doing. His presence in this impossible place made my head whirl.

Alice bumped into my back.

Vince looked up and smiled. "Hey, Kevin!"

Eric said, "Detective Holtzmann, right?"

I took a deep breath. "Ex," I said. I wasn't sure if it was ex-detective or ex-Holtzmann.

"Not sure why we needed a detective before," Vince said with a smirk. "Dunno why anything should change now."

I stepped in, Alice and Ceren right behind me.

"Haven't seen you here before," Eric said.

"First night," I said.

Eric nodded. "We're, like, the welcoming committee." He jerked a thumb over his shoulder. "Get a bowl from the counter, Jack will fill it up for you. You wash your own dishes at the back. Leave dirty dishes, you don't get to come back."

"You have this all organized," I said.

Eric shrugged. "Jack had a couple dudes thought they'd pay with Visa. Started trouble when he laughed them off. I offered to bounce."

"Bouncer, huh? So, do we meet the dress code?"

Eric chuckled. "I don't know that I'd've let those two out dressed like that."

Ceren crossed her arms and raised her chin. "And what's wrong with it?"

"You're about ten years too young for that look, girl," Eric said.

Alice shifted her feet nervously.

"This is Alice," I said. "Ceren. They're with me. We're neighbors."

Eric studied them. "I'll make sure people know that."

I opened my mouth to thank him, but Ceren said "We can look out for ourselves."

"'Course you can," Vince said. "But Jack doesn't like trouble. Best if everyone knows not to start any."

"What, is Jack in charge now?" Ceren said. "He's the mayor or something?"

"Ceren," said Alice.

"Mayor was never in charge," Eric said. "Jack's the cook. You wanna eat? Or you want to find your own meal every night from now till doomsday?"

"Doomsday was a few weeks ago," I said.

Ceren snorted. One side of Eric's mouth twisted up.

"Best t'be polite," Vince said. "You don't want me t'use ma leet ninja skills to mess you folks up, do you?"

Alice forced a smile. "Oh, polite we can do."

Ceren said, "Until we can't."

Eric said "You need to be rude, you let me know." His sausage fingers rolled into a surprisingly tight fist. "I do rude pretty good. Doing rude would do me some good."

My stomach let out an unexpected rumble. "Thanks, guys. If you'll excuse us, I think my innards are about to rebel."

Eric held a hand aside as if to steer me.

Jack stood behind the darkly gleaming polished wood bar, wearing a white apron spotted with brown. A five gallon steel pot stood on a table beside him, steam rising from it. Four more big steel pots sat on a portable cooktop near the back door. The bar itself held stacked towers of melamine bowls, cups of water, and a row of canned beers.

"Officer Holtzmann," Jack said in a slow drawl. "Welcome to the Frayville Supper Club. If you've come for that bottle, you gotta wait til after the dinner rush."

Veronica Boxer's face rushed back to me, pale in the dim church, full of the calm certainty of her mental connection with the other people of Acceptance. *When you can't live with yourself anymore, we will help you live with Acceptance.* My pulse ratcheted back up. Jack saving that half bottle might be the most thoughtful thing anyone had done for me since I woke up. "Just dinner this time," I said through the acid in my gut. "What's on the menu?"

"Let's see…" Jack rubbed his chin. "We got…let me think here… chili…chili…and, if you're really hungry, there's chili."

I took a blue bowl from the stack. "I think it's chili, then."

"Good choice. Tabasco on the counter, leave the bottle there. Bread?"

"Sure."

"No sour cream, but the bread will soak up the burn if'n you need it."

"Thanks."

"And you, miss?"

Alice handed him a bowl. "The same?"

Ceren said, "Make it three." She tried to make her voice confident, like she belonged here, but didn't quite succeed.

Jack piled the rich chili high and added a warm roll the size of my fist. I considered grabbing a glass of water, but decided not to push my luck. I'd been hit in the head. If I reached the table without spilling dinner all over myself, I'd come back for a drink.

I scanned the room. Most of the tables had people at them, and I didn't know anyone. A month ago Frayville had a population of almost ten thousand, and if these few were all that Absolute had resurrected I was lucky to find Eric and Vince.

From a booth at the back of the room, Jesse waved.

I raised the hand holding the roll and gave a small smile. The battering I'd taken must not have hurt me as badly as I'd feared. My bruised skull ached at the motion, but I was lucky to escape without a bruised brain. With the two girls in tow, I weaved my way to the booth. "You have room for us, ladies?"

Jesse and Teresa sat on one side of a dark wooden booth. Teresa was pulling her bowl over to her side, and reached out to gather her silverware from the side she'd vacated. "We're making room," she said. She eyed the girls. "Grab an empty chair, put it at the end, we'll all fit."

I stood aside to let Alice and Ceren have the bench, put my dinner at the end of the table, and snagged an unused chair from a table where three men sat. "Thanks."

"Sure," Jesse said from her huddle against the plastered wall. Her chili bowl sat empty between her elbows, her hands cradling her jaw. In that shadowed corner, I couldn't see the gray salting her short spiky hair or the color of her eyes. "Any time, Kevin."

"This is Alice," I said. "Ceren."

"Pleased to meet you," Alice said.

"Pleased to meet anyone," Ceren said.

Teresa smirked. "I hear you."

Jesse said, "How's your investigation coming along?"

I felt Alice's eyes lock onto me. I picked up the roll and broke it in half. "Alice here is Doug's daughter." The bread wasn't quite fresh enough to steam, but the inside still tasted soft and warm and melted on my tongue.

"I'm sorry to hear about your dad," Teresa said.

"Sure am," said Jesse.

"What happened to him?" Teresa said.

Alice lowered her spoon without touching her chili. "He…he changed."

Jesse and Teresa glanced at each other. "Like Paul?" said Jesse.

"Who's Paul?" said Alice.

"He used to panhandle down at Main and River," said Teresa.

"*That* Paul?" Shock must have shown on my face. " He's around?" Ever since Paul Drennel came home from his hitch in the Middle East, entering a building made him scream in terror. He wore all his clothes even in the steaming humid bowels of summer, and scraped a living off the biggest intersection in town with an outstretched cup and a cardboard sign. Now and then he felt together enough to visit the shelter for a hot shower and a change of clothes, but most days and nights he remained outside. He wouldn't sleep in an empty cell, and wouldn't take more than a dollar or two. His VA benefits would have covered a place in a room and board, but Paul's damage wouldn't let him handle four walls—or even just a ceiling.

"You wouldn't recognize him," Jesse said.

"Go by the intersection," Teresa said. "He'll be happy to see you."

"I walked up there today," Jesse said. "He's still panhandling, though nobody's driving."

"It's worth the trip," said Teresa. "Bring him a dollar."

I'd driven the opposite direction today. "I'll do that."

"What else have you seen?" Ceren said, blowing on a spoonful of chili.

"Biked out to see Legacy today," Jesse said.

"That's a weird one," Teresa said. She nibbled at the crust of her roll.

"Haven't made it there yet," I said.

"Not as shithouse-rat-fucked as Acceptance," Jesse said, "but pretty damn weird. Fills most of the mall. There's a couple of geeks out there playing with it now. They've been living with the damned thing since they came out."

"They say it's the future," Teresa said. "Looks like petrified snot to me."

"Electric snot," said Jesse. "But they say they're learning things, about us."

I chewed, trying to clear my mouth to ask about Legacy. Before I could, Teresa said "I heard a cop car today. Was that you?"

"Afraid so," I said.

"What happened?" Jesse said.

"I…" I paused, thinking. "I had reason to worry about Doug."

"Why?"

I chewed my lip, pondering the headless chicken. "Have either of you had any meat? Fresh meat, that is?"

"Y'ever notice," Jesse said, "that when it comes to havin' a conversation, nobody can change the subject like a cop?"

"It's like he doesn't want to tell us anything," Teresa said.

"They take information," Jesse said, "but don't tell you a damn thing."

"Okay." I raised my hands. "Okay. You got me. Habit." I took a bite of chili. Peppers and beef exploded on my tongue, scattering cinders of cumin and garlic.

"So," Ceren said in horrified fascination, "what does fresh meat have to do with Alice's dad?"

"I was following up on Doug," I said, "and ran into a couple people who tried to cut the head off a chicken." Maybe I needed another piece of bread, to soften the chili's kick?

"And?" Ceren said.

I put my spoon down. My tongue tingled, but the burn didn't grow any worse. "The head ran away."

"No shit," Jesse said.

"The body went nuts, all tentacles and claws. I thought that headless chicken was going to kill Becky and—" *what was his name* "—and Mick. We finally bludgeoned it into an old metal drum."

"Wow," Ceren said.

"So. Have you had any fresh meat?"

"Don't think so," Jesse said. "If we did, Jack fed it to us."

"So what did that have to do with Doug?" Teresa asked.

I didn't want to say that Doug was also missing a brain. Not in front of Alice. I took another bite to delay. "I'm still trying to figure that out."

"You came racing into town," Jesse said, "sirens blastin' through the roof, and you're trying to figure it out?"

"I'm still investigating what happened to Doug," I said. "I really can't tell anyone what happened until I have a better idea myself."

"Afraid it'll cause panic in the streets?" Jesse said. "Aren't we past that?"

"Word gets around," I said. "If someone did this deliberately, I don't want them to know what I know. They might panic." *They might sneak up behind me with a baseball bat.*

"Look," Jesse said, "I get that. I'm not askin' for the details, but look, if someone's going around hurtin' people, I'd like to know what to look for."

"For our own safety," Teresa said.

"All I know is, it could happen to me," Jesse said.

Ceren snorted at Jesse. "Not likely."

I glared at her. "Ceren."

"What?" Ceren said.

"Please," I said.

"He turned into a cock!" Alice shouted.

Alice had dropped her spoon in her bowl, and fresh tears ran down her cheeks. "My dad's head vanished and he turned into a cock as big as me." Her whole body shook with anger. "A dick. Literally, okay? You wanted to know?" She shoved herself out of the booth. "Now you do." Then she ducked between two men and disappeared into the crowded bar.

Ceren suddenly looked very small. Embarrassment flushed her face.

Teresa and Jesse both looked stunned.

"Pardon me," I said, holding my voice very flat. "A hurt little girl needs my help."

Alice had slipped between two tables, whose occupants had interrupted their conversation to stare after her. I marched across the ceramic tile floor through the abruptly quiet room. I got to the front door while it was still swinging shut and set out after my dead daughter's last living friend.

Chapter 18

I SCANNED the street, scrambling to find Alice before she vanished. The line of one-story buildings cast shadows across the first two lanes of Main Street, leaving the other side glittering in the lowering sun. The flavor of Jack's chili still filled my nose, but I still caught hints of grass and hot asphalt. A group of three people walked down the sidewalk towards me, hands and arms gesticulating as they talked between themselves.

Alice hadn't gone far. She leaned with one arm against the oak tree in front of Jack's, quivering. Her chin was tucked to her chest, and her hair cascaded down to conceal her face. Her sobs made me feel like I'd breathed powdered glass.

I walked up next to her. "Alice?"

She didn't answer.

Teenage girls: more volatile than sweating gelignite. I made myself sound calm. "This sucks," I said. "There's no other way to say it. You're having a harder time than the rest of us. We all lost everyone. You, though—you get extra suckage. I'm sorry."

When she didn't answer, I put my hand on her shirt, over her shoulder.

Alice swirled with youthful speed, wrapping her arms around me and burying her tears in my tweed sport coat.

"Easy," I said. I instinctively wanted to stroke her hair, but remembering how Acceptance had formed with a touch, I settled for putting one arm around her and gently patting her shirt between her shoulders. "It's okay, kid. It's okay." She just shook harder.

The people coming up the street, two thirtysomething women each holding onto an arm of the man in the middle, fell silent as they came within hearing range. I caught sympathetic expressions from all three as they disappeared into Jack's. Alice kept sobbing, and I put my attention back on her. "I know, Alice. I know."

"Hey," Ceren said behind me.

I looked over my shoulder.

Ceren had lost her aggressive posture, leaving only a teenage girl. "Alice. Listen, I'm sorry. I shouldn't have—I mean, she was being—you need to—your dad—"

I nodded with a tight smile.

Alice looked up for half a moment, then reached one hand for Ceren and pulled her into our hug. I found myself with two girls hanging onto me, and each other, both crying. I put an arm around each and found myself making meaningless soothing sounds as I gently rocked them both.

Sometimes, all you can do is hold someone while they cry.

Eventually, Alice drew a shaky breath and pulled back a few inches. I immediately dropped my arms and stepped back. Her bright red face gleamed with tears, and a trail of snot traced a path from her nose over her lips.

Ceren grimaced. "Gross, girl. Here." She pulled a lacy handkerchief from a pants pocket. "Blow." As Alice mopped her face Ceren said, "Jesse and Teresa wanted to say they're sorry, too, but I told them to stay where they were until you damn well felt like talking to them, if you ever do, because it doesn't matter how sorry they are, you're the important one and they can go fuck themselves."

Alice blew her nose again. "Thanks."

"You okay?" I said.

"How okay can you be?" Alice forced a tremulous smile. "Nobody should ever be okay ever again, ever." She took a deep breath and ran her fingers through her hair. "But I'm hungry. Let's go see if they fed our leftovers to the dog."

"That's the girl," I said.

A few faces glanced up when we came back in, but nobody broke off their conversations for us. The hubbub made my head throb harder. Across the room, Teresa saw us and stood up from the booth, and hurried towards the bar. By the time we got to the booth, she had returned with a tray. "I had Jack throw your dishes in the microwave," she said, setting a steaming bowl in from of Alice. "Listen, honey, I'm sorry. I wanted to push Kevin here, because he's a cop and so he's a jerk. But you don't deserve that. I'm sorry about your dad."

"It's okay." Alice picked up the spoon. "Thanks."

Teresa nodded at me. "Back with the others in a minute."

Jesse said "Me too. Detective Kevin is a closemouthed bastard, but if anyone can find out what happened to your dad, he can do it."

Alice swallowed a mouthful of chili. "If he can't, I'll find out myself."

"I'm sure you can."

We ate in silence for a moment. As I scraped the last of the sauce from the bottom of my bowl I said, "So, the chicken."

"Yeah?" Jesse said.

"Becky cut off a tentacle with the hatchet. But when we threw the tentacle in with the rest of the body, it reattached."

"Coool," breathed Ceren.

Teresa's eyebrows arched. "That's…weird."

"I'd wondered if we can change," I said. "Now I'm wondering if we can reattach severed limbs."

"Whack off a finger and find out," said Jesse.

"On the other hand," I said, "they told me that a friend of theirs shot a deer and it died."

"Huh," Jesse said.

"Are they sure it died?" Alice said.

"They said they ate it," I said. "I didn't see it myself, though. And I did see the chicken. The point is, if you run over a squirrel, be careful. It might try to rip your face off."

Jesse and Teresa both looked serious, while Ceren looked thoughtful.

"And don't go cutting a squirrel in half to see what happens!" I said to Ceren.

She smirked. "Yes, Detective Holtzmann."

Detective Holtzmann. The words stabbed at me, and I fumbled my spoon into my empty dish to cover. "Anyone else done? Let me take these up."

"You gotta wash, then," Jesse said. "Let me give you a hand."

I scrubbed dishes in a washtub of lukewarm soapy water, handing them to Jesse to rinse in another tub and racking them to dry among a couple dozen others. Ceren and Alice still sat in the booth talking with Teresa, so I detoured to the bar for a glass of water.

I reached for another warm roll from the mound on the polished wood counter.

"Good evening, Officer Holtzmann," a familiar voice said behind me.

Chapter 19

THE WOMAN in a black dress and veiled face perched on the barstool, precisely where she'd sat during my visit this morning.

"Hello," I said. This second bread roll was warmer than my first. How was Jack baking at a bar and grill? A room jammed full of people, and he'd done five vats of chili and enough rolls to feed us all?

"I heard you wailing down the road this afternoon," the woman said.

I knew her voice. "I'm afraid you have the better of me," I said.

"I suppose I would," she said, brushing the veil with her long fingers. "I'm Rose." She must have caught my blank look. "Rose Friedman."

"Rose!" Rose Friedman lived half a block west of Kevin, in half of a duplex. She'd been Julie's kindergarten teacher, but had retired a year or so later because of her...heart? No, stomach, that was it. "How are you doing?"

"About as well as you might hope." She picked up a can of beer and whirled it in her hand, testing for lingering remnants. Finding it empty, she put it down in front of her. "I keep drinking, but it doesn't seem to do anything."

I remembered Rose at a block party several years ago, perched on the edge of a lawn chair, working on a glass of iced tea. The heat had shimmered up from the asphalt driveways, and we all had an extra bottle or two just to try to keep cool, but she'd politely refused even a single beer of her own. She'd told her students about the dangers of alcohol and drugs, claiming she never touched either. Now, she hid behind that veil and reached for a fresh can. "One for you?"

The base of my skull and my temple ached through the ibuprofen. "I better pass tonight, thanks."

"No reason to." Rose cracked the top of the can, deftly raised it beneath the veil and drank without catching the thin mesh or exposing her face or her hair.

I probed the back of my neck, triggering a dull surging throb. "Already killed enough brain cells today."

"Fair enough." Rose lowered the can. "You can do anything you want, young man. There's no reason for you to play cops and robbers. Why don't you find something better to do?"

The water in my glass tasted flat. "Like what?"

"Just about anything. Farming. Mechanic. Juggling." She chugged another mouthful. "I was a teacher. Raised two boys. Competition shooting on the weekends. Almost made the Olympics. Almost. Then I was a Red Hat lady. Toured the country by train." She drained the can and smacked it to the bar. "Now I'm going for alcoholic."

"Sounds like you might have had enough to drink."

"I'm sober as a stone." Rose pushed the can away. "That's what happens when the world ends. You can't pretend it hasn't."

"It's changed," I said.

"Any time now, Absolute is going to come along and pull us all back in." I got the sense she stared at me through the veil. The Rose I remembered wore an inexpensive French perfume, but all I smelled on her was chili and cheap beer.

"Maybe." I bit the crusty roll. Crumbs trickled from my lips. "But if you assume that, you might as well keep drinking."

"It's over," Rose said. "Stick with the past, you'll just get hurt more."

Sudden melancholy burned my gullet. "The past is all we've got." I turned to return to our table.

Rose reached for another can. "We don't have a past."

We have a past. It just isn't our past.

I weaved past an arguing group of college-age people, catching fragments of words. "Why would Absolute—" I didn't need any more of that conversation right now.

Jesse had joined the group around the jukebox, leaving Teresa with the girls. Teresa stood as I came back. "Thanks for dinner," she said. "I'll leave you to your dates."

I stood to the side, holding out an arm to usher her past. "You should have asked me out first."

Teresa nodded with half a smile.

I returned to the booth and settled in opposite Alice and Ceren. "Adequate dinner?"

Ceren nodded. "Better than my cooking."

"You do hot dogs," Alice said.

"*And* mac and cheese."

"We're out of mac and cheese."

"We're out of hot dogs, too."

"There's another pack in the freezer?"

"They're tofu dogs. Not a bit of real dog in them."

I leaned back into the wooden bench, folding my hands across my chest. They weren't my kids, but I still felt proud. Not everyone can substitute banter for bravery. "Sounds like you had it all covered, then."

"Chili was pretty decent, though," Ceren said.

"Good." I drained the water in my glass. I'd had a big bowl of chili, more than I usually ate, but my gut still felt empty. I hadn't had a proper meal in—in ever. Who knew what I'd eaten while Absolute held my reins? Since waking up in my living room, I'd only grazed on stale leftovers and the old cans of soup and whatnot from the cupboard. "I think I might check for seconds."

"Sure." Ceren raised her chin. "I think we're going to the dart game." A group of kids a few years older than Ceren and Alice clustered in the back of the room.

"Fine," I said. "Before you go, though—"

"You're not going to give us that lecture on being safe, are you?" Ceren said.

"You can take that as given," I said. "Someone has already gone after Doug. I don't want you to be next."

"We're fine," Alice said, scooting towards the edge of the booth.

"Do you know why your dad changed?" I said.

Alice stopped, her face taut, trapping Ceren in the booth.

"Do you?" I asked.

Alice shook her head.

"It might be something he did," I said. "Or something he knew. Someone he hurt. Or for gain. And on some on those, his attacker might come after you."

"I don't know anything," Alice said.

"You don't know what you know," I said, keeping my voice soft. "It might be as simple as your dad's bank card PIN number. I want the two of you to stay together. Stay where there's lots of people. Be home before dark."

"You're not going to make us stick with you?" Ceren said.

"If I'm going to figure this out, I can't stick with you. Normally, I'd tell you to stay home. Call a relative to stay with you. Post an officer outside your house. But either we all go to ground and stay there until the perp comes to us, or you lie low while I go hunting." I raised my water glass, realized it was empty, lowered it again. "So please. Stay with a group. Go home before dark."

"All right," Alice said.

I glanced at Ceren. She glared at me, then gave a single sharp nod.

"Thanks." I scooted out of the chair. "I'll be by your place tomorrow. Give you the latest." With any luck, Alice at least would spend the day at Ceren's waiting for me. I'd show up in time to take them to dinner. Then show up early the day after. Keep her guessing, encourage her to stay home. It was a jerk move, but I didn't have better.

Half a dozen bowls remained on the bar. I took one, met Jack's eye, and pointed my chin at the pot. "Any chance of seconds?"

"For our finest boy in blue?" Jack smirked. "Our *only* boy in blue?"

"Plain clothes."

"Wha'eva." He took my bowl and scraped his ladle through the dregs in the bottom of the kettle. "Just don' call it a bribe."

"I have to ask. How do you bake rolls on a grill?"

Jack smirked. "That would be tellin'." He set my bowl, mostly filled, on the counter before me. "Enjoy."

"Thanks." This bowl smelled better than the first. "Listen, Jack, I have to ask a favor."

"Seconds aren't enough?"

"The seconds are fantastic." I shook a drop of hot sauce in the bowl. "I get the idea you're here all the time."

"Noon to close," he said. "Sometimes working in the back. Tryin' to build a still."

"Good idea. My problem is, there's no 911 anymore. I'm talking to a lot of people, but there's no way for them to call me back."

Jack raised his hand. "Everybody else is using me as the message board. You might as well, too."

"Thanks. Oh, I ran into some people today who had extra meat. They killed a deer. I told them to bring it by, you might be able to use it."

Jack's smirk deepened. "Well, that's more to pay the phone bill than anyone else's offered."

Ceren swept past. "Going home. Straight home. Both of us."

"See you tomorrow," I said.

I took my bowl to an empty stool and concentrated on slowly eating every savory bite, trying to make the pleasure of eating compensate for the pulsing aches in my brain. The ibuprofen seemed to be helping. I thought of going to talk to Vince and Eric for a few moments, but decided to rest. I tried to forget Acceptance, Doug, the beheaded chicken, everything, just float on the blended babble of the crowd and the gentle burn of the peppers. Eventually I washed my empty bowl, nodded to Jack, and stepped out into the twilight street.

A shadowed figure stepped out from under the willow tree. "Kevin."

Chapter 20

EVENING SHADOWS swallowed the storefronts. Main Street made a black river beneath unlit streetlights. Stars shone around scattered clouds, hinting at later brilliance. Heat rose from the concrete sidewalk, but the air above it already felt cool. The backlit sign over the door diffused softly into the darkness.

At the sound of my name, my weight shifted onto the balls of my feet. I glanced into the deeper shadows beneath the willow tree, then over my shoulder at still darkness. "Who's there?"

Someone took two steps forward from the building's black corner. My left hand rolled into a loose fist.

Teresa. Her pale skin gleamed in the weak light, her shoulder-length hair casting a deeper shadow over her face. She dropped something at her feet as she came closer, wiping her hands against each other. "Kind of dark out here," she said, stuffing a napkin into her pocket.

"It is." Had she been the one who swung the baseball bat behind Doug's house? I still couldn't remember a face, and I couldn't imagine why she would have. I couldn't imagine why she was lurking out here, either.

"I got kind of nervous," Teresa said, with a faint chuckle. "Don't suppose you'd care to walk me home?"

I blinked. For the last twenty years or so, when people asked for a ride home they usually went in the back of a squad car—mine, or one I called. I'd walked Sheila to her apartment, her car, her office more than once, many years ago. Painful memories flashed through me.

But I wasn't Kevin. They weren't really my memories.

"I can do that." My voice sounded more forceful than I intended. I relaxed my fist, let my weight settle back onto my heels. Softening my voice, I held a hand aside. "Lead the way."

Teresa slipped her hand through my jacketed elbow. "I'm a couple blocks back from the bar."

"I thought you and Jesse lived in the same apartment building." This part of Frayville only had single-family homes.

"I picked a new house." Teresa tugged me towards the corner. I let her guide me. A faint fruity perfume drifted around her; melon? pear? "We lived out in the Orchards."

The inexpensive apartments on the very west border of Frayville—Apple Orchard, Cherry Orchard, and a few others I never could remember—housed the people at the bottom of Frayville's economic pyramid among the Section 8 housing for the poor and disabled. "I'd move out of there, too. But what about—"

"If the family who owns this house shows up, I'll pick another one."

I looked around the empty street. Maybe one house in five had a light on. I suspected most of those remained lit from before Absolute's final attack. A month ago, these homes had been homes. "You probably don't have much to worry about."

Teresa squeezed my arm. "I'm glad you think so."

"I wish I didn't. I mean, look around. It's empty. Where is everybody?"

"Absolute took them."

"Right," I said. "Absolute attacked every coastline simultaneously. Out of every lake, the rivers—probably the storm sewers. Half the population of the United States lived within fifty miles of a body of water."

"Meaning us."

"Yes." We—Kevin and his family—had barely made it over the Mississippi before everything went bad. My heart thudded in my chest. I took a deep breath to try to slow it. "He needed, what, a week? Five days, maybe, and he absorbed and duplicated everyone?"

"About that," she said.

"And we woke up here. I heard it on the radio as we drove west, Michigan was taken in about four hours or so." I waved my hands at the buildings around us. "I know we fought, but there's no way we killed ninety-five percent of Absolute's puppets. But there were a few dozen people at dinner. I met an old guy today who's busting his back trying to get the main power back on. A couple who wanted a chicken dinner. This town had ten thousand people in it."

"Absolute had us move away," Teresa said. "We—" Her voice caught. "We helped take other places."

"Utah for me," I said. "But I ended up back here. How?"

Her head shook in the dark. "No idea."

"And why do it?" I said. "I mean, say you're an alien."

Teresa's hand clenched my elbow. "I'm—"

I stopped. "I'm sorry."

"I know." Her hand squeezed once, more gently, then loosened. She kept hold of my elbow, however. The warmth of her hand seeped through the tweed.

"Say you're Absolute," I said. "You come to Earth. You start devouring and duplicating people. You set the duplicates to taking other people. You win. Then what? You let everybody go? Why? What's the point?"

Crickets chirped in the night. Copies of crickets.

"I never worried about the point before." Teresa veered around a fire hydrant at the edge of the sidewalk. Swerving aside with her felt more natural than anything I'd done since waking up. "You're born. You scrape out a living. You die. Sometimes an alien infects you."

"It's one thing if there's evolution," I said. "Or you believe in God. Either one of them gives you some kind of answer, tells us it's either random chance or divine plan. But Absolute remade the world in his image, and then put it back the way he found it. It's a divine plan without a purpose."

"It might just be us," Teresa said. "Maybe if you leave Frayville, you'd see the rest of the world is shapeshifted to hell and back. Maybe we're a nature preserve."

"Could be," I said. "But why have so few people? If you're going to have a nature preserve, don't you want more than a handful?"

"I don't know." She squeezed my arm again. "Right now, I'm just trying to figure out where I belong. Why."

"Sorry," I said. "I shouldn't rant. It just doesn't make sense." I breathed in rich cool air and consciously relaxed my shoulders. "What did you do, before? What kind of place are you looking for?"

"Cashier at McDonald's," Teresa said. "Don't know what I should be doing now."

"It could be worse." I gently squeezed her hand between my elbow and my ribs. "You could have decided to reopen a fast-food place. On behalf of the other residents of Frayville, I thank you for your restraint."

Teresa laughed quietly, more reaction than I deserved. "It kept me and my son okay, when we shared a couple rooms with Lucy and her son."

"You have a son?"

"*Had.*" Pain tightened her voice. "I haven't seen him since Absolute took us."

My jaw clenched. "I'm sorry. Really."

"He's thirteen months old. I can't see him being much use to Absolute. I keep hoping he'll turn up." She drew a shaky breath. "We searched the apartments. But there's no babies. I haven't seen anyone younger than twelve or so."

"My daughter was fourteen," I said.

"That's a rough age."

"Not anymore."

"I'm sorry," she said.

"Yeah." *Kevin, you utter bastard. I'm proud of you. And I'd kill you myself for what you did.*

We passed another couple houses before Teresa said "How goes your search? Really?"

"I don't know yet." I shrugged. "I'm still asking the questions. It's not like your average murder, where you know who did it and just have to gather the facts to support it. What you figure out in investigations like this always seems unconnected, until suddenly you get the piece of information that makes everything else you learned fit together. Heck, half the time you get answers for the wrong crime."

"You knew who did murders? Really?"

"Usually, yeah. It's the husband, or the boyfriend. Maybe it's revenge. Or greed, for control of the trust fund or the company. The kind of murder where you really have no idea who did it is pretty rare. Working this feels more like a robbery than a murder. Even if someone could've changed Doug, how would they know how to already? This might not even be a crime. He might have triggered some screwed-up trap Absolute left. I just keep asking and asking and eventually something will turn up."

"What if it is a crime? If you do figure it out? You can't send anyone to prison."

My stomach suddenly felt uneasy, and the bruises on my head throbbed anew. "I don't know. See if I can get a jury. Wing it."

"Maybe I could help you," she said. "I mean, I'm not doing anything."

"Thanks," I said. "I'll remember that."

"That's what people say when they don't want to say no," Teresa said.

"No, it means I really have no idea what you can do to help, but when something comes up, I'll ask." I jerked a thumb over my shoulder. "I have poor Jack acting as my answering service, at least until someone gets the phones working again. Who knows what I'll need tomorrow?"

"I kind of hope they don't," Teresa said.

"Don't what?"

"Get the phones working." She hugged my arm. Even through my jacket it felt nice enough that my heart started beating more quickly. I leaned closer and smelled her sweet perfume in the cool night. "It's kind of nice to walk down the street in the dark. Nobody can call to interrupt. Nobody having half a conversation so loudly that you can't hear the person in front of you."

"That *is* nice."

"The good thing about not having so many people is that we'll know each other," Teresa said. "Eventually. We'll have to work together. Have to be friendly, or at least civil. Maybe a hundred, or five hundred, people can get along better than ten thousand."

"You think more will show up?"

"I think there's a lot of people still hiding in their homes." Teresa turned her head to look up and down the dark street. "What got you out of your house?"

"Alice knocking on the door."

The air carried scents of pine and distant wood smoke. Our feet scuffed the concrete in near unison. Somewhere, a dog barked.

"Maybe that's what I should do," Teresa said. "Go knock on doors. 'Hi! I'm the outside world, and I don't completely suck.'"

"Getting them out of their house is only half the problem," I said. "Getting them out of their own head, that's the real challenge."

Teresa was quiet for a few steps. Insects chirruped around us. A few lit windows cast just enough light to make out the pale sidewalk against the surrounding grass. I'd run across the grass in front of St. Michael's, and it hadn't eaten me. But the grass might change its mind at any time. Or Absolute could change it for me.

"That's why you're investigating," Teresa said.

"Hmm?"

"To get yourself out of your own head."

"It's either that, or drive myself nuts asking all the questions I can't answer."

"What does Absolute plan for us?" Teresa said.

"Is he going to take us back?" I said.

"Am I just a copy?"

"Will I ever see my friends again?"

"What else did he change in me when he took me?" Teresa said.

"If I'm not who I remember being, who am I?"

"What do I do now?"

My tongue choked on *Why did I kill my family?* Asked and answered.

I heard Teresa's quickened breath. "I know. Jesse and I been talking about where to go and what to do, but you know? It doesn't seem like there's a reason to go anywhere. It's like, before we had a place in the world, and the world kept us in that place and gave us a few chances to climb up and a whole lot of chances to fall down. Now, though, there's no point in trying to be the richest person in the world. Money is useless, there's so much of everything around. I can't go to school, there isn't a school. Jack made himself a barkeep. You decided to keep being a cop, but if Alice hadn't knocked on your door, you'd be just as lost as me."

She stopped in front of a small house barely visible as a deeper blackness against the quiet night. "This is my place."

I stopped and turned to face the house. If I'd straightened my arm Teresa's hand would have fallen, but I carefully kept it bent.

"We'll figure it out," I said. I freed my arm from her hand and looped it over her shoulders in a gentle one-sided hug, my hand on the shoulder of her jacket, carefully not touching her skin. I hoped she'd be okay. At least I had an investigation, a line to hold on to. She didn't have anything.

Teresa pivoted, pressing her whole length into me. The top of her head came to just beneath my nose. Startled, I inhaled a quick sniff, stopped, and slowly sniffed again: fruity shampoo and vanilla soap.

She tilted her head back, rose onto her toes, pressed her lips into mine.

Her lips were hot and hard and soft and liquid all at once, sending electric shocks through my nerves and down my spine. My breath stopped. I involuntarily wrapped my arms around her and pulled her closer.

Teresa broke the kiss in a heartbeat, pulling back so that her lips barely brushed mine. "I know you had someone," she said. "But... she's gone. They're all gone. I can't stand to be alone again tonight."

She kissed me again, sending sparks through my nerves. Her hand trailed up the back of my head, leaving a tingling trail on my scalp. *So much for not touching anyone.*

"I need to feel alive. Stay here. With me."

Chapter 21

WE STAGGERED in her front door, Teresa's warm hand burning in mine, kindling flame in my bones, setting fire to my skin. Our clumsy entrance triggered several small lamps, and I glimpsed a sectional leather couch, an empty fireplace, boring beige walls. A broad picture window opened onto the darkness. Then her palms clasped my chin, thumbs before my ears, fingers in my hair, and everything faded away but the glow of her pale skin and the searing heat of her lips. Her fingers trailed fire down my chest as she reached down to yank my buttondown shirt out of my pants and scratch her nails up my bare back.

My hands bunched up the back of Teresa's silk blouse, raising it to her shoulders and exposing the clasp of her bra. I fumbled with the unfamiliar snaps. Sheila's bras had closed with an hook-and-eye, but Teresa's seemed fiendishly more complex.

The memory of Sheila slopped into my brain like a bucket of sludge. I felt soiled. Sheila was dead. Maybe because I was a copy of Kevin, I'd never really known her. I wasn't Kevin, but I contained his memories. His heart. Kevin wouldn't jump into bed with the next willing warm body.

He wasn't here. My hands still worked at the bra.

My pulse hammered in my ears, pounded in my groin, shook my hands with tension and overwhelming desire. That damned clasp would just not come loose. Every kiss Teresa left on my neck, the flowery smell of her hair, her fingers on my skin, everything pushed my desire.

Sheila and I had our wild moments. But this was something else. The back of my brain *demanded* I take Teresa, thoroughly and completely and without a moment to think about anything except getting her out of those clothes. My hands clenched. Buttons and snaps and cloth popped. The back of Teresa's bra flew open.

Teresa laughed. Sharp teeth nipped at my neck. She took her hands off me to finish the job, ripping her blouse off. Her nipples pressed burning points into my chest, leaving an electric tingle like licking a battery. She half-stepped back from me, her hands rising up to frame her breasts. She smiled.

"Here," she said, "taste these."

My knees buckled. Her skin tasted salty and had its own scent of smoke. My blood hammered, and my pants felt far too tight.

"Too…much," I managed to gasp.

Teresa steered her nipple to my mouth, and I couldn't help locking my lips over her breast, desperately sucking as if I could breathe her in. "No," she gasped. "It's fine. It's all going to be fine."

My tongue flicked a hot hard knob of nipple.

Teresa arched.

I pulled my mouth away. "It's too much," I said, coughing the words out. My hands were on her bare buttocks. She'd worn sweatpants. I'd yanked them down around her knees without realizing it.

Teresa crouched, lowering her mouth to mine. "It's not enough," she whispered between my teeth. "Yet."

Her lips electrified mine.

This wasn't just hormones, I realized. Her skin gleamed white like alabaster. Soft, yes. The tingle where her breasts touched the bottom of my ribs, where her hand gripped my hair and pulled me into her, her buttock clenched in my hand, wasn't just desire and unfamiliar flesh. A burning charge flowed between us.

I felt desperate to drown in Teresa, desperate to drown out loneliness and fear and loss.

Earlier today I'd met a woman desperate for death but unable to kill herself. She'd met another man desperately screaming to be punishment for his own sins. They'd touched and become one being, Acceptance.

I felt just as desperate as they had. I wanted Sheila, who I had saved by murdering her in cold blood. But Teresa was here, and we hovered on the brink of the greatest intimacy two people could share.

What had Acceptance felt before merging into one?

Maybe an electric charge?

Guilt over Sheila couldn't have stopped me. Maybe it should have, but it couldn't have. Perhaps the overwhelming intensity of what I felt couldn't have stopped me. But the two blended together gave me the strength to yank my mouth away from breast, grab the softly bony sides of Teresa's ribcage, and push her a foot away. My heart was a jackhammer, my skin suddenly soaked in sweat.

Teresa's eyes burned into mine. Her face flushed red, her breath stopped and started irregularly. Her skin under my hands quivered and trembled. She grabbed my shoulders. "Don't you stop now."

"We have to," I gasped, desire and guilt and fear and longing making my voice just short of a shout.

"You. Will. Not. *Stop*," she hissed. "Not until I say."

The electric charge surged through her hands into my shoulders, making my breath catch in my gut.

It wasn't electricity, I realized. It was desire. I felt her *need* echoing against my own.

Teresa hurtled herself onto me. Her forehead caught my chin. I toppled to the side, clumsily falling off my knees onto the rough carpet.

Her whole body pressed against me in a flood of soft heat. Her lips found mine again, then her hands found my belt.

I wrenched my lips away from Teresa's, only to lean over and bite her shoulder. She gasped, clenched her hands around me, and fell back, pulling me onto her. I smelled sweat on her skin, her touch demanding I bite harder, push harder, claw and plunge and taste and feel everything she so freely offered.

Her hands deftly unfastened my pants and reached within.

I bit harder. I couldn't stop.

"I won't let you," she gasped. "Let you—stop."

Teresa pulled her shoulder away from my mouth.

I strained my neck towards her.

She knelt above me, her thighs and calves burning against my sides.

I put my hands over the bottom of her ribcage. Took a shaky breath. Summoned guilt and fear. And made one last, heroic effort to push her away.

My hands burned against her skin.

They wouldn't push.

I pulled them back to try again.

My palms wouldn't leave her skin.

My fingers raked her ribs beneath her breasts, but the palms stuck fast.

I felt my own hands on her skin. We'd merged together.

Just like one of Absolute's puppets. Or a physical version of Acceptance's coalescence.

Teresa, kneeling above me, reached down and impaled herself on me with a low groan.

I cried out. My hands dropped off her ribs, but we were more intimately attached.

Teresa's breath heaved out in short little gasps as she twitched each inch further down. Her hands clenched my sides.

I grabbed her thighs and shuddered.

In excruciatingly delicious seconds, she'd taken all of me.

We both moaned.

"There," Teresa said, dropping forward. "You're a—decent man," she breathed into my mouth. "But too—many—"

She moved over me.

I wheezed out a breath. The fear and guilt dissolved into pleasure.

"—questions—"

I lost control. I bumped my hips up and to the side, toppling Teresa and riding her down.

Something in the back of my head remembered Acceptance and wondered what we would become.

Our breath synchronized with each thrust, drowning out every other sound.

Then the crash of breaking glass filled the air.

The picture window shattered in a barrage of shrapnel.

A brick smacked the carpet inches from our heads.

A vodka bottle sailed through the hole, flame billowing from the neck. Crashed into the television, bounced off. Hit the floor. Glass shattered.

Stinking, burning diesel splashed my back.

Chapter 22

THE SEX drive is strong. The don't-burn-alive drive is even stronger. Liquid pain lashed my shoulder blades and the small of my back. My lust evaporated.

I shrieked and thrashed. Teresa's ankles locked over my hips kept me clamped tight against her as I flopped onto my back and tried to smother the pain against the rough white carpet.

Teresa screamed, trying to wrench her feet free even though I lay on them. She didn't hold me only by her ankles, but more intimately, and that grasp seemed tighter than humanly possible.

My hours and hours of emergency training dissolved in the pain. Even the old-fashioned *stop, drop, and roll* was too complex. I bucked and thrashed. I sucked in a chestful of air, only to convulse coughing at fresh cinders and fumes of melting plastic laminate.

Teresa flailed her feet free from beneath me, braced her hands on my chest, and pushed. Air flushed between us even as she pushed it from my lungs. She kept her hands on my chest and got to her knees. I still felt myself inside her, somehow.

My back pressed against the carpet. Flames flared against my skin, then dulled as my weight smothered them. I gasped in relief, sucked in burnt carpet fumes, and coughed.

Teresa scrambled up my body, pulling herself off me. She got her knees to my armpits before rolling to the side and to her feet.

Fire burned around us. A pool of liquid fire oozed across the carpet in front of the television. Burning diesel had ignited streaks on the couch, splashed flame onto the bottom of a shelf of old paperbacks, sparked tiny fires across the carpet. Flames licked the slats of the antique rocking chair. The woven seat crumpled into glowing ash.

Teresa glared at me. "We are *not* done." Glanced at the fire. "You don't get away that easy."

She hurtled herself at the door.

I rolled to my feet, unsteady, delirious from my earlier injuries and the shocks of the last few moments. My heart pounded impossibly hard. The heat of the blaze instantly evaporated the sweat pouring off me. Her taste still filled my mouth, my skin still tingled with her touch and her transmitted need, but every breath of choking smoke and the pain of my burned back overrode everything.

Out. Get out. Or burn.

Naked, I staggered through the front door. The firelight through the shattered front window didn't illuminate the sidewalk, let alone the street, but would soon. For now, the night was only black shadows against black shadows. Even what I saw shimmered, as if I had a monstrously high fever. I stumbled down three cement steps onto the walkway and staggered towards the street.

Dizzy.

Where did she go?

Hurt.

Black moved against black at the edge of my sight. I staggered towards the motion. Stumbled to a halt. My burned back flashed with agony.

I couldn't think.

I knew what to do now. I'd learned before. But I couldn't remember. The knowledge juddered and shook just out of reach. The blow to my head? Hadn't that been earlier?

Hunger stabbed my guts, throbbing in synch with my pile-driver heartbeat. I coughed again. I'd just eaten, but the sudden ravenous vacuum inside my guts seemed stronger than the diesel burns covering my back. Something smelled rich nearby. Maybe an apple or a pear. The aroma pulled me into the shadows near the street.

A shadow moved before me. A figure with arms and legs. It made sounds. Maybe words. Maybe just inarticulate grunts. I couldn't tell the difference.

It shrieked. Swung at me.

I jumped forward. Shoved. *Get through it.* It was between me and food.

Maybe it is food.

It tottered back. A scrape. A thud. It tripped over the curb and fell onto the street.

Don't eat people. Not that hungry.

Not yet.

I forgot it. Forgot the burn on my back.

Nothing but the stabbing, twisting pain in my gut.

Food.

Warm concrete under my feet. Then cool grass.

I reached out. The fingers—too long.

A shape in my hands. Didn't know what it was. But the smell: fruit and roast meat and other things I've eaten. Things I knew but couldn't remember.

I bit.

Impossible flavor exploded in my mouth.

Chapter 23

SUNLIGHT WARMED my face.

My tongue tasted like bad brandy somehow gone worse. Wet grass cooled my cheek, my flank, my buttocks, my outstretched arm.

I'm naked on the lawn.

The thought spasmed through me, lifting me to a sitting position even before I could get my eyes open.

"Easy," someone said.

A hollow metallic pop and hiss sounded behind me.

My hands found a blanket. Someone had covered me. I clutched it to my chest and worked my gummy eyes open.

A heavyset man knelt before me, one knee on the cracked sidewalk, the other pressed to his chest as he leaned into my face. I needed a moment to recognize the flat chin and broad nose flattened by a fist many years before. "Fred?"

Fireman Fred Pearson's slow, thoughtful nod hadn't changed from before. "Kevin. How do you feel?"

I worked my jaw side to side, expecting pain but feeling none. My hand touched my chin. The blister still lurked beneath the chin, and something sticky tacked my hand around the beard stubble. "I'm—"

I'd been *burned*. I remembered the sheet of pain across my back, the crisp smell of my own flesh searing like bacon. Now I just felt a chill across my back where I'd sat up and let the cool morning air under the blanket. I fumbled to pat my back and shoulder blades, expecting char but touching only cool soft skin.

"I think I'm fine," I finally said.

"Good." Fred leaned back. "You know who I am?"

"Fred...Pearson. FD."

"Good. Do you know the date?"

Name, date, and president. The standard orientation questions for an injured person. "I just did this," I muttered. "It's June… third, I think? And I think Jack is president. He's the one feeding us."

In the last day I'd been beaten until my brain concussed and then splashed with burning diesel fuel. I should be writhing on the ground and begging for morphine. If I was really lucky, the flames would have killed my nerves and I wouldn't feel anything at all. But I felt impossibly good. The skin on my back was smooth and soft. After all the running around I'd done yesterday, I expected at least the slow burn of sore muscles. Instead, I had a blister on my chin and grass stains on my ass.

Fred studied my face. Behind him, the carbonized shell of Teresa's home smoldered, stinking of burned plastic and glue and all the other toxic chemicals that make up a building. The wind carried the worst of the smoke away, but enough came my way to wrinkle my nose. The building still creaked and popped as it cooled, accentuating the hollow hiss behind me. I sat beneath a willow tree, heavy melons swaying precariously overhead.

"I'm fine," I said.

Fred nodded absently. "We'll decide that." He'd checked my orientation to see if I had a brain injury, but that finished, he said nothing else. Crouching on his heels, he studied my face and shoulders.

"What's going on?" I said.

"Covering you up was probably a mistake," Fred said.

I hugged the blanket around my shoulders. "I appreciate it."

"Drop it."

I furrowed my brow. "Excuse me?"

Fred stood, his face hard. "Remove the blanket."

"What's going on?" I asked.

He stepped back. "Kevin—I believe you misunderstand the nature of this conversation."

Something clunked behind me, and the hollow hiss became much louder. A dry warmth prickled across the back of my head. My gut suddenly felt hollow. I turned to look.

The nozzle of a flamethrower gun, a few feet away. I had a clear view down the opening. A blue halo of heat shimmered around the gaping maw.

Chapter 24

MODERN FLAMETHROWERS don't differ much from those used in World War Two. The backpack has a tank of compressed nitrogen and a tank of fuel, either propane or a modern mixture of gelled gasoline they still call napalm. Pressurized nitrogen drives the fuel up into the gun, into the nozzle, past the igniter, and out at the target.

Either type can ignite living body fat, reducing people to greasy bones.

The nozzle pointed at me had the rounded opening of a propane model. It wouldn't shoot more than ten or twelve feet, creating a cloud of diffuse flame. More than enough to swallow me, unfortunately. It was only a couple feet out of my reach. I didn't recognize the skinny kid wearing the backpack, but I recognized the almost panicked way his leather-gloved hand trembled over the release lever.

My pulse went through the roof. I tried to take a deep breath to calm down, but the smell of propane made that impossible. I was sitting on grass. Beneath a tree. The propane would ignite everything. The emergency blanket wouldn't protect me, and beneath it I was naked.

Fred still stared.

"Fred," I said, "what's going on?"

"You tell me," Fred said.

"We saw you." The kid's eyes hid behind smoked glass goggles. "We saw what you are."

I knew the kid's tone of voice. I'd heard it before, down in Detroit, usually from nervous kids who hadn't thought any further than "show them the gun and they'll give you the money" and didn't know what to do when the victim refused.

"The blanket," Fred said. "Push it to the side."

"Okay." Very slowly I took the edge of the silver blanket in one hand and pulled it off me. Cool morning air coursed over my bare skin, raising goose pimples and an involuntary shiver.

The flamethrower nozzle wobbled in the air. I blinked, and made myself look at the kid's hands. The blue cloud of pre-lit flame surrounding the nozzle wasn't the danger. If the kid's hand tightened, I'd have to try to throw myself beneath the flame. I'd end up at the kid's feet. Maybe I could kick up, knock him back, get his hand off the trigger long enough to do something.

Or get covered in flame for the second time in twelve hours.

"See?" I said.

"What were you?" Fred said.

"Burning," I said. "Fred, I don't know what you saw."

"He's Absolute," the kid said.

I stopped. "Excuse me?"

"You were *changed*," the kid hissed. "You're Absolute, and you're gonna give us answers."

I raised my hands, palms open. "Hang on. I'm—I'm not Absolute."

"Nobody else has changed," Fred said. "But we saw you."

"We all changed," I said.

"Not since he released us," Fred said.

"Look." I licked my lips. The flamethrower nozzle drifted hypnotically, never quite leaving my face. "I don't know what you saw. Someone threw a bottle of burning diesel at me last night. I was screaming in pain. I staggered out here. Someone hit me. I hit them back. Then I woke up."

Fred studied my face. "No."

"What?"

"We've seen some weird shit," Fred said. "But what you were, I hadn't seen since that last night, when Absolute moved. You're something else."

Maybe I was. I'd struggled against Teresa's seduction even as I cooperated with it. Enthusiastically cooperated. I'd felt her lust, let it feed my own. Maybe we would have merged into one being. I'd felt Teresa's every touch much more intensely than anyone else. The sex had felt wonderful, but something else had ridden along with it.

Teresa's words: *We're not done.* A weird time to say that, surrounded by a burning building.

I'd heard many things during sex, but *too many questions* was new.

My memories had blurred after that. Someone had attacked me. My hands had been shaped wrong, bending unnaturally when I fought them off. I remembered walking wrong, too, my knees too stiff but my hips swinging impossibly wide.

I shouldn't be lying here, staring at the flamethrower nozzle. The choking fear of burning alive—again—had a sudden twin, the fear of what I'd become when burning alive the first time. "Look," I said, "I've seen weird things too. Have you killed anything?"

"Just you," the kid said. His hand trembled on the trigger. The flamethrower huffed, a ball of burning gas haloing a few inches around the nozzle. My stomach clenched with the reek of burnt propane.

"I saw some people behead a chicken," I said quickly. "It lived. It went nuts, just like Absolute's Taken could, not even thinking about it. But someone else shot a deer, and it died."

Fred watched me.

"Last night's a blur to me, but—but I was hurt. I was going to die." Broken memories of staggering across the lawn and clawing at a nameless faceless figure, agony arcing through my blistered and blackened back, skittered through my mind. "Burn alive."

My brain skittered through what I knew, trying to attach one bit of knowledge to another and explain what had happened. If I didn't have an explanation, if I didn't give Fred something he could understand, the kid would burn me alive. Again.

I took a deep breath. "I think I did the same thing the chicken did."

"That's reaching," Fred said.

"Have you seen anyone else get badly hurt?" I said. "Do you know what happens?"

Fred's eyes flickered. I'd struck something.

"Have you?" I demanded.

"No," he said.

I carefully kept my gaze on Fred's eyes. If I said these words to the kid, he'd pull the trigger. "Up to you, Fred. Tell your boy to put down the flamethrower and we'll talk. I don't know what happened, but I know we're all the same thing. We can work out what happened."

I paused to let the words sink in.

"Or you tell him to burn me down. Your choice."

Fred watched me. His eyes flicked to the kid, then back to me. "Harry," he finally said. "Turn it off."

"But he—"

"We don't know," Fred said. "We don't burn a man alive because we're afraid. Not now."

I slowly turned to look at the kid. "Harry," I said. "I don't know what you saw, what happened to me. But it do know it could happen to any of us. Please. Let's figure it out before someone gets killed."

Harry's jaw clenched. His shoulders trembled. Then he stepped back and released the flamethrower handle, letting the flame curl back into the gun and die with a hollow pop.

I let myself exhale, suddenly aware of the pounding in my ears. "Thank you."

Harry lowered the flamethrower gun, but kept it in his hand rather than hanging it on the hook dangling from one side of the fuel pack. "Yeah."

Fred and Harry kept staring at me.

I forced myself to exhale deeply before drawing another slow breath.

Finally Harry looked at Fred. "I guess he isn't going to change."

"You sound disappointed," I said.

Fred snickered.

I reached for the blanket as I stood. It went around my body twice, and I had to fold the upper end to make it short enough that I could stand without tripping on it. "That's better."

"What happened?" Fred said.

"I told you," I said.

"Not that." Fred waved his hand. "The fire. Harry and I've been taking shifts up in the belfry down at First Baptist. We saw this one last night, came as fast as we could." Anger tinted his voice. "If someone's starting fires, I want them stopped. One fire would take out the whole town."

"I'm glad you were," I said. "Thanks."

"Don't thank us," he said, bitterness hardening his words to points before launching them at me. "You got yourself out of it. What I want to know is, who started the fire?"

Standing, I studied the smoking shell that had been Teresa's new home.

"Who, I don't know," I said. "I can tell you what. A Molotov through the picture window."

A few charcoal spires stood, steaming as deep embers met morning dew. The smells of burning plastic and wood filled my nose, and my skin felt gritty with smoke and ash. The houses on either side had scorched walls, but Hank and Fred had poured enough water over them to prevent an inferno. Frayville's smaller fire truck stood on the curb. Above me, the willow creaked in the breeze.

The willow. I glanced up into its melon-laden branches. Had I eaten one of those melons last night? The memory of the taste filled my mouth, fruity but with the rich texture of red meat. I'd bitten straight through the rind, somehow opening my jaw wide enough to eat a soccer-ball-sized melon like an apple. I still felt hungry, but not ravenous.

"When did you get here?" I asked. "You said you saw me?"

Harry nodded.

Fred said, "We got here a couple minutes before the flames broke the kitchen windows. You were right about here, eating."

I didn't want to ask. I had to ask. I forced out the words.

"What did I look like?" My mouth felt like parchment.

"Like one of Absolute's monsters," Harry said.

"Shriveled," Fred said. "Your hair had burned off your head, and your back was burned black. I had Harry watch you with the flamethrower while I hosed down the houses." He glared at me. "If this had been on the west side, we would have lost the block. At least."

These homes, in the wealthier part of town, had enough space between them to slow the fire. "What was I doing?"

"You don't remember anything?" Fred said.

"Fighting." I shook my head. "Hunger."

"You were eating melons." Harry had slung the flamethrower gun back on the hook jutting off the backpack. Exhaustion laced his voice, as if his grip on the flamethrower was the only thing that had kept him alert. "Just pulling them out of the tree and taking bites out of them. Your mouth was big enough to eat them like pears, one after the other. Each one made you change."

Mutagenic melons? My stomach roiled and twisted at the thought. What had Absolute left us, hospital fruit?

Fred said. "Those burns should have hospitalized you. And infection should have killed you in hours. Instead, your skin kept growing. Your body kept filling out. You look like Detective Holtzmann now, but then..." He shook his head. "You looked like a chimpanzee with talons."

The kid smirked. "A three-legged chimpanzee."

The seething in my guts froze. "Excuse me?"

Fred sighed. "Don't listen to him. We didn't see anything else important."

"No," I said. "Hang on. Harry? What did you see?"

"You were hung like a horse," Harry said with locker-room bravado. "I mean, like, horses would be jealous."

Fred said "Young man! There is such a thing as taste."

The cold spread from my guts into the rest of me.

Uncontrolled transformation. But it wasn't unknown. I'd seen the same thing only yesterday.

I'd almost become another Doug.

Chapter 25

THE IDEA of traipsing across town wearing an emergency blanket and a scowl left me cold. And drafty. Fred offered to drop me off at home on their way back to their watch steeple. I rode in silence, glowering in the fire truck's front passenger seat, questions washing through my brain.

I should have burned to death. Had something in the melon healed me? Had Absolute seeded the town with hospital fruit? That thought chilled me. It implied that the creature that had eradicated life on Earth had plans for our future.

But *recovery* wasn't quite the word. The bruise at the back of my head, where someone had tried to use a baseball bat to split my skull, had completely healed. I'd skinned a knuckle some point in the last couple of days. Even the scab was gone. The quarter-sized blister on the bottom of my chin remained, as if I needed something else to remind me I'd failed to kill myself before Absolute claimed me. Or Kevin. Whoever I'd been. Was.

The melon couldn't have changed *me*, not the me inside my head. Teresa gleamed in my memory, her pale skin shining above me in the darkened living room, her fingernails clawing my shoulders. My hand had stuck to her. No—I'd felt my own hand, through her skin. I'd told my arms to push her away, and they had ignored me. Like they belonged to someone else. Had she triggered the physical change in me? Had we triggered a change in each other?

Riding in the fire truck's front passenger seat, with Harry right behind me and Fred driving, I resisted the urge to reach under the silver blanket and check my crotch for defects. I couldn't get her last words to stop playing on a loop in the back of my brain.

We're not done here.

Had she triggered that change in me deliberately? Or was it just that people couldn't have sex at all? Had I entirely misread the scene in Doug's bedroom? Maybe the woman who'd been there had somehow merged with Doug? If I checked Doug's spare bedroom, would I find a headless woman with a vagina built for a four-foot dick? Sex is one of the most primal human activities, right after not getting eaten by sabre-tooth tigers and not burning alive.

And who had attacked me on the front lawn? Presumably the person who started the fire. Was it the same person as the baseball bat? My body might have healed, but I couldn't remember any face behind the bat. Presumably the healing melon couldn't restore what wasn't in my brain.

Maybe only one person was against me—Teresa? It could be as many as three: Teresa, Bomber, and Baseball Bat.

I'd lost my mind.

Doug had lost his brain.

"Turn left," I said as Fred reached Main Street. "Then right on Ducasse."

If we hadn't stopped, what would have happened?

Thoughts whirled around my brain while Fred took me home. "Brick house on the left," I said. He slowed, and I hopped out before the wheels quite stopped. "Thanks," I said.

"Any time," Fred said.

"But maybe with pants next time," Harry said.

"Glad you're on watch," I said.

Fred studied my face. "We'll talk later."

"Dinner?" I said. "I'll be at Jack's."

"Sure."

I slammed the door and thumped it twice. Brakes hissed, and the truck lumbered into motion.

I looked at the lines of silent houses for a breath. A car motor purred in the distance. Clouds cloaked the June sun, leaving the concrete warm underfoot but not hot. A hammer pounded nails somewhere, maybe on the next street over, maybe a mile distant. Not as silent as a tomb, but perhaps as silent as a morgue.

Questions swirled through my head. I tried to push them aside to find two words drifting forward to replace them. *Immanence. Legacy.*

Those words had circled me after I'd awoken, and only yesterday's flurry of activity had driven them away.

I shook myself and walked up my sidewalk. I'd locked the front door on my way out, but the trick rock in the backyard yielded its emergency key.

First things first: I couldn't keep walking around naked. My tweed jacket was gone, burned up in the fire, but I had an older linen jacket. My backup sidearm had burned with my clothes, but it hadn't been terribly useful so far. I studied my second-best leather shoes for a moment, then tossed them back into the garage and pulled on my comfortable athletic shoes. Something told me I'd best be ready to run.

All the questions I'd been asking centered on Doug. I'd approached this like any other case, talking to friends and family looking for loose strings to pull at. But this wasn't like any other case. It couldn't be like any other case because the ground rules had changed. If I wanted to make progress on learning what happened to Doug, I needed to understand how things worked now. I needed to understand the new rules governing this new game. I needed new questions.

Had anyone else had sex? Was what happened with Teresa normal now? Not easy questions to ask, but at least I knew where to start asking: Jack's.

And I'd heard of one place where people said they were getting answers. That gave me the answer to one question. The answer was now.

Now was time to find Legacy.

Chapter 26

THE POLICE cruiser squatted before Alice's house at an angle that blocked half the road. Somebody should have given that guy a ticket. Before driving away, I detoured to knock on Ceren's front door.

No answer.

A sick feeling sifted into my gut. It was hard to not take a Molotov cocktail personally, but maybe the attack wasn't about me. Perhaps Teresa was the target, and I had my fingers a little too close to the match. I pounded on the door and leaned on the bell.

No answer.

Frustrated, I looked around Ceren's bare yard but saw nothing usable to break in. The house next door, though, featured a raised flowerbed ringed in rocks. I took a step towards it—

Click. Clang. The deadbolt turned, the door swinging open an inch. "Yeah?"

"Ceren?" I said, releasing the breath I didn't realize I'd been holding. "Are you okay? Are you *both* okay?"

"Yeah." She opened the door a little wider, revealing her blue sweatshirt and one tired eye. "Just sleeping."

"Right," I said. "How late were you up?"

"How late is sunrise?"

"You came home when you said, right?"

"We did. We watched movies." Ceren yawned.

Footsteps approached from behind Ceren. "Who is it?" asked an unfamiliar voice.

What the hell? I pushed on the door, surprising Ceren into a two-step stumble. A boy, maybe Ceren's age, maybe a little younger—the boys all look younger at that age—stood behind her wearing blue jeans and a wrinkled anime T-shirt. In the living room beyond half a dozen forms sprawled in the gloom, asleep on couches and carpet. One girl somehow managed to curl up like a puppy in a big overstuffed armchair. "Are you having a party?"

Ceren glared. "You said come back before dark. We were having fun, so we invited folks back with us."

I turned my coldest Angry Police Detective stare on the boy. His face faded to white and he stumbled back to bounce off the foyer wall.

Memories of my own daughter clenched my jaw. I wanted to call Ceren's parents, call the school, call Child Protective Services. My left hand twitched towards my belt where I'd kept my phone. I forced it to relax. Someone had tried to kill me twice in the last day. That had to take priority over busting a teenager party. I promised myself I'd talk to Ceren later, if only to make myself feel better.

"So long as you're all okay, I'm okay."

"Alice wants to get in her house. She needs some clean clothes."

"Tell her I'll be back later," I said. "We'll all go together."

"Good, 'cause I don't have anything left that'll fit her."

I glanced at Alice's silent house. "Don't let her go home without me."

Ceren tried to glare harder, but it looked more like a pout. She needed a few more years of disappointment and anger. "You get back to take her. I'm not having her wear Mom's stuff."

The boy had disappeared into the living room.

I said, "Just… Be careful, Ceren. Okay?"

Ceren yawned, disguising fatigue as boredom.

My teeth tried to clench, and muscle spasms rippled up my back. If she was Julie, I would have broken my own rules and tanned her hide. "I'll be back in a bit."

"Go on." Ceren waved a hand. "Us growing kids need our sleep."

I turned around before I forgot my own rules, and concentrated on pushing my anger away. Winchester Mall was a five minute drive from here. I'd need all my emotional energy to deal with whatever I found at Legacy.

Chapter 27

I DROVE the police cruiser down Main Street at a gentle ten miles an hour, barely above an idle, one hand on the wheel and one elbow out the window. The early summer sun burned dew off the sidewalks and grassy medians in a cool mist, leaving a fresh smell. A man in dusty denim pants and a tatty leather jacket walked briskly south, the most purposeful motion I'd seen yet. He cast more than one nervous glance at Saint Michael's, and I steeled myself to not look that way. I didn't need to know if one of the people who composed Acceptance watched me from the vestibule.

In front of Jack's adopted bar, a shiny blue pickup truck with a federal diesel sticker in the rear window blocked the sidewalk, its tailgate open to the front door and front tires in the road. My stomach rumbled at the sight, but Jack did dinner, not breakfast.

Besides, I had to think I'd eaten enough last night to last me for a while. I didn't remember eating, but just thinking of the melons that hung heavy from the willows invoked the sweetness of cantaloupe, the tartness of tamarind, and the satisfying feel of crisp bacon in the back of my mouth. I wanted another bite even as I didn't want to touch anything Absolute had left for us.

As I rolled south on Main Street towards Winchester Mall, someone shouted my name.

Jesse, Teresa's older friend, watched me from the sidewalk, her arm raised in a half wave. She caught my eye and beckoned. "Kevin!"

I pulled to the curb and parked.

Jesse trotted towards me.

As she closed in, my gaze flicked towards the police shotgun racked between the seats. I simultaneously chided myself assuming Teresa had deliberately attacked me, lumping Jesse in with Teresa, and for not checking the load.

"Kevin," Jesse gasped, lumbering to a halt. Her chest heaved as she caught her breath, straining her fuzzy sweater.

"Jesse. How are you?"

She waved a hand impatiently. "You seen Teresa?"

"Not since last night."

She frowned. "I got to her place this morning, it'd burned—"

"She wasn't in it," I said.

"How would you know?"

My mouth flapped open even as I told myself to keep control of the conversation.

"Oh!" Jesse said. "She invited you? She said she might. What happened?"

"Er—"

Jesse scowled. "I mean, what happened to Teresa?"

"The fire started and we got separated. She got out before I did. I looked for her, but no luck." *Technically true.* "I'd really like to find her." *Very true.*

"It looks like it burned a while ago. I walked around and shouted for her, but she didn't answer."

"The fire started...maybe nine o'clock last night."

Jesse chewed her lip. "She'll probably turn up back at the 'partments."

"Maybe."

"But if it burned last night, she's had lots of time to get back."

I shook my head. "She could have walked halfway, found a place to crash, and gone to sleep. Lots of empty houses between here and the Orchards. I wouldn't worry yet. But if you see her, tell her we need to talk."

Jesse smirked. "I bet you do. Don' worry, I'll let her know."

"Thanks."

I waved and put the cruiser back into gear, thoughtful. Maybe Teresa had suffered her own transformation. Maybe she had tried to change me. Maybe she was mad, or hurt, or anything. I had to find her.

At Frayville's south end, the businesses stopped and the ground plummeted into the Sand River Valley. Main Street became a dusty concrete four-lane bridge fifty feet above the valley until it merged into the side of South Hill. The police cruiser easily climbed a few hundred feet of densely wooded hillside to the plateau where the K-Mart and Frayville's one indoor mall sat.

Tourists came to Frayville for fishing and camping. Frayville's teenagers came to Winchester Mall for the closest thing to big city life they'd find this far up Michigan's Huron shoreline. The mall sat at a crossroads, lurking at the back of a vast expanse of cracked concrete marked with light poles all just a few degrees off straight, and a gas station at the corner. I saw maybe a dozen rattletrap cars scattered around the parking lot, and another three up near the door.

The gas station sign shone too brightly for the morning sun alone. They had enough solar for the lights at least. I looked at the cruiser's fuel gauge and saw an eighth of a tank. I could roll the cruiser back down the hill, but a tank of diesel would make the rest of the day easier. The Winchester station was old-fashioned, with two service bays in addition to the snack shop. I pulled to a stop by a pump island, carefully parking so the white-and-rust awning overhead would shade the driver's seat. Familiar diesel and gasoline fumes offered a shred of comfort.

Before, I would have used a federal diesel card to fill the tank, or a charge card to fill the family car despite the savage gasoline taxes. The bright blue LED screen showed that someone had set the software so anyone could fuel up freely, but I didn't fiddle with the pump. I didn't want only a tank of fuel. I wanted to know who was providing the fuel. I was the closest thing to a police officer we had; that had to count for something.

"Hello!" I shouted.

A muffled call drifted from the nearest repair bay. A few seconds later, a lanky man in gray mechanic's coveralls with grease-stained knees meandered out the open door. He walked like his joints were overlimber, arms and shoulders all swinging too freely.

He saw me standing by the car. Stopped.

I'd seen him before. Yesterday afternoon, at Jack's. He'd been sitting at the bar.

He stood still. Eyes on mine.

No. He'd looked familiar then, too.

His head rose, tension straightening his spine.

That walk. I'd seen that walk before. Detroit?

No, Frayville.

Possession. Intent to distribute.

Aaron? No, Ian, that was it. As in *Ian Reamer, this court finds you guilty*. The fresh convict screaming obscenities at me, arms pinned and legs flailing ineffectively. Three bailiffs dragging him from the courtroom as he shouted *You will pay, Holtzmann! You will so fucking pay! I'll piss on your corpse, fuckhead!*

Reamer launched himself backwards, dashing around the corner of the gas station and out of sight.

Damn, but a straight-up chase felt *good*.

Chapter 28

I DIDN'T know if Reamer had hit me over the head with a baseball bat. I didn't know if he'd been the one to pitch a jar of burning diesel through a window at me. The first time I'd gone into Jack's, he'd ducked out when I came in. But when he realized I recognized him, he fled.

I'm a cop. I didn't need any better reason to chase him.

Reamer's long legs devoured the weedy parking lot, his feet striking cracked blacktop hard enough to cast echoes against the K-mart's brick front.

After only a few steps, I could feel that the days of aimless wandering around Kevin's house had drained my stamina. In a hundred yards I had a stitch under my right lung and my hamstrings tugged and ached at each step. I made myself exhale, pushing dead air out so I could cram more in. My shoes pounded asphalt as I tucked my elbows to my side and raced after Reamer.

The lot looked even more desolate on foot. A few scattered cars marked random dots near streetlights, and a couple concrete-bordered dirt beds held scraggly starved trees. Reamer dodged around those few obstacles, running straight for the closest entrance to the sprawling Winchester Mall. He hit the broad glass doors at full speed, instantly disappearing into the darkness within.

My hand touched the door handle maybe forty-five seconds behind him. The tip of my tongue burned from oxygen deprivation and my pulse pummeled my temples and throat. I focused on my breathing, concentrating on that stitch in my side to keep it from blossoming into a full-blown cramp that would cripple my breath. If I stopped to breathe, the chase was over.

The door swung easily. I plunged into gloom.

Coming from the bright sunshine into the dim mall, my eyes barely made out the shadowy shapes of a wooden bench and an information kiosk. The drier, cooler air sucked the moisture out of my mouth. I knew Winchester Mall, I'd been here hundreds of times, but everyone said that Legacy—whatever that was—was here. I slowed to let my eyes adjust to the light leaking through the crusted-over skylights two floors overhead.

The stores on both sides were blocked, the fence gates lowered and padlocked. Despite the dryness the air carried a fetid loamy scent, like a greenhouse. I glanced up the paralyzed escalator, but didn't see any signs of motion up the stairs or on the mezzanine.

Sucking in another deep breath I plunged forward.

A shout broke the silence. Echoes made the words unintelligible.

I bolted past sealed shops I'd seen countless times on duty, rounded the familiar curve to the central plaza, took two steps, and stopped in bewildered amazement.

The plaza had been a hexagonal open space, with a great glass dome to cast filtered light down on the captive trees and planters and food stands. The benches and chairs that had once sat artfully around the foot stalls were mostly overturned or pushed against the walls. The foliage was gone, leaving only bare earth in barren buckets. The north hall, which had once led to the pet supply shop and the Olga's, now overflowed with monstrous green foam. Bubbles as large as beach balls had boiled out of the hall, an opal gleam in the teal and viridian tones, forming a spill that ran in irregular channels halfway across the courtyard.

In a cleared space in the middle of the courtyard sat two people. They ignored the complicated computerized equipment surrounding them to stare up the central escalator to the upper level. I followed their gaze, and glimpsed motion on the upper level.

Reamer. Running north. Right into the bubbles.

I didn't have enough air to speak to the people. I bolted past them and launched myself up the steep escalator stairs.

I'd memorized this building years ago, but I felt lost looking at the mezzanine's south, west, and east empty halls. The mall should have skylight illumination *or* closed storefronts, not both. But the north hall looked like a giant pressurized canister of green insulation foam had burst, filling the hall below and overflowing up here. Gleaming aqua and teal bubbles foamed up from the lower level and climbed the walls. Some surfaces hinted at iridescence. Smaller bubbles clung to the ceiling, going up to but not covering the skylight. The air tasted even drier, and my panting made my tongue and the inside of my mouth feel gummy. I couldn't help looking closer, spotting a few islands of normalcy: half a mannequin here, a rack of pants there, a glass wall clear on the hallway side but with bubbles pressed up against the far side.

This had to be Legacy. The only thing I knew about it was that Reamer had run straight into it. And that Absolute had left it for us. If Absolute wanted us to play with it, I wanted to set it on fire.

I forced a breath, gritted my teeth, and plunged after him.

A layer of fine bubbles covered the floor. I didn't see where Reamer had stepped, but either he'd gone on safely or the bubbles had already eaten him. I pushed for more speed as I approached, then tromped straight out onto them.

My shoes slipped a little. I wobbled.

The bubbles had no give, but the gleam wasn't a finish on the bubbles. A thin layer of slime covered the floor.

My hand automatically reached for a wall to catch myself, but I stopped before slapping my hand into the gleaming coating. That stuff could be acid, or some sort of biological nightmare.

I forced myself to take a deep breath through my clenched teeth and carefully set out after Reamer.

The bubbles on either side sometimes left open space near the wall, and sometimes came within a few feet of the green-encrusted railing, but I always had room to slip through.

I didn't touch the bubbles with my hands. I wanted Reamer—he'd run for a reason, and it couldn't be a good one—but I didn't want to experiment with Legacy. The bubbles somehow radiated a dry warmth, like summer-drenched concrete at twilight, despite the mucous covering them.

The corridor turned, and suddenly thin strands of green and yellow fiber criss-crossed the air before me. They stretched from floor to ceiling, from the ceiling to the wall, from the mass of bubbles that bulged up against the short glass wall that separated this level from what had been open air to the level below. Droplets of slime ran down them like rain. The central mass now bulged up so high I couldn't see the opposite wall.

Maybe a hundred feet ahead the bubbles smothered the mall's north entrance, a solid mass rising to join the ceiling. The yellow fibers seemed to converge in the center of that bulk, in a giant ball of viscous snot.

Reamer stood only a few feet in front of that mess. He'd crouched to slip beneath a navel-high tendril blocking his path.

"Reamer!" I shouted.

He glanced back, his expression a mélange of fear and anger. Whirled away and tried to hurry forward without touching any of the strands.

"Stop!"

He dropped to his hands and knees, heedless of the slimy floor, wiggling his way beneath another tendril.

Reamer thought the tendrils were dangerous. I had to assume the same. Absolute had left them for us; the tendrils might be harmless, or might tear us apart. Again.

I turned sideways, slipped between a tendril and the wall, took a high step to avoid tripping on another, then did a sideways crouch-and-shuffle to evade two more.

Reamer ducked right. Towards the rest rooms?

No, towards the facilities closet. When I'd toured the mall, shortly after starting with Frayville PD, the overweight and overhairy security guard guiding me took me into that closet.

With the ladder.

And the trap door leading to the roof.

If Reamer got to the roof and jammed the trap door behind him, I'd never catch him. No way I could cover all the exits from the roof by myself. He'd easily get down and away. And in this empty city, with thousands of vacant homes to hide in, I'd never find him.

I jerked off my linen jacket and wrapped it around my left hand as a misshapen mitten. Teeth gritted, pulse pounding even harder, I reached my shaking hand out for a tendril.

It didn't give.

My chest and mouth still hurt from a shortage of air, but I didn't dare breathe. A slow degree at a time, I pinched the tendril between my thumb and palm.

It still didn't give. Through the layered linen, the wispy tendril felt like steel or concrete.

I launched myself forward, using my jacketed left hand to pull myself around the maze.

Nothing tried to eat my face as I swung through the web, and seconds later I followed Reamer into the darkened service corridor.

The bubbles stopped a few feet down the broad corridor, leaving the faded tile floor and white concrete walls. A solar-powered emergency light hanging from the fiberglass ceiling made a single point of painfully brilliant light, casting enough illumination to reveal the restroom doors but not enough to read the OSHA posters in the glass display case. At the end of the hall, the metal door to the maintenance closet hung a few inches ajar.

I slowed my steps, trying to reduce the slap of gym shoe on ceramic to a soft creak. My lungs still hadn't caught up, but I made my breathing slower and deeper and quieter. The silence grew freakish: no air handlers, no fans, no buzz of fluorescent lighting, no murmur of crowd or soft music. Not even an unintelligible human voice or the whistle of wind on sand. The loudest silence of my life.

Metal clanged on metal. From the maintenance closet.

Keeping each step quiet, I trotted forward. The white metal closet door felt cool on my hand, then I shoved it violently in and stomped forward.

The room felt larger than I remembered, but more crowded. Shelves along the wall held gallon bottles of cleaning chemicals with big POISON labels. A workbench in the opposite corner held tools in neat racks. The single LED emergency light in the middle of the ceiling cut sharp shadows from everything. The stench of bleach cut through the air, so that soap and wax could follow it.

At the opposite end, a ladder climbed to the ceiling ten feet overhead. Reamer stood with his head against the ceiling, hanging on with one arm while banging on the trap door with the other. When the closet door crashed against the wall behind it, he glanced over his shoulder and scowled at me.

I charged forward.

Reamer started down the ladder, dropping his feet as fast as he could.

I squeezed between the floor waxing machine and a rack of gallon bottles.

Reamer's feet hit the concrete floor.

I danced around a collection of wheeled buckets.

Then Reamer spun to face me, a five-foot wooden mop handle in his hands.

I charged forward, trying to get inside his reach before he could attack.

Reamer raised the wooden handle.

Ready to swing it into my skull.

Again.

And this time, there weren't any teenage girls to help me out. Just me and a felon, at the silent end of an abandoned mall overrun with alien matter.

Better than a flamethrower, at least.

Chapter 29

HIS BACK to the concrete wall, Reamer raised the mop handle, holding it like a baseball bat, with the cloth head close to him, ready to crack my skull.

I threw myself into park, feet scrabbling on the tile to stay out of his reach. The rubber soles on my shoes squeaked on the ceramic floor, my arms windmilled, and I lurched to a halt inches outside Reamer's range. A broom handle isn't a flamethrower or even a baseball bat, but it isn't harmless. You can grab someone who's waving a weapon—if you have a partner, or some way to catch the weapon. Working alone, I'd have to wait for him to charge and hope I could both evade his swing long enough to move in and seize him.

Reamer's wide bloodshot eyes glanced at me, at the open door behind me, back at my face, towards the ceiling, and back. "Leave me alone!" He waved the mop handle, sweeping the space between us.

I took a step back and raised my hands. "Put the mop down, Reamer."

"I knew it! I knew you remembered me," Reamer said.

I kept my hands upraised, before my face. "You're hard to forget."

"You've got no rights now," he said, words tumbling out. "You can't touch me, you're not a cop anymore, you're just like the rest of us."

His words hit me like he'd jabbed my gut with the end of the mop. My breath shuddered, and tension rippled down my back. The smells of cleanser and wax and the moldering tang of disused cleaning equipment suddenly seemed stronger. I blinked and gathered what little dignity I had left. "I'm the closest thing to a cop we have around here."

"That doesn't matter," he said. "The law is gone. Everything's gone. You've got no right to get after me."

My throat felt tight. Reamer was right. I hated it, but he was right. Not that it mattered. I wasn't trying to arrest him. All I needed was answers. If I had to beat him to keep Alice and Ceren and everyone else safe, I'd still sleep well tonight.

Someone had hit me over the head. Tried to burn Teresa and me alive. And Reamer's threats were the closest thing to a motive I'd found.

Reamer's Adam's apple bobbled. The mop whistled as it sliced the space between us. He swung too far, whacking into the metal storage shelf to his left. Gallon plastic bottles rattled. An empty jug of floor wax toppled to the tile. Reamer jumped at the hollow thud.

If I couldn't get to Reamer, I needed to make him come to me. I took another step back, then a second. My heel kicked a wheeled mop bucket. I needed some room, so I stepped forward. "You wanted my head."

"You sent me to prison!"

"I did." He wasn't going to come forward and take a swing at me. Not unless I made him angrier. "That's where you belonged."

Reamer gritted his teeth. "You bastard."

"You were selling pills to high schoolers."

The mop shook in his hands. Reamer's jaw slid sideways against his teeth.

"We should have beaten the shit out of you before we locked you up," I said. "Let the parents line up to take a swing at you."

Reamer trembled even harder.

"All so *you* could support your coke habit," I said. "Do you know how many kids' lives you ruined?"

His legs bent a few degrees at the knees. Reamer planted his feet and shifted his weight forward.

He'd move. Any moment now.

Then Reamer choked out "Twelve." He held the mop handle to one side, ready to swing. "Twelve kids."

I blinked.

"Is that what you want to hear? Twelve kids, okay. Eight of them bought Percocets, four Ritalin. I taught Jeri to grind up the Ritalin and snort it. Is that what you want to know?" His voice rose to a shout. "What about the parents, huh? Most of my customers were grownups. I know their names, too. My *customers* cursed me for selling the same shit to their kids. And not a fucking day goes by that I don't think of every. One. Of them."

Reamer's chest shook. Tears formed in the corners of his eyes.

"I've been clean for two years now," he said. "But you bastards won't let me make up for it. Make up for *any* of it. Won't let me be clean. Just keep pushing my face in the dirt. I know what I did. Okay? I'm fucking *sorry*."

I studied Reamer's agonized face.

"Dammit," I said. "It's not you."

Reamer's brow furrowed. "What?"

"You're not the one who cracked my skull yesterday."

"Me?" His eyebrows rose into his hair. "I'm staying as far away from *you* as I fucking can."

I exhaled, trying to relax.

He stared at me.

I took a step back. "Listen," I said. "I'm going to walk away now."

Reamer looked puzzled.

"You didn't try to set me on fire last night," I said. "When I saw you at the gas station… You ran, and I remembered you swore to get me, so I thought—I thought—look, I'm leaving. You go your own way." I shuffled my feet around the buckets. "Far as I'm concerned, we're done."

I retreated another step, then turned. *Now*. If Reamer was going to attack, it would be while my back was turned. My ears caught every creak and tiny ringing within the metal shelves along the walls. I held myself ready to spin and dodge the coming blow.

Reamer didn't make a sound, maybe even didn't move as I walked out the door and back into the alien hallway. I didn't see him while I wove through the giant green bubbles and tendrils of Legacy back to the mall's courtyard, back into a tangle of questions and without even one answer for company.

Chapter 30

WALKING DOWN dead escalators is harder than running up them. The steps are too tall, even for me, and too narrow to comfortably stand on. Each lurch down dragged my spirits with it. For a few glorious minutes, everything had seemed so simple. I investigated Doug's transformation. Someone attacked me to stop it. I saw a guy who had threatened to get me. He ran. I chased. But he'd fled thinking that I meant him harm, not because he'd tried to kill me and failed.

Simple dissolved into complex too quickly. No reasons for the transformed father. No reason someone would attack me. Twice. Teresa, a woman who might or might not want more from me than sex, missing. And just as a bonus, two teenage girls who were and weren't my responsibility throwing wild parties.

The people in the courtyard stopped working, turning to watch me lurch down to their level.

"Hi," a woman said as my feet touched the floor. Pale, with pink streaks through her black hair, she nodded at me from her office chair. Her hands hovered over the computer keyboard in her lap, paused mid-word.

The man nodded his plump face at me. He hadn't shaved in a couple days, but his polo shirt, windbreaker, and cargo pants looked tidy.

"Hello," I said.

"What's going on?" the man said.

"Nothing," I said.

"Where's Ian?" the woman asked.

"Up there," I said. "He'll be along, I'm sure."

They glanced at each other, then back at me. The man's weight shifted forward, and I caught hints of aggression in the set of his shoulders.

"I'm Detective Holtzmann," I said. "Frayville PD."

The man nodded. "And where's Ian?"

"Up by the restrooms." I jerked a thumb over my shoulder. "We talked, that's all. I needed to ask him some questions. He's up there, he's fine."

"Fine. Right," the woman said, her nostrils flaring. "So why didn't he come down with you?"

"He didn't want to talk to me," I said. "Didn't want to walk back with me, either."

The man grunted.

I decided to prod a bit. "Is this thing Legacy?"

The man shook his head. "Tell me something. You come in here. You chase Ian through here. You come back. He doesn't. You know what this looks like?"

"Really," I said. "I'm police. Frayville PD."

"Where's your badge?" he said. "Where's your department?"

"Lost it in a fire."

"Uh-huh," he said. "There's a couple ways this can go. Brandi, can you go check on Ian?"

"Sure." Brandi stood up, and I realized that my eyes came to her chin. I couldn't help glancing down. Flat shoes. She had to be at least six foot eight. I suddenly remembered seeing her around Frayville, but never had reason to interact with her—just one of those faces you get used to seeing in a small city.

She didn't take a step, though. She stood and watched me.

"All things being equal," the man said, "I'd rather not shoot you. Stand there while she checks on him, and I won't have to."

He carried his weight on the balls of his feet, and his shoulders were relaxed. A bulge in his jacket pocket was about the right size for a small handgun. Most people get a little loud when they threaten to shoot you, but his voice hadn't changed. Either he was a sociopath or he'd grown used to threatening people.

"I'll stay here," I said.

Brandi nodded at the man, circled around me, and climbed the escalator, calling for Reamer every few seconds.

I held myself still, hands empty at my sides.

The man didn't take his eyes from me.

"You look like you'd know what to do with a gun," I said.

"Four years MP," he said.

I was outclassed. Military police regularly subdued trained fighters, selected for their ability to subdue trained killers. I normally subdued drunks. And this man carried himself like a fighter.

The question was, what would Reamer tell Brandi? I'd tried to leave Reamer in peace, but I had chased him through the mall. Pursued him through Legacy's alien web. Trapped him in a dimly lit room, behind an alien growth. Terrified him.

People don't enjoy things like that.

My badge wouldn't have helped. I'd been running around under the guise of Police Detective Kevin Holtzmann, but that was doubly wrong. I wasn't Kevin, no matter how much I felt like him. And I wasn't a police detective. A police detective needs a police department. With no department, no badge, and very much an impostor, I might as well have been exactly what these people thought I was—an intruder chasing one of their own.

A year ago I would have called for backup. The man would have contacted his superiors. We'd do the bureaucratic two-step and go on our way. Now, he might shortcut all of that and shoot me in the gut.

I forcibly dropped my shoulders as if I had relaxed. "Ian's a friend of yours."

The man shrugged.

"I didn't touch him," I said.

"Then we'll talk," he said. "Once I know you're telling the truth."

My throat tightened in fear. Maybe if Reamer had a few minutes, if he could think about what I'd, he might say we were okay. Right now, though?

Most likely outcome, Brandi returns. Things get ugly. I get hurt.

I studied the space, trying to find something I could use. Half a dozen eight-foot folding tables around us held complicated electronic equipment. They'd brought in several computer displays, most of them broad enough to qualify as family televisions. One table held soldering gear and storage cabinets with dozens of tiny clear plastic drawers. Cables of different colors and thicknesses, confined into neat bundles with Velcro tape, connected the tables. Heavy-duty electrical cables ran across the floor towards the nearest food kiosk.

And the man's attention didn't flicker from my chest.

My best bet was to wait for an interruption. Use Brandi's return to close in. Get inside his reach before he could pull his gun.

Someone had already pointed a flamethrower at me today. I didn't need another fight.

"He's okay," Brandi shouted from overhead.

My feet shifted to launch me forward, but her words penetrated my brain just before I moved. The gun hadn't twitched, but I thought I saw his finger tighten a hair around the trigger.

"What was that?" he shouted.

Brandi appeared on the mezzanine. "He's okay. Mad as hell, but Officer Friendly didn't hurt him."

I looked at the man.

He studied me for another moment, then relaxed.

My breath rattled out, and the world stopped fading to gray. Maybe Reamer really had changed. He could have launched Brandi and the man at me. If they had shot me, thrown me in a dumpster, and set me on fire, nobody would have said anything.

I hadn't realized how much I relied on my badge, on the implied authority backing it. When I'd felt insecure, the familiar touch of that shield against my palm had centered me. Without it, without the mantle of law, I only wanted to get out of the mall and find a place to think. Maybe down a few beers. I'd come out here to learn about Legacy, though, and I didn't see anyone else here.

I took a step sideways and leaned my hand against a cafe table. Cold sweat drenched my back.

Brandi trotted easily down the steep escalator stairs. "So," she said with forced lightness, "Ian says he's not coming out until you're gone. Why did you chase after him?"

I studied Brandi, then the man. "Yesterday, someone hit me over the head with a baseball bat. Then threw burning diesel on me." Brandi flinched, but the man's expression didn't change. "Reamer—Ian—threatened me for putting him in jail. Said he'd kill me. Just by chance, I stopped at the gas station where he was. He saw me, and ran. I chased."

The man nodded. "I'd have done the same."

"Steve!"

He shrugged again. "That's how the world is, babe."

"Ian's clean," Brandi said. "Been clean for years now."

"He threatened an officer. Makes him a suspect." He turned to face me. "Steve. Steve Lightner. This is my wife, Brandi."

Part of the tension drained from my stance. "Kevin Holtzmann, detective, Frayville PD." My back tightened and I added "Former."

"Didn't think they needed a detective out here," Steve said. He sat down in a wheeled office chair and held out a hand to a cafeteria chair between us.

I sat. "Most of the time, they didn't."

Brandi crossed her arms. "Ian is working really hard, and you scared the snot out of him."

I nodded. "I told him we were done, that I didn't suspect him."

"You could try apologizing," she said.

I blinked.

Steve looked at me, looked at Brandi, opened his mouth, and closed it.

I thought about telling Brandi that wasn't how things worked, but maybe they did. Now. Besides, I needed her to talk to me. "Right now, he doesn't want anything to do with me. When I see him again, if he seems to be up for it, we'll sit down and talk."

"He's got enough to deal with," Brandi said. She looked ready to hit me. "He doesn't need you running him down."

I still felt proud about putting Reamer away, even though the felon didn't serve out his whole term. Nothing I could do about that unless I wanted to spend my days as a prison guard. And I suspected Reamer would have preferred time in prison to death by Absolute.

"As far as I'm concerned," I said, forcing my tone to stay level, "what happened before is over."

"Just don't get after him."

I held my silence.

Eventually Steve said "If you weren't gunning for Ian, what brought you out here?"

I nodded towards the towering green bubbles that had overflowed the north end of the room, their coat of slime gleaming in the filtered sunlight. "I take it that's Legacy?"

Steve nodded. "Yes."

"What is it?" I said.

"Far as we can tell," Steve said, "it's Absolute's idea of a library. It's a legacy."

Chapter 31

MY FACE must have given away my surprise. The great green slimy bubbles mounded to the ceiling, filling the abandoned shopping mall, didn't resemble any library I'd ever thought of. Brandi snickered and sat in another office chair, spinning her back to me and pulling her keyboard back into her lap.

"What kind of knowledge?" I finally said.

"We don't know yet." Steve shrugged. "Found a couple ways to get at it, though." He jerked his head towards the green bubbles. "Go in a bit, you'll find a little alcove with two handprints. Spray-painted red around them. Put your hands there, ask a question, see what happens."

"Absolute talks to us?" I said. Anger flashed through my gut and my throat clamped almost shut.

"Doesn't feel like a person," Steve said. "Feels like a machine. A machine that doesn't understand us, so gives answers we can't understand."

"Can't understand yet," Brandi said.

"So what's all this gear?" I said.

Steve stood up. "Come on." He led me around the back of the table and followed a bundle of different cables to the leading edge of a stream of bubbles. "Look at that."

The cables ran straight into the front of a green bubble. Up close, the giant bubbles had tiny bubbles all over their surface as if they'd gone from simmering to petrified instantaneously.

I blinked.

Legacy had USB connectors.

And video ports.

Steve and Brandi had cables in half a dozen connectors, but this stony organic mass had dozens more. I recognized some of those connectors, from computers back when I was growing up. Back then computers had special ports for keyboards and mice, for network devices and printers and hard drives and everything else you might want to attach. Looking closer, I realized that Legacy had all of these and more, connectors I'd never seen but were clearly human, mounted as firmly as if Legacy had been injection-molded around them.

The fiber optic connectors even had little green protective caps, attached to Legacy by small flaps.

The area was even free of slime for about a hand's width all around.

"Huh." I said. "We're supposed to plug in."

Steve gave a single impassive nod.

"I don't suppose you can just hook up a TV?"

"Sure," he said, "but all we get is gibberish. The problem is, we don't understand the encoding."

Brandi looked at him. "Yet."

"Yes, Brandi. Yet," Steve said. "I did signals intelligence before I went MP. Brandi's a hacker." His flat voice picked up a note of pride. "A damned good one."

"What have you learned?" I said.

"Lots about encoding," Steve said, leading me back to the chairs. "Nothing actionable."

"Yet," Brandi said.

"Yet," Steve said.

"We will crack this thing open," Brandi said. "Rip out everything in there."

I'd heard less determination from ultra-marathoners. "I think you will." I felt glad to see people working with a purpose, but that didn't help me now. I'd wanted to learn something about what happened to Doug, but Legacy didn't seem able to share any answers I'd understand.

"So, Officer Friendly," Brandi said, "care to try your chance in the Booth of Befuddlement?"

"Excuse me?" I said.

"Put your hands on the prints," Steve said. "People don't get much, but we've learned a few things from it."

"Like what?" I said.

Steve walked back to his chair and picked up a spiral-bound notebook. "First few folk we saw asked about people they knew before. Didn't get much."

"I haven't seen anyone younger than twelve or so," I said. "Anybody ask about that?"

Steve's finger ran down the page and shook his head. "Someone asked how we can die."

My eyebrows arched. "Really? Who?"

Steve pursed his lips. "Don't think that's your business. She has enough troubles."

"Doctor-patient confidentiality?" I said. Steve opened his mouth and I waved him off. "No, I get it." I leaned forward. "Did she get an answer?"

"She said she 'sensed forever.'"

Forever.

Jared Collins, the sick bastard, had told the truth. He'd said he'd "dumped the old mortal clay" before driving Kevin into suicidal, homicidal despair. I felt sick to my stomach. Four years ago, before Absolute ate the Southern Hemisphere and the northern nations had burned half the planet to glass in self-defense, if someone had offered Kevin immortality with his family he would have snatched it. Back then, the idea of immortality would have been a blessing. Now, alone most likely forever, Sheila's and Julia's absences stabbed at me. Kevin, that lucky bastard, didn't have to deal with it at all.

"What about..." I paused to organize my thoughts. "Changes. Can we change our bodies? Can we be changed?"

"Nobody's figured out how," Steve said. "But I'm sure we can."

"Why so sure?"

"We're made out of Absolute stuff now," Steve said. "We'll figure it out, one day."

Someone's figured out how. Either they haven't told anyone how, or he can't. "Any clue why?"

"Did they teach you to ask specific questions at Police Academy?" Brandi said. She sat with her back to me, hands clattering on the keyboard. "Because there's an awful lot of whys out there."

"Why Absolute did this," I said.

"No," Steve said. "Not a hint."

I scowled in frustrated curiosity. We all wanted answers, Legacy might have the answers, but getting them out was beyond my abilities. Steve and Brandi might master Legacy, but it wouldn't be today. And even if eternity waited for me, I couldn't wait for answers.

"It doesn't sound like you have much concrete," I said. "It'll be easier if you just told me what you learned."

Steve skimmed the page. "Most people report very abstract answers. There's a sense that we have eternity. People who ask about danger get a sense that something's coming for us, that a threat is—imminent. There's no sense of hostility from Legacy itself. Only the maddening idea that a danger is coming. And there's maybe half a dozen people who've tried and come out dazed but without anything useful."

"Legacy attacks them?" I said.

Brandi snorted. "Absolute attacked us. Legacy just knocked them around a bit."

"Everyone gets a little dizzy when they use the handprints," Steve said. "Seems like the people who push harder for answers get really confused. Can't stand up for a while afterwards. That's why we mark the handprints in red, when we find them. Touch the wrong part of Legacy and you take the ride." He pointed at a darkened storefront with his chin. "We opened up the furniture shop. Let people lie down for a few hours if they need it." His eyes looked distant.

"It's alien," Brandi said. "Really, really alien. We all thought Absolute was alien, but plugging your mind into Legacy shows what the word *alien* really means. You want answers? Go put your hands in his mouth. Try to follow what he's thinking. You won't be able to, and you'll turn your own brain inside out just trying, but you'll get a sense of something."

I considered trying Legacy myself. Putting my hands on the spots and asking what would transform a man. If Legacy gave firm answers I might have tried it, but I didn't have hours to recover in exchange for a feeling. Doug wasn't going anywhere, but my mysterious assailants were still out there. I didn't want them to find me on a shopping mall bed, sprawled on stale bedding unable to stand.

Now I knew what Legacy was. Fine. But that knowledge didn't help me at all.

Chapter 32

THE LAST of the mist burned away under the midmorning sun, leaving a day that promised more warmth than the one before. Winchester Mall's asphalt lot blasted its captured heat against my face during the trudge back to my ride. Someone wanted me dead, and I had no idea who. Something had transformed Doug. While my guts screamed it was a crime, my gut didn't understand the ground rules. His change might be a natural consequence of something he'd done. Just like what Teresa and I had done had changed me. The firebomber might have saved me from becoming another Doug. I'd chased Reamer, only to find him innocent. Another bad assumption, leading me to the back end of nowhere. I needed an ice-cold beer and one of Sheila's massive burgers out on our—Kevin's—deck. I had a headache and an empty badge holder.

The police cruiser still sat under the service station's metal awning next to the diesel stand.

"What the hell."

On a whim I pulled the pump out of its slot. The blue LED screen lit up. I twisted off the car's fuel cap, stuffed the pump into the fill line, and hit the button. Fuel flowed. The bitter tang of diesel filled the air.

Where to now?

Jack had opened for drinks earlier in the day yesterday. Maybe this was the time to attack the sex question. If Doug's transformation was part of the new natural order, I would at least have something to tell his daughter and I could put the mystery out of my brain. I hoped it wasn't that easy. A world without sex depressed me even more than the idea of telling Alice why her dad was gone. It's not that I wanted sex—the bare word made me think of Sheila, and the memory opened a screaming chasm inside me. Teresa had distracted me, but I missed Sheila with a passion far beyond mere sex. I didn't feel like sleeping with anyone, but a world without sex would be an uglier place.

The fuel pump clicked off. I got in the cruiser, started the motor, and coasted down the hill back into town. The open windows carried the smells of wood smoke, trees, and a hint of burning plastic. Teresa's home still cast a hazy gray column into the sky.

And that's when I saw the monster escaping the convenience store.

Chapter 33

A FEW businesses clung to the hillside where Sand River Bridge ended and Frayville proper began. A vacant, boarded-up restaurant on the left overlooked the lush wooded valley beneath the bridge, a gorgeous view if you ignored the gravel pit and the train yard in the middle of it, all sadly abandoned. Just like us.

Across Main Street, the pizza place and the Quick-Stop, fine purveyors of off-brand Real Hunter Meat Stix and liquor and cheap porn magazines and plastic bags of surplus comics for rednecks headed north, competed for the Ugliest Building in Town prize. Over the years I'd grown accustomed to seeing kids hanging out in the Quick-Stop parking lot, skateboarding and dancing and working on sugar highs from slushies and candy. The empty town was bad enough, but the thought of the empty parking lot raised a fresh knot in my chest. I didn't expect to see a man with a tangle of snakes haloing his head climbing out through the broken glass door.

I stomped on the brake. Tires squealed on concrete.

At least a dozen of the snakes snapped towards me, their heads shifting like jaws opening and closing.

I slammed the cruiser to a stop at an angle that blocked Main Street's two northbound lanes.

The cloud of shifting snakes obscured the man's head. He reached behind himself to tug the bottom of his long gray overcoat free of the broken glass jutting from the doorframe.

Kevin had trained for this. He would know what to do. *Step out of the car. Open the cruiser's rear door. Turn around. Slip into the flamethrower's shoulder straps. Stand up straight. Buckle the belt. Pull the nozzle. Burn.* Willow trees growing hospital melons were weird. Doug the Dick of Doom trapped in his bedroom was weird. But this piece of weirdness shook its leg free and hopped out of the Quick-Stop, where weirdos and kids constantly came and went.

My first thought was: Absolute. Or his minion.

But the debacle with Ian Reamer still smarted. I'd jumped to an assumption—a logical assumption, one I'd jump to again in the same situation—and never landed on the far side.

The creature carried a bulging plastic bag on one hand.

He cradled a cardboard case of beer in the other.

I forcibly pushed out the air trapped inside my lungs.

Weird, yes. Monstrous, yes.

But maybe I could live with the kind of monster that wanted a bag of munchies and a few beers.

The creature raised its bag to wave at me.

I backed the car up and turned into the parking lot. By making a broad circle, I turned the car back around towards the road and stopped maybe ten feet away from the creature. My foot rested lightly on the brake, ready to slip down to the accelerator and rocket me out of there.

I leaned my elbow out the driver's side window. What do you say to an alien?

"Hello."

My voice didn't squeak. I felt kind of proud of that.

If it twitched wrong I'd shoot away in the car. Grab the flamethrower. Burn down the block if I had to.

I didn't expect it to say "Detective Hertz-man!"

I blinked. Only one person ever called me that. I flashed back to Teresa and Jesse drinking beer and telling me I wouldn't recognize Paul Drennel.

"Paul?"

Schizophrenia ran in Paul's family. He'd joined the Navy out of high school, served overseas, and received a medical discharge after his first psychotic break. The police and social workers had arranged a long-term group home bed for him more than once, but every time we got him shelter he refused it.

The snakes facing me bobbed up and down in a vague approximation of a nod. Now that I was closer, I saw that the things weaving out of his head weren't snakes. They were stalks, with an eye on the tip of each,

each eye different from the others. Eyes the size of my fist. Tiny eyes suited for a mouse. Scleras of white and yellow and bloodshot emerald, irises in blue and brown and red and mauve, and black pupils, mostly round but some slit like cat's eyes, all bobbing and weaving at the end of tentacles that looked too slim to support them.

The figure laughed. "You sound surprised! I su-*prized* you."

This didn't look like Paul, even if you discounted the eyes. Paul always wore every piece of clothing he owned. He zipped his winter coat shut in the muggiest bowels of summer, and tied rope and rags around his legs and arms to hold his clothes against his skin. This man wore a loose gray overcoat, jeans, and a T-shirt.

Paul had been massively overweight, a side effect of the antipsychotic medication and his appalling diet. I could only see the chin and hands of this creature, but they didn't seem to have a spare ounce on them.

The Paul I knew wouldn't willingly have gone into the Quick-Stop. Surrounding him with walls and a ceiling would have made him scream and fight. He wouldn't have stopped screaming and fighting until he lost himself in open air again.

But he had Paul's voice.

"How are you doing?" I asked, keeping my voice soft and level.

He laughed, somewhere behind the tentacles. He had Paul's laugh, too. "I am doing *so* fine! Haven't been this totally excellent since service. I'm a new man, Detective Hertz-man. You won't be running me in at *all*."

"What happened to you?"

"I'm not coming apart anymore!" He bent at the waist and set his beer and bag on the asphalt beside him. "You gotta see this." With both hands, he grabbed the bottom of his T-shirt and yanked it up.

I was right. He didn't have a spare ounce of flab on him.

White chains and leathery straps crossed his abdomen, completely obscuring his skin. I couldn't figure out what they were made of; too dull for metal and too tightly fitted for off-the-shelf anything.

I blinked in surprise.

Those straps and chains and ties were made of Paul.

"I'm tied up, see?" he said. "I'm cured! The nurse said if I kept taking my meds I'd feel better, and she was right, I'm all good now. Don't even need my coat to keep me from coming apart. And I can *see*,

see?" The tentacles swirled around his face like a school of fish, moving to some aquatic rhythm I sensed but couldn't feel.

"Oh, I see it all right. How'd you get into the Quick-Stop?"

"Nurse Nealie told me I could." His voice caught a note of doubt. "That's okay, wasn't it? The door was open and nobody was there, and I've been so *hungry*. All the healthy stuff is gone, like the sandwiches and eggs and stuff, and the ice cream's all melted and the slushie got all nasty, so I got me some chips and *quee*-so and spice drops. Lots of spice drops. I left a bag of spice drops, though. You can't take them all. That's rude."

"I know you don't want to be rude," I said. "I meant, you don't like going into buildings."

"Oh! That?" he said. "I'm cured. I told you I'm cured. I can see now."

"You weren't blind before," I said.

Paul's chin drooped, and a few eyes glared at me through half-closed lids. "They can't sneak up on me. It doesn't matter if they can go through walls, I can see through the walls, I can see them, and they *know* I can see them. I can even see them when I sleep. I'm cured now. Mostly cured. I can be better, but I'm doing better. Lots better."

"Yeah," I said slowly. "I can see you're doing a whole lot better, now."

This had to be a copy of Paul Drennel. I'd given him a bag of spice drops and a big coffee a couple months ago, when he wouldn't come into the homeless shelter before February's ice storm. He'd kept his voice, his manic charm, but lost the blanketing fear. If Absolute had decided to infiltrate or assault those of us he'd freed, he would have chosen a less broken puppet.

"You want a candy bar?" Paul said, bending over to grab his bag. "I've got lots."

"No, thanks, Paul. You go ahead." My heart quickened in excitement. If this was Paul… He'd changed his body to become what he wanted, or what he needed. Could we all do this? Did you have to be crazy to pull it off? How did Paul do it?

Paul's eyes parted around his chin to expose his mouth. I recognized the ragged yellow teeth. He peeled the wrapper back from a Snickers bar and stuffed the whole thing into his mouth. I saw his jaw work from side to side as his hands peeled another. He swallowed the candy after too little chewing and fed another into his maw.

"Hungry?" I said.

Paul swallowed the second bar. "Starving." A handful of spice drops went in after it.

Suspicion twinged in the back of my brain. "You've lost a lot of weight," I said.

Paul nodded. He crouched, then sat on the dirty asphalt, feet sticking straight out in front of him.

"When you got cured," I said carefully, "were you hungry?"

Paul swallowed again. "Starving."

After last night's fire, when I'd changed, I'd felt ravenous. I'd awakened a few pounds lighter.

We could change. Paul proved we could change intentionally. I didn't know how he'd figured it out, but he had. And, figuring out how to change, he'd solved his most immediate problems.

Change isn't free. It's never been free. Change required energy. Animals got their energy from food. Maybe we did too.

As I watched Paul eat, his eyes twitched and shuddered. His chin began swelling.

I reflexively leaned back in the car. My hand tightened on the wheel.

A bubble of skin formed on Paul's chin. He didn't seem to notice, but focused on tearing open a pack of beef jerky.

The bubble twitched and stretched, extending from Paul's chin like a growing plant.

I watched, fascinated, the flamethrower forgotten.

When the unfolding tendril was almost a foot long, the end swelled into a pool-ball-sized lump. A slit formed in the tip. Then the skin rolled back like a peeling banana to expose a glistening, multifaceted insect eye.

"Ah," Paul said. "That's better."

The stalk twitched. The eye peered around.

Paul started in on a family size bag of salt-and-vinegar chips.

I began to smile.

Maybe I'd screwed up. Maybe I'd fumbled around all day. Maybe sorrow and solitude loomed over me. Maybe I wasn't Kevin, wasn't even me.

But the world still had rules, like conservation of mass and energy. If I kept my eyes open and used my brain, I should be able to understand the world again. If I knew the rules, I'd figure out what had happened to Doug. Find my attackers, and stop them. Whatever I was, I would either lose and die or become stronger and smarter.

"Detective Holtzmann" said a voice behind me, inches from my head.

Chapter 34

I SPUN so quickly my elbow cracked on the steering wheel. Pain flashed down my arm, and white sparks flickered in the edge of my vision.

A boy in his late teens peered in the passenger side window, bent over, hands braced on his knees. Neatly combed black hair hung over his right eye, but the left side of his scalp was shaved to fuzz. Silver rings shone in his nose and left ear. I smelled hot peppers and too much chocolate body spray.

At my movement he stepped back, hands raised. "Hey! Chill, dude."

I glanced back over my shoulder. Paul's numerous eyes watched every direction at once, but he seemed intent on methodically working his way through the bag of chips right there in the parking lot. "S' okay," I said. "You surprised me." *That wouldn't have surprised Kevin.* No, I still had lingering adrenaline from seeing Paul and chasing Reamer. The kid probably would have gotten Kevin, too.

His gaze held my face. Wrongly.

I knew how teenagers and college-age kids look at authority figures. There's rebelliousness, resentment, insolence, and that excruciating can't-you-see-I'm-innocent wide-eyed mask. Rarely, thankfully, there's a horrified desperation after something gouged the innocence from their soul.

This kid had none of that. He had the face of a Buddhist monk, waiting tranquilly for what I would do next.

I stopped rubbing my elbow. "Acceptance," I said.

"And Rick." He gave a mocking bow. "At your service, Officer."

"Does Rick need the police?" I said.

"We all need the police."

Acceptance had offered to help me, when I couldn't stand being me. I'd had a taste of that last night. I'd been too weak to resist it. "What does Acceptance want, then?"

"We've been watching you put things together." The boy spoke slowly and carefully, his eyes looking over my shoulder at an invisible teleprompter.

I glanced around. "You're following me?"

Rick laughed, renewed life in his voice. "Do you think we wouldn't have someone watching Legacy? Or hanging around Jack's?" He waved a hand at Paul. "Or keeping an eye on our most inexplicable resurrection?"

My spine tingled. I'd grown accustomed to working in the gaze of omnipresent video cameras, but nobody looked at that footage unless something went wrong. Unwatched camera footage was different than the single mind of Acceptance watching me in all these locations. "I'm not that interesting."

"Au contrary." His tone made it clear he'd twisted the word for effect. Rick took a couple steps towards me, loudly scuffing his feet. I got the feeling he deliberately made that noise, mocking my earlier surprise. "All those dudes woke up and did what they wanted to do. You're the one who came out and stuck his nose into other people's business."

"I'm a cop. So what?"

Rick bent back down, resting his elbows on the bottom of the passenger side window. "We got a guy who wanted to cook. A chick who knows the water plant. Two nurses, no doctors. A couple of electricians. A janitor. No judges, no social workers, no damn lawyers. All these people with real skills. Most of them're getting up off the couch and doing what they do."

I thought of Fred and Harry, watching for fires. Nobody'd asked them to. "So?"

"It's like Absolute had a plan," Rick said. "Like it had some idea what we needed to keep things together."

I'd danced around the same idea, but hadn't thought of it in terms of people. The melons might have healed me, or helped me heal myself, but the population made a difference too. How many people knew how the electrical grid worked? Not many, but we had Chad Brockett out at the substation replacing transformers. And he'd known how to check the main power plant, too.

Absolute had released a few people.

But had he chosen ones who could help us survive?

"But then there's weirdos," Rick said. "Like Paul."

I glanced over my shoulder. Paul sat on the curb now, his back against a streetlight, downing a beer. His myriad eyestalks waved as if drifting on an invisible current. Three empty beer cans sat around him. The emptied chip bag now bulged with candy bar and jerky wrappers.

"I'm not sure what job he's supposed to have," Rick said. "And there's you."

"Me?"

Rick nodded. "Does Absolute think we need a cop to keep us on the straight and narrow? All law-abiding and shit? He can't trust us to just chill?" His voice sounded too calm and stable for his slang. Rick's smile straightened. "Or do you have another job? Something we should worry about?"

The vinyl seat beneath me suddenly felt clammy. I didn't trust Acceptance, but the thought of Acceptance not trusting me twisted my guts. My tongue felt like a dry sponge. I was just a police officer doing his best. Acceptance was a group of suicidal people who'd formed a mutual support network that let them communicate with each other, feel each other, constantly reassure each other that they were okay. I don't know that humans should have that kind of constant assurance. Compared to that, a police officer sworn to serve his community should merit trust.

"You know more than I do," I finally said.

Rick nodded. "Yep. That's why I'm here to say, go ask about the deer."

I blinked. "Excuse me?"

"He's still at Jack's," Rick said. "Jack opened up early. Gave Larry the very last bottle of Baying Beagle Winter Pale—the bastard. Veronica sees him still there. Hurry up, go ask about the deer. He won't hang forever, he's got shit to do." Rick stood straight. "Later, dude."

"Hold it!" I said.

Rick bent to peer in the passenger window again. "Yeah?"

I licked my lips. "You already know what I'm looking for."

"Mayhaps."

"So why don't you just tell me what happened to Doug?"

"Where's the fun in that?"

"This isn't fun," I said. "This might be serious. If anyone who tries having sex turns—"

Rick laughed. "Dude, I wouldn't take *that* casual-like. Really."

"So tell me."

His smile evaporated. "You know, I had trouble for a while, a few years back. There's a line between being interested in a girl and being creepy. I was, like, thirteen or fourteen, trying to figure out where that was. I was creepy. Didn't want to be. But I was. I figured it out, but still had the rep."

I didn't say anything. Silence makes people uncomfortable. They'll throw words into the gap, trying to fill it. Sometimes those words are useful.

Rick didn't look discomfited at all. He was too calm to be a college kid—placid saint, or indifferent psychopath? After giving me that chance to speak, he said, "Acceptance… All of us… We're still human. But we *are* different. If we get a bad rep, that's hard to come back from. We don't know where the line is between creepy and friendly, but we all want to be on the right side of that line. Flat-out telling you shit nobody could have figured out without being in a dozen places at once? That's *waaay* over on the creepy side of the line."

Rick wasn't the first witness to give me a hint when he knew more. But he was the first to blatantly tell me he would only hint. I didn't like a plainly labeled hint any better than the more oblique sort, but leaning on him wouldn't do much good. Interrogation plays on the subject's emotions, and the constant reassurance Acceptance gave Rick would keep the kid from spilling his guts. Instead I said, "You think we each have a job to do."

"Looks that way."

"What was your job supposed to be?" I said. "What aren't you doing that you should be?"

Rick's face split in a brilliant grin. "Looking awesome, dude. And hanging with the chicks." He straightened up and turned towards Main Street. "It's a tough job, but I'm good at it. We'll be seeing you, Officer Holtzmann!"

Immortal Clay

Rick walked around the corner of the Quick-Stop and was gone.

I put the car back in gear.

How many people were in Acceptance? And if everybody had a job to do, what weren't those people doing?

"Take care of yourself, Paul," I said, leaning my head out the window of the cruiser. "You need me, leave word up at Jack's."

Paul raised a beer, a peanut butter cup, and half a dozen eyes in salute as I pulled out of the parking lot.

Chapter 35

FRAYVILLE WASN'T quite coming back to life, but it didn't echo quite so emptily. Two young men maneuvered a dolly loaded with a pair of stacked kegs down the sidewalk. A woman in shorts and a tank top came out of the darkened pharmacy with a bulging shopping bag in each hand. A civilian car, a little blue-and-yellow two-door with tinted windows, puttered towards the mall at a sedate fifteen miles an hour.

Seeing the car took me back. In the three years between the northern nations' saturation nuclear bombing of the southern hemisphere and Absolute's final assault on humanity, gasoline had been tightly rationed. Most of the fuel production switched over to diesel, taking official vehicles like my police cruiser with it. They stank, but nobody worried about global warming back then. Even if you had a gasoline permit, you still needed cash. The roads weren't empty, but we had a lot of buses, carpools, and bicycles. Now we had a different kind of rationing; what we had was all we'd ever have. Michigan had oil wells, but no refineries—and besides, we'd be lucky to get the heat on before winter. I wondered where Reamer had found diesel.

If Acceptance was right, these people weren't the last survivors, digging through the wreckage to eke out a few more days. We were the sprouting seeds of something new. Something Absolute intended to survive. But survive as what?

There might be a future worth surviving to reach, maybe even worth working towards. I let out a thin smile.

I felt somewhat surprised that I wanted to survive. I wanted to find something to live for, something to strive for, a way to make a difference for others. I wanted life—but on my own terms, not as a gear in Absolute's master plan.

Or part of Acceptance's plans, either. But I pulled to a stop at the curb in front of Jack's anyway. The oversize, gleaming blue pickup still sprawled perpendicular across the sidewalk with its tailgate down. A squat brass antique pot or vase the size of a basketball propped the door open, letting a block of sunlight into the dim interior.

As soon as I opened the door of the police cruiser, Jack shouted "Come on in, Dee-tective" from inside.

I had just cleared the doorway, blinded by the change from brilliant sunlight to dim interior, when the thick stink of cold blood stopped me. I shaded my eyes and took half a step back, taking a breath to let my eyes adjust.

Heavy plastic bins sat on the bar and on most of the tables. Jack and a scrawny man made mostly of gristle and bone sat at a clear space at the bar, each with a brown bottle in his hand. "Jack," I said.

"Holtzmann, Deckard." Jack gestured at each of us with his bottle. "Deckard's a fearless hunter. Holtzmann's our fine po-lice force. Specializes in missing peoples."

Deckard snorted and stuck out a hand. He wore a new flannel shirt and heavy, battered denim pants. "Well, *that's* a hole with no bottom. Pleased to meet you."

I took his hand out of habit before I realized what I was doing. His callouses scraped my palm, and the muscle and bone underneath made it obvious he could crush my hand if he tried. I let go after a single shake. My hand didn't stick to his.

"Not to question your cooking," I said, "but I do have to ask—what is that smell?"

"Dinner!" Deckard said. "I do the fun bits, and Jack cooks."

I peered into an open-top plastic bin and saw several pounds of meat, roughly cut into slabs. "You're the deer hunter."

"And you're th' one who told him," Jack said. "Come by for supper, I'll hook you up with a nice venison tenderloin. The best in town. Beer?"

I shook my head. "I just put out the word."

"And Becky passed the word on to me," said Deckard. "Worth a tenderloin."

"I won't argue," I said. "I ran into Becky and—Mick, wasn't it?" Deckard nodded. "They were trying to kill a chicken."

Deckard snorted. "Mick told me. That head almost had you, did it?" His words bounced across throttled laughter.

"I'd tell it another way," I said.

"Oh, Becky kicked him twice while he told me the story," Deckard said. "Mick's a decent guy, but if you ask him he's always the hero. He would have stopped Absolute if the feds had let him."

Acceptance, through Rick, had said we all had a job to do. I wondered how Mick and Becky fit into the organizational chart. "Maybe you can answer a question for me," I said.

"Sure." Deckard tipped his beer back.

"They cut the head off the chicken. It changed shape and went berserk."

Deckard nodded, rolling the beer around his mouth.

"But you killed a deer."

Deckard began nodding, still savoring his drink.

"So," I said, "why did the deer die, but not the chicken?"

Deckard swallowed. "I've got ideas," he said. "But they're just ideas. Not all the deer died, though."

"Oh?" I said.

Jack leaned forward on his stool, his curiosity piqued.

"I shot one through the head," Deckard said. "Nice six-point buck with one twisted antler. It fell. I walked up to it. Its legs just, *unhinged*. Its hooves turned to razors and it tried to stab me. I had to run like hell. Dropped my rifle and everything. It was maybe ten feet behind me when I got the truck started. It punched holes in the tailgate before I got out."

My blood chilled. "You mean to tell me—"

Deckard raised a hand. "I got a flamethrower—north fire station—and went back. Didn't see my dead deer. I did see a buck that looked an awful lot like the one I shot, though. Looked an awful lot alike… only this one still had all its head."

Hunters always claim they can tell deer apart. I was mostly sure that the ones with the horns were male. Antlers. Whatever. "So, you think it reverted back to a deer?"

"Maybe," Deckard said. "I didn't see it happen. And I'm keeping the flamethrower in the truck."

"So, what was the difference between these," I said, waving my hand at the buckets of venison, "and the one that tried to kill you?"

"The one that went nuts, I shot in the head."

I frowned, chewing that detail in my mind. They say that a good shot to the heart can kill a man instantly, but that's not quite right. They're dying, yes, but there's still a few seconds of awareness behind their eyes. You blow a hole in someone's brain, though, and they're gone even if their heart keeps beating for another twenty years.

"You ever hunted?" Deckard said.

I shook my head. "I've seen people die, though." Down in Detroit, I'd held a couple people as they died. Up in Frayville, I usually arrived after the dying.

"Animals are different." Deckard took a quick sip of beer. "The bigger ones, at least. Shoot a deer in the chest, you've killed it. Even if it needs a few seconds to fall over. There's an awareness. It looks at you. It *knows* you've killed it. It *knows* it's dying. I think that's the difference. The one I shot in the head never got a chance to *understand* it was *supposed* to be dead, so it didn't die."

"Makes sense," I said, rubbing my chin. My fingers scraped fresh stubble, then my blister, and I felt a stab of pain. "You chop off the chicken head, the chicken doesn't know it's dead."

"A chicken don't know it's alive," Jack said. "I raised chickens. They don't *know* shit. Damn things're insects with feathers."

"Deer know they're alive," Deckard said. "They might not have much brain, but they're at least as smart as a dog."

"I've known some dumb dogs," Jack said.

"A working dog," I said.

Deckard nodded. "A deer has to avoid predators. Like me. He's got to live by his wits. Dumb deer don't last."

"That sounds good," I said.

"Can't think of how to test it," Deckard said. "I mean, I could catch a deer. Gas it unconscious. Shoot it in the chest. If it doesn't know it's dead, maybe it isn't."

I thought back on my first encounter with Acceptance, as Veronica, in the church. Veronica had tried to slash her wrists, and they'd healed. I'd almost burned to death, and had woken up healed. No—I'd changed after the fire hadn't killed me. I'd lost my mind in delirium and hunger. I'd fought someone off for food. *Then* I'd woke up healed.

"There's always something in people that fights to live," I said.

Veronica had mentioned the first person she'd touched had tried to blow out his skull with a handgun. Where had the bullet passed through his brain? Had his forebrain told his body to rebuild a stem?

A warmth kindled in my gut. Things were starting to make sense. I might not be able to do any advanced calculus, but I'd started to find the numbers and discover addition. The rules might not look anything like the rules we'd lived with before, but they existed.

A smile cracked my face. "I shouldn't drink on an empty stomach," I said, "but if you've got something to put under it, I'll take one."

Jack grimaced. "Rolls from last night. Pretty hard now."

My stomach grumbled. "I don't care," I said. "I skipped breakfast, and all of a sudden I'm starving." They say hunger is the best spice. That's true, as far as it goes. Without hope, all the spice in the world isn't enough to make you hungry.

Hard didn't begin to describe the rolls, but the first taste of stale bread woke my stomach right up. I spent the next few minutes methodically tearing through tough crust to get at the soft core, licking crumbs off my fingers, washing them down with warm Strohs and listening to Jack and Deckard discuss deer recipes.

"Garlic's the key," Jack insisted.

"Garlic is like spray paint," Deckard said. "It covers up everything. Salt. Pepper. You're done. Roast. Flank. Steak. Even liver and heart. Garlic's good with brain, though."

Jack looked around.

I pressed my finger against my shirt to pick up stray crumbs and debated a sixth roll. Each roll was the size of my fist. I really ought to wait a few minutes to let my brain catch up to my stomach.

"No, I didn't bring you the brain," Deckard said. "I will next time. I'm doing the brain up for Uri tonight. Fry in butter, a bit of garlic—yum! You can't eat it all the time, though, it's mostly fat."

I picked up another roll and tore off another mouthful.

"Fat's good," Jack said.

"It's not good for you," Deckard said.

My mouth suddenly went dry. I tried to talk, but could only make a dry cough. Half-chewed bread swaddled my tongue. Deckard and Jack turned to look at me as I fumbled for my beer and washed my mouth clean.

"Mostly fat," I said.

"Yeah," Deckard said.

I'd burned. I'd healed, but it had come at a cost. I'd dropped weight overnight—not that I'd had a lot of extra weight, but I'd had a few extra pounds around my gut. The fire hadn't burned it off.

Ideas twirled around my brain. I didn't dare look at them too hard, for fear of scattering them.

Jack and Deckard traded puzzled glances.

"What?" said Deckard.

My partners had known that look on my face, but Deckard and Jack didn't. I held up a finger. "Hang on..."

Something metallic clattered outside, and a figure ran in through the door.

By the time I identified the figure through the halo of bright sunlight, Ceren was already talking.

"Alice. Have you seen her?" Ceren spoke quickly, panting for breath.

Jack lifted his head. "That girl you were wi' last night?" He shook his head. "Nope."

Deckard raised his eyebrows and looked mildly curious.

"I thought she was with you," I said, dropping the uneaten chunk of bread on the bar.

Ceren shook her head. "I was in the shower, and Darren said she'd gone—gone to get clothes."

Her clothes?

Her clothes were inside her house.

With what was left of Doug.

That damn kid.

"Let's go," I said.

Chapter 36

I DIDN'T bother with the cruiser's siren. Or my seat belt. Or proper side of the road. I threw myself into the cruiser, gave Ceren half a second to slam the passenger door behind her, and scarred black asphalt with blacker tracks.

I'd told Alice to stay out of her house. She shouldn't have to deal with what was left of her father. I didn't think Doug's remnants could actually rape her, and I'm sure she'd seen pictures of a naked man if not the real thing, but there's certain things about your family nobody needs to see. I didn't know where the line was, but Doug fell firmly on the far side of it.

Couldn't the damn kid have waited? I'd told Alice I'd escort her into her house for clothes today.

I nurtured the anger. Anger outweighed the fear.

I slammed the cruiser to a halt between Alice's and Ceren's homes, this time bouncing over the curb before yanking the brake up and flinging the door open. Climbing out of the car and into the June breeze, my skin chilled and I realized how much I'd been sweating.

"Stay here," I said.

"But—"

I leaned back into the car and put my hand on the stock of the shotgun racked between the seats. Staring into her eyes I said "Stay. Here." I backed out of the car with the shotgun and slammed the door behind me. "I don't want you getting shot," I called over my shoulder as I marched up the walk. "But if you come in there, you will."

The house looked just like it had yesterday morning. Red brick. A steeply slanted roof of solar shingles, with a second floor nestled inside it. Small, tidy windows. A month ago, flowers had choked the beds beneath the windows. Now, they were bare stretches of dirt. Absolute had restored the grass and changed the trees, but apparently hadn't known what to do about the flowers.

I pondered the flamethrower for half a second, but I couldn't go around torching random houses. The shotgun would have to do.

The front door was unlocked. I stepped into quiet dark stillness, blinking to let my eyes adjust. Family photos hung thick on pale walls. Sunlight through the windows cast parallelograms on shaggy dark blue carpet.

I held the shotgun tight across my chest, the cool plastic stock slippery in my sweaty hands. The room seemed to wobble with each jackhammer beat of my heart. My teeth ached with the adrenaline-fueled need to do something.

Doug didn't terrify me that much, but I knew exactly why my nerves felt scorched. Kevin had lost my—his daughter. That fresh incision burned in my soul, only a few days gone in my memory.

And now, another teenage girl was missing.

If I'd had a police department behind me, I would have called in every officer. Instead, I made sure the safety was off on the shotgun.

"Alice?" I called.

Silence.

"Alice, it's Detective Holtzmann." More or less. "Are you here?"

Nothing.

I started up the stairs, trying to watch every direction simultaneously.

The third step creaked.

I dropped the barrel of the shotgun to point between my feet, barely managing to not pull the trigger and blast the stair out from under me. My jaw burned on clenched teeth and my vision jumped.

Deliberately, I grabbed the bannister and made myself breathe in and out slowly, trying to cool my overheated skull. A jumpy cop kills people. Alice might be upstairs, or in the basement, or she might not even be here.

I moved up the stairs and back into silence all the way to the hall at the top. Beams of sunlight illuminated sparks of dust drifting through the stagnant air and glanced off bright white paint.

Something scratched behind Doug's bedroom door and my guts clenched around themselves.

I'd left the door closed. It was closed now.

That proved nothing.

Even if Alice had come here, I had to believe she wouldn't have gone into Doug's room. Not after I warned her specifically. She'd been, once, before she knocked on my door. She wouldn't want to see him again… would she?

I tugged on the doorknob. The door was firmly closed, the bolt set in the frame.

Something slammed into the other side of the lightweight door, rattling the frame.

I flinched, but made myself swallow. Doug had nothing resembling hands. He couldn't work the knob. Unless I struck out everywhere else, I wouldn't need to go in there again. I decided to leave his room for last and check Alice's room first.

The first room was a guest bedroom tucked under the eaves, with a tiny bed crammed beneath the sloping ceiling and a minuscule round window overlooking Ceren's home. A dozen cardboard boxes labeled for cereal and fruit filled the space, now with hand-written labels for DRESSES and SUITS and WINTER. Women's shirts towered out of a banana box. Doug hadn't sold or given away any of his wife's clothes.

The master bedroom door shook again. I imagined Doug crouching behind that door on misshapen limbs, deflated skull dragging behind like a beaver tail, that absurd penis swaying with every lopsided lurching step.

Compassion and revulsion blurred my thoughts. I didn't want to know how he knocked on the door.

The last room on the hall had to belong to Alice. Doug had refurnished her room not long ago to fit a teenager a little better. Once the bombs had started flying and the scorched-earth policy against Absolute had gone into effect, new furniture had been hard to get, but Doug had found a gently used bedframe with a headboard and footboard carved in swooping curves. The angular dresser obviously didn't belong with the bed, but someone had carefully painted both pieces pure gleaming white and traced scrollwork in delicate gold trim. An oval rag rug covered most of the hardwood floor. The room smelled of talcum powder hiding underneath a fading note of sickly-sweet teenage perfume.

Immortal Clay

Almost exactly like my daughter Julie's room. I tried to swallow past the lump blocking my throat.

Those weren't my memories, but they hurt.

Holding the shotgun stock in my right hand, I opened a dresser drawer with my left. Tidily folded shirts filled it, and pants the drawer beneath it. No missing clothes. The closet looked well-filled. Alice hadn't been here. Relief and worry streamed through me.

"Dammit kid," I muttered, "where did you go?"

Doug's door thumped again. Something scratched.

If that girl had decided to hike up to the mall and pillage a store, I would kill—be *very* angry with her.

Wood splintered behind me.

I spun back towards the hall.

The next sound fell somewhere between snapping lumber and tearing paper.

Shotgun level at my hip, finger over the plastic trigger guard, I put my back against Alice's open door, staring down the empty hallway towards a window. I glimpsed a bathroom across the hall, its mirror displaying a shower stall with a limed glass door.

Something hit the other side of Doug's door. Wood cracked again.

Doug wanted out.

I wanted him to stay in.

Cheap wood crunched.

If I wanted to know what made that sound, I'd have to stick my head around the corner. Most of the time, a slow peek into a hostile room is an invitation to get shot. You're better off charging straight in.

I pivoted into the hall, facing the stairs and Doug's room.

One limb stuck through a ragged hole in the bottom of the closed door. A foot? No, it couldn't be a foot—but it wasn't a hand. It had to be a long, sharp foot attached to a shin. Half a breath later a second limb punched through the door. Fragments of hollow-core door sprayed down the hall as what remained of the door's lower half hit the opposite wall. The doorknob assembly bounced off the floor and rolled into the guest bedroom.

Then the creature that had been Doug crawled over the wreckage and into the hallway.

I blinked. I wanted to launch myself forward. Or flee screaming. But I couldn't make my brain send commands to my legs.

The creature's form still echoed Doug. His torso hung between four limbs, belly towards the ceiling. His thighs had shortened, his shins lengthened, so that his spine barely brushed the carpet. His feet were narrow, the toes fused into hard planes. His shoulders had rearticulated to support his weight a few inches above the ground. His ribs made stark ridges against his emaciated chest. The overall effect resembled a praying mantis, except for the penis, which had grown thinner but not much shorter, the tip bobbing a foot above his knees.

Doug took another step, moving fully into the hall. The penis flexed halfway up, swiveling to menace me.

The last time I'd seen Doug, he'd waddled. He'd transformed further. Lost weight. Streamlined. He more closely fit what he was becoming, whatever that was. But "waddling" didn't describe him anymore. Certainly not "agile"—not yet at least.

Yesterday, he'd looked ridiculous and obscene.

Now, with skin stretched over misshapen bone, he looked too gaunt to be anything but horrifying.

I couldn't breathe, but my brain started firing again.

Paul Drennel had needed food to grow all those eyes.

I'd dropped weight after my attack last night.

Decker had said that deer brains were mostly fat.

Human brains weren't that chemically different than deer brains.

Did Doug burn up his own brain to fuel his transformation?

Had he done this to himself, willingly or not?

His transformation hadn't stopped with yesterday's appalling but dopey form. He'd kept changing. Burning calories and proteins and maybe even bone to transform himself.

Doug was *hungry*.

The head of Doug's penis swelled, doubling in size in a heartbeat. The narrow slit at the end spread wider. The two edges curved inward and picked up an unnatural gleam, then serrated into jagged ill-fitting teeth.

Chapter 37

THE HALL'S gleaming white walls formed a funnel, with a ravenous deformed Doug at one end and me at the other. Sunlight streamed through the window at my back. The cartilaginous maw at the end of Doug's penis snapped and clacked at me.

Doug wasn't even vaguely funny anymore. Disgust sloshed in my guts, and I fired the shotgun from my waist. The recoil knocked the barrel up and wrenched my shoulders.

Shot sliced the air above Doug's torso.

The window at the far end of the hall shattered.

Doug screeched. Bloody slashes appeared along the penis, near the mouth, where stray shot had grazed him.

I pumped the shotgun and raised it to my shoulder.

Doug dropped closer to the ground, stretched his mouth towards me, and charged. The leading legs ate distance with each step, but fortunately the arms in the back scrabbled to keep up, the repurposed hands taking two or three lurches forward for each step the legs took.

Shotgun nestled properly against my shoulder, I fired again.

Shot drilled bloody wells into his torso and sliced slivers of flesh from his penis and legs.

Doug shrieked again, a high-pitched keening like metal rasping on metal, utterly unlike anything I'd ever heard from a living creature before. Doug stumbled forward and staggered into the wall.

Cordite and coppery blood stung my nose with each breath.

I crouched in the doorway to Alice's bedroom, working the pump again.

Doug's arm-legs kicked the floor behind him, the palms beating irregular rhythms on the carpet. His legs, stretched out before him, quivered in pain. Blood quickly slicked his abdomen and oozed down his side.

If I stretched out my arm, Doug's new mouth might just scrape my fingertips.

Or bite them off at the first knuckle.

Doug shuddered. His gut bulged, the skin straining, distending and tearing the tiny buckshot wounds more open.

"Dammit." I threw myself headfirst into Alice's room. My feet felt trapped in tar.

Doug's gut split from groin to ribcage, a raw bloody gap creaking open.

The world shifted gears, dropping into something lower and slower. I floated through the suddenly solid air, my vision locked on the appalling horror that used to be my neighbor.

My feet barely cleared the doorframe before a tentacle slashed through the hallway where I'd stood. Then another.

I hit the hardwood floor face-first, knocking the air out of my lungs.

Footsteps pattered in the hall. Doug screamed again.

I rolled onto my back, straining my hand for the door but knowing I couldn't get there in time. The barrel of the shotgun knocked the edge of the door, and I shoved to swing the flimsy wood into place.

The door clicked shut.

Something wet smacked the other side of the door.

I rolled to my feet and leaned against the door, blocking Doug outside.

Government training programs from before the end of the world told us that firearms wouldn't work on people taken by Absolute. I remembered Kevin learning that the hard way driving across the country in his doomed effort to try to save Sheila and Julie.

The shotgun only slowed Doug, but ultimately made him more dangerous.

I should have brought the flamethrower.

I couldn't breathe quickly enough to get enough air into me.

Lopsided footsteps outside the door, coming closer. The stink of blood and shit and other things meant for inside a body leaked through the gaps in the frame.

He'd knocked one door apart.

I couldn't stay in the bedroom.

A double-hung window in the gable opposite me looked like the obvious way out. Even leaning against the bedroom door, I saw the lock twisted closed between the window frames.

I fumbled at the doorknob.

No lock.

The door exploded between my feet, launching fragments of cheap wood and corrugated cardboard filler everywhere. Splinters filled my khaki pants and bounced off my leather shoes. One of Doug's legs, toes sharpened almost to spears, stuck into the room.

I wrenched the shotgun down and fired.

The noise stunned my ears in the tiny room, but the barrage of shot dissolved most of Doug's calf.

Doug shrieked again, the sound still excruciating even through the door. He might have eaten most of his own brain to fuel his transformation, but still had enough hindbrain to feel pain and get really, really angry.

The bloody stump jerked back into the hall, trailing a foot attached only by ribbons of muscle and a battered spar of bone, leaving a smear of gore behind it.

One foot braced against the door and the shotgun in my right hand, I stretched out my left and grabbed Alice's dresser with my left hand. The slick paint resisted my grip. The dresser was heavier than it looked—quality wood furniture, not cheap cardboard crap. Unfortunately.

Doug shifted his weight in the hallway

Gritting my teeth, I threw myself away from the door and behind the dresser. I rammed my shoulder into the dresser. The shock of impact rattled down my spine, but the dresser moved a foot.

I slammed myself against the dresser again. And again.

Four shoves, and it blocked the door.

I leaned against the dresser to snatch a deep breath.

Doug slammed into my blockade.

The dresser rocked against me. I'd shoved it into place one godforsaken inch at a time, and it wasn't heavy enough to stop Doug.

If I was going to escape, it had to be now.

I sprinted across the room, twisted the window lock, and threw the window open. A flimsy screen blocked my way, but one good smash with the shotgun stock knocked it clear.

Doug body-slammed the door again.

Wood scraped on wood as the dresser shifted.

I leaned through the window and set the shotgun on the shingles, to the right. I stuck my head out, sat on the sill, and convulsed through. A few painful twists later I was on the roof, my feet wedged between the solar panels onto the asphalt shingles underneath.

Below, someone shouted my name.

I snatched the shotgun and shuffled down to the edge of the roof.

The lawn was maybe ten feet below the gutter. A twenty year old kid might step off that edge into open air, but not a guy in his forties. Sure as hell not me. I grimaced, flipped the safety on the shotgun, knelt, and tried to gently toss it to the ground below. It hit the grass a couple yards from the house and bounced, but didn't go off.

Something crashed in the bedroom behind me.

It sounded like a dresser shattering.

I sat on the edge of the roof, feet dangling in empty air. Grabbed the gutter beside me with both hands. Took a deep breath, and spun my butt off the roof.

The sickening plunge unhinged my stomach for half a second, then my weight hit my hands. The edges of the gutter bit my fingers, the metal squealing under my weight, but it held just long enough.

I reflexively opened my grip. My heart stayed where it was and the rest of me plummeted through a mile-long three feet of empty air.

The ground slammed up into my feet. My legs crumpled, and I fell to the side, chin tucked, arms outspread to diffuse the impact. Just like they taught in unarmed combat classes. My joints still jammed against each other, and I felt something pop in my back.

Glass shattered overhead.

Small shards rained down on my upturned face.

Ceren shouted "Kevin! Run!"

Broken wood and a scrap of plaster pattered down on me.

Doug shrieked from the roof, right overhead.

"Get out of the way!" Ceren shouted.

I grabbed the shotgun, flailed to my feet, and took two steps towards the car before I realized what I saw.

Ceren stood on the sidewalk beside the car, stooped by the weight of one of the flamethrowers from the back of the cruiser. Her left hand held the forward grip. Her right hand wrapped around the trigger. The nozzle pointed straight at me.

My eyes bugged.

I dashed sideways. "Ceren, get in the damn car!"

"I got this!" Ceren said.

Something hit the ground behind me.

I didn't want to know what horrors Doug had for me now.

I started to turn anyway.

Ceren grimaced and pulled the trigger.

A haze of wet spray spattered from the nozzle. Liquid flamethrower fuel drooled out of the barrel and onto the pavement.

"Oh," Ceren said.

"Get in the damn car!" I shouted.

Ceren fumbled with the nozzle. Fresh flamethrower fuel gushed out, splashing her feet.

Chapter 38

CEREN HAD grabbed the flamethrower to rescue me, and instead doused herself with toxic, sticky fuel. She stood by the police car, her face slack with surprise and one hand on the trigger, as incendiary sludge oozed out of the flamethrower's unlit nozzle, down her hands, drooled down her pants, and pooled on the asphalt around her feet.

It didn't matter that Doug was ready to eat me. I couldn't let her burn alive.

"Ceren!" I shouted, staggering sideways across the grass. "Drop it!"

Behind me, Doug growled.

Alice's house looked tidy enough, with its clean red brick and solar shingles, nestled up against the contrasting homes on either side. Suncatchers and broken glass shattered the afternoon sun into rainbows, and the grass could use a trim but didn't yet rate a ticket.

Doug sprawled on the lawn just below the window. His chest had split open, releasing four or five flailing tentacles, each smacking wetly at the ground around him again and again and again. The mouth at the end of the penis-neck now resembled a beak, brutally curved and designed to slice flesh. The mouth turned from side to side, upraised, like a dog sniffing the air. His arms and legs lay askew. One foot kicked in the grass. Had he broken that leg in the jump? The other ended in a red ruin from my shotgun blast, but the meat churned and thrashed as it grew back together.

Ceren coughed in flamethrower fumes.

Doug levered his hands beneath him, trying to regain his footing.

Ceren shouted wordlessly and shrugged one shoulder out of the flamethrower, struggling to release the second strap. The kid finally realized that triggering a spark while standing in a pool of spilled flamethrower fuel was a really bad idea.

The flamethrower nozzle hit the ground with a clang.

Doug's mouth weaved towards her.

"Doug!" I shouted.

Doug took one step towards Ceren.

I glanced behind me to see a few clear feet of grass. "Doug!" My thumb flicked the shotgun's safety off.

Doug took another tentative step towards Ceren. His tentacles arhythmically flailed the ground. His elbows and knees bent to crouch.

He didn't have eyes. What was he hunting by, smell? Sound? Feel?

I'd give him something to feel.

The shotgun bucked against my shoulder.

Doug roared, swiveling towards me.

I tottered backwards and fired again.

Doug's roar grew deeper. His feet caught the ground, and he bolted straight at me.

"Get in the car!" I shouted at Ceren.

I hoped she'd listen. Then I turned and ran.

Chapter 39

NEVER BEFORE had I needed to shoot someone in the dick more than once to get their attention.

I sprinted down open road, littered with branches and boxes and blown trash from a month of neglect. Scattered tidy houses and occasional trees on either side. And chasing me, a ravenous misshapen creature that had once been human.

I risked a glance over my shoulder. Doug galumphed behind me, using the half-dozen tentacles flailing out of his abdomen the way a blind man used a cane. His front legs still took longer steps than the rear, but the repurposed arms that served as rear legs seemed to be growing longer to keep up. Not good. The head of his penis still made a jaggedly toothed mouth, but the shaft swayed and bent like a neck. The foreskin formed a grotesque shawl around the mouth.

I had a Mossberg 590 shotgun with two shells and comfortable running shoes. The shotgun hadn't helped. Time to try the running shoes. I pushed all the air out of my lungs, pulled in a deep breath, and ran faster.

I didn't dare outdistance Doug. If we ran straight, I'd get to Main Street and other people. If Doug couldn't eat me, he'd happily tear into someone else. Once he got food in his gut, who knew what he would become? I had about half a mile to figure out a better plan.

At my last department physical, I'd run a six minute mile.

Three minutes to figure something out.

Doug fell further behind. I slowed my pace. Call it an eight minute mile. Four minutes to make and execute a plan. When serving in Detroit, I'd had entire firefights in less time.

Maybe I could set a house on fire. Lure him into it. Trap him, burn him alive. I didn't have a lighter, but if I picked the right house I might find something. I needed a house without anyone hiding in it. And an unlocked front door, or I'd pinch myself between Doug and a wall.

Or a different weapon. Maybe one of these garages had an ax. Or a circular saw. If I chopped enough pieces off of Doug, he might stop moving.

Or Frayville would have bits of Doug scurrying around like rats. Hungry, carnivorous rats.

I needed something better.

A motor roared behind me.

I glanced over my shoulder.

My police cruiser thundered up behind Doug's galumphing form at a rocketing twenty miles an hour. I glimpsed Ceren behind the windshield, sitting up straight to peer over the dash, hands tightly gripping the wheel. She veered to the far side of the road to avoid flattening Doug. The tires scraped off the opposite curb, bouncing the whole car back towards the middle of the road. I grimaced even before she rolled slowly past me and stopped thirty feet ahead. The front passenger door popped open.

I bolted, launching myself into the car and slamming the door behind me.

"Oh my God," Ceren said.

"Go!"

"Did that thing eat Alice?"

Doug, sensing opportunity, picked up speed.

"Not too fast," I said, gasping. "Don't want to lose him."

Ceren sat perched on the front edge of the driver's seat, stinking of petroleum. Flamethrower fuel saturated her clothes. She nodded at me with wide eyes and took her foot off the brake, letting the cruiser coast forward.

I glanced back to see Doug only a few yards behind. "Little faster."

Ceren goosed the accelerator, almost dangling from the steering wheel as the car's motion shoved her back.

I sank into my seat. "Careful!"

"Sorry," she said. Her eyes flicked down to the dash, then back to the road. She turned the wheel a degree.

"First time driving?" I said.

"Yep."

"You're doing fine."

I glanced behind. Doug followed the car as readily as he had me.

"Is that him? Is that Mister Tander?"

"No." I shook my head. "Not anymore."

"Did it eat her?"

"No." The Doug-thing wouldn't be so ravenous if he had.

I scanned all the different homes for something I could use as a trap. A van. A cage. Anything.

No—maybe trapping was the wrong idea. We needed distance.

"Get us up to the intersection—the far side of the intersection—and stop. On the wrong side of the road."

Ceren blinked. "Why?" She glanced over her shoulder towards the Doug-beast.

"We've got to stop him. Do it!"

Ceren goosed the accelerator again. Rubber screeched on concrete. I fell back in my seat, and the cruiser ate road. Too much road—we shot through the intersection and veered towards the curb.

"Brakes, kid! Brakes!"

Ceren stomped on the pedal, twisting the wheel to the side.

I shoved my free hand out in front of me barely in time to jam it against the dashboard, and bounced across the seat into Ceren. My coat suddenly felt damp with gelatinous fuel, and my eyes watered with fumes.

The car jerked to a halt sideways, twenty feet too far.

"Park!" I shouted as I scooted across the bench seat to the passenger door.

The Doug-beast raced towards me.

I threw myself out of the slowly drifting car. My jacket stank of flamethrower fuel, soaked up from Ceren. If I fired a flamethrower, I'd turn into a candle.

Instead, I raced back towards Doug.

Doug changed as he charged. Each of his steps seemed a little smoother than the one before. The probing tentacles moved with more certainty. He must have been burning something of himself to make those changes, but whatever he lost didn't slow him down. Maybe it was like exercise, and the Doug-beast first burned the parts that slowed him down.

I ducked my head, tucked my elbows to my side, and sprinted.

Something thudded behind me.

Ceren had let the cruiser coast into a tree.

All four corners of the intersection held a home. A rusty yellow fire hydrant jutted from the sidewalk on the opposite corner. I sprinted towards the willow tree laden with melons on the closer corner. I dashed beneath the low-hanging fronds and melons, reached up, and without stopping seized a melon with both hands. The slick, slimy rind slipped in my grip and remained attached to its branch, almost dragging me off my feet.

I stumbled, stepped back under it, jerked harder, yanked it free, and chucked it overhand.

The melon plowed through the willow's dangling fronds and fell short, just to the side of Doug's path. It broke on impact, the bottom pulverizing and the remainder splitting into two bouncing halves, leaving a slick wet trail as it bounced.

When I'd been starving, burned to the point of mindlessness, the melons had drawn me. Maybe they'd snare Doug.

I grabbed another melon. This one I aimed more carefully, launching the melon directly at him. The second one also fell short, maybe twenty feet from me, but came apart into chunks right in his path.

By the time I had my hands on a third melon, Doug reached the broken remnants of the second.

Doug hurtled over it, straight at me.

My heart stopped.

Air petrified in my throat.

I'd left the shotgun in the car.

Doug skidded to a stop. The questing tentacles whipped around to play inquisitively over the slabs of melon scattered behind him.

I forced my petrified lungs to exhale.

Doug skittered backwards, seized a chunk of melon in three tentacles, and dragged them to his groin. His neck bent, and he chomped a mouthful of fruit, then another. The tiny mouth worked efficiently, as if he didn't need to chew. Knobs of fruit began visibly working their way down through the neck-penis.

"Ceren!" I shouted. "Get out here!"

The uppermost few degrees of tension drained out of me. Whatever had driven me to the melon willow last night also drew the Doug-beast. I didn't know if it was some trigger Absolute had planted in the human brain or if the melons had some subtle chemical trigger that said *this is food*, but I'd use it.

I'd stopped Doug. For a moment.

But he'd eat all the melons I could throw. And use them to heal himself, just like I had. Maybe even transform himself further.

What shape would a malignant, mindless penis with teeth take?

I couldn't let him finish.

"Ceren!" I shouted. My voice screeched higher than I wanted it to. "I need you!"

I launched another melon. It landed a few feet short of Doug, slightly off to the side, and shattered. Doug's questing tentacles found it in seconds, and he lurched towards it.

The tree had another eight or nine melons within easy reach. After that I'd run out of ammo.

"What?" Ceren sounded thin and shredded, trotting jerkily up behind me.

"Grab a melon," I said. "Can you get near him from here?"

Staring at the Doug-beast, Ceren wrenched a melon out of the tree, held it over her right shoulder, and lobbed it with both hands. It hit maybe fifteen feet from us but didn't break, rolling straight into the cleft between Doug's front legs.

Doug's head dove down. Sharp teeth punched straight through the rind.

"I got it!" Ceren shouted. "Got it, got it, got it!"

I grimaced. Ceren's eyes shone wide. Any second she might break and run.

But I needed her.

"You have this," I said. "Keep him busy. Don't throw until he's almost out. I need him tied up for a couple minutes."

"Got it."

"And stay back!" I shouted, trotting back to the cruiser.

I dropped my fuel-soaked jacket on the road by the cruiser before getting the second flamethrower out of the back. Slipped it on. Tightened the shoulder and hip belts. Pulled the valve to mix the pressurized air with the fuel.

Immortal Clay

Ceren watched Doug, throwing melons directly at him whenever he swallowed the final chunk of the previous one. She shook with tension. Her mouth opened and closed mindlessly.

The Doug-beast snarfed another chunk of melon. A tentacle stabbed the last piece.

Ceren threw.

The melon hit right between the Doug-beast's legs.

I pulled the flamethrower nozzle off the hook.

Doug attacked the melon. His scrawny muscles filled out with each mouthful.

I walked back towards the Doug-beast in a broad arc, staying well out of Ceren's way, until I stood about ten feet from his flank.

He chomped another mouthful.

I flipped the igniter on.

Aimed.

Doug swallowed.

I studied the Doug-beast, flamethrower in hand, a halo of flame surrounding the nozzle. Did anything remain of Alice's father? Could he come back from this?

I'd recovered from getting burned. Could Doug perhaps do the same?

Doug's form filled out as he ate. His neck grew thicker and stronger. The taut skin stretched between his ribs eased. Muscles started to ripple along his mismatched limbs. The limb I'd shot began to lengthen.

When I'd recovered, I'd transformed back into a man.

Doug wasn't heading towards anything resembling human.

Might he be able to think, though?

Doug was gone. Anything could happen, but most of the options would be horrible and threatening.

I took a deep breath and pulled the trigger.

The flamethrower's incendiary spray caught Doug in the middle of his chest, enveloping him in a cloud of flame.

He crawled fifteen feet away before collapsing in a puddle of fire.

I added occasional spurts of flame until all that remained of Alice's father was crumbled bones, greasy ash, and tarry smears indistinguishable from the stinking molten asphalt.

Chapter 40

I SAGGED in the driver's seat, exhausted and discouraged, catching my breath through my teeth to minimize the reek of expended fuel. Ceren sat beside me, withdrawn and pale and stinking of flamethrower fuel. Yesterday, she'd seemed a brash and aggressive teenager, but Alice's disappearance and Doug's attack had deflated her. A couple people had emerged from homes along the street, but didn't approach. Nobody wanted to confront a man with a flamethrower, or study the heap of carbonized flesh smoldering in the intersection.

The wind shifted, bringing the column of smoke from Doug's remains towards us. I coughed at the sticky black haze and turned the cruiser's ignition. Ceren hadn't stopped the cruiser well, running the nose into a tree at three miles an hour, but the engine turned right over. Clean air swirled into the car as soon as I put it into drive. A block closer to Main Street and clear of the smoke I parked, shut off the engine, closed my eyes, and sank back into the vinyl seat.

Ceren's eyes were wide. She'd stopped hyperventilating, at least. After a quiet moment she said, "That thing almost ate me. I mean, it could have killed me. Killed me."

"You're okay now."

Ceren shook and shivered, but eventually got herself back under control. Finally, she drew a shuddering breath. "What did I do wrong?"

I took a deep breath and swallowed my first dozen responses. "You got out of the car." It was kinder than what I wanted to say.

"What do you expect?" she said, her voice just above a whisper. "I heard the shots."

"Do you know how many dumb Detroit kids I saw shoot themselves?" I wanted to shout, but restrained my voice. She didn't need someone yelling at her. "A weapon you don't know how to use belongs to the enemy."

"I couldn't let something happen to you."

"I understand. Really." I opened my eyes, immediately locking gazes with her. "But I jumped out of that window thinking all I had to do was get behind the wheel and we'd drive away. And there you were, dribbling jellied gasoline down your legs." The wind brought a hint of burning asphalt and bone, but it couldn't cut through the nasty petroleum flavor coating my mouth. "Do you know what would have happened if you'd gotten the igniter going?"

Ceren's face grew even paler, but she nodded, her head barely moving. She looked ready to fall apart.

"You did good with the melons, though. Better aim than me."

She smiled, stretching her lips tight over her teeth, but it hardly eased her shudders.

I grabbed the shotgun and pulled it into my lap. Once I found the ammo box, I started feeding shells back into the magazine.

"So, what now?" Ceren said.

"Now, we get you cleaned up. I don't have to worry about—about that thing, I'll search Alice's house. Thoroughly. While you get a shower."

"We've got to find Alice!" Ceren's voice frayed further with every word. "We don't have *time* to shower."

"That stuff you poured all over yourself is toxic as hell." I snapped the reloaded shotgun back into its rack, trying to keep my voice level and unemotional. "Half an hour from now, if you don't get it off you, you'll have blisters everywhere. A couple hours from now, you won't be able to stop screaming from the pain."

"Oh, God," Ceren said. She started shaking again.

I eyed her. "Slow down, kid. It's over. You're safe." I made my voice hard. "Focus on your breathing. Unless you need me to wash you. I'd rather not. We have to get it off of you, though."

A flash of indignation dulled the edge of her hysteria. "No. No, I can do it."

"I know you can. Use dish soap, the lemon stuff if you have it. Use every drop you can find. Scrub, rinse, and scrub again. Take a couple of those Tylenol, too. Not the special ones, not yet. Be sure you scrub your back, everywhere the fuel might have touched. Use a loofah—you have one? Scrub twice, three times if you're not sure. And say something if you've got any burns on your skin. We can get you some silvadene cream and antibiotics." I didn't know if we could get an infection any more, but I'd rather play it by the manual until we knew better.

Ceren took a deep breath. "What then?"

I sighed, watching the couple down the street go back into their house, wishing I could join them.

"Then—if I don't find Alice in her house—we make a list of places Alice might go. We rank them in order by the chances she'd go there. And then, we check every one of them."

Chapter 41

WE SEARCHED for Alice with methodical desperation.

A few friends' homes were abandoned. Others had occupants, but none who had seen Alice that day. The high school was locked, and I didn't want to break a window to get in. Once someone broke the first window, the other windows would follow in quick succession. The St Vincent de Paul store sat unlocked, the air heavy with the musty aromas of secondhand clothing and bleach. We roamed the aisles, but it wasn't until I kicked a pair of moldy tennis shoes away from the last changing room that Ceren said, "If she'd been here, she would have taken that blouse by the door. She wasn't."

I drove Ceren out to Winchester Mall and introduced her to the Lightners. We paced the mall shouting Alice's name and peering into clothing stores. Nothing.

By the time we left, the sun was well down in the sky—it had to be at least five o'clock. I sat down behind the cruiser's steering wheel, tipped my head back, and closed my aching eyes.

The passenger door slammed as Ceren climbed in. "Where now?" I said.

Ceren didn't say anything for a moment, and I didn't need to open my eyes to see the pique on her face. "You're the cop." After this morning's debacle she'd quickly reassembled her brash shell, but her eyes still twitched too quickly and every so often her voice shook.

"We've checked every place on your list," I said.

"It's not my fault she's not there. It's every place I could think of, so back off."

"Chill, kid. I'm not blaming you. You're the only one with the clue. Just take a moment." I concentrated on relaxing my petrified neck muscles. "The next step gets more complicated. If there's any other place we can check before we get there, even if it's a long shot, it's worth it."

I enjoyed the silence for a few breaths. Then Ceren said "I can't think of anyplace else. I just can't."

"Okay, then." I opened my eyes and reached for the ignition.

"What's the next step?"

I gave her a thin smile. "We get help."

"That doesn't sound very complicated."

"If I had a police department behind me, it wouldn't be. We get to round up help the old-fashioned way."

I had barely stopped the cruiser outside Jack's when the smells of roasting meat with garlic and peppers blew through my open window and hooked my nose. My stomach roared. Occupied by finding Alice, I hadn't even considered lunch. Ceren followed me in.

We found Eric looming at us from a chair by the door, exactly as he had the night before. He'd clearly claimed his spot. "Holtzmann. You're short a girl tonight, aren't you?"

"That's the problem," I said. "Alice is missing."

"Missing, or *missing* missing?"

I glanced at the wall clock. Five-thirty. "About seven hours now. She's supposed to be with us."

Eric shrugged. "She probably wandered off with a friend."

"There might be people trying to find her," Ceren said. "Probably are."

"They'll find her," Eric said.

"Her father was—" I stopped. "Her father was attacked." I still wasn't certain it was an attack. My uneducated gut said so, but I hadn't found anything resembling proof. Even if I was wrong about the attack, though, we still needed to find Alice. If people helped because of the wrong idea, well, there are worse reasons to do the right thing.

"I told her to stay home. Whoever attacked him might go after her."

Eric nodded. "Sure."

"She said she was going for clothes," I said. "And hasn't been seen since."

Eric frowned. "Worrisome."

"Put the word out, will you? I don't care if she doesn't want to talk to me—I mean, yes I care, but maybe I upset her or something. Long as she's okay I'll deal."

"Alice sticks to the rules," Ceren said. "It's really annoying. She wouldn't go off on her own. Not without telling *me*."

"I'll tell people," Eric said.

"Appreciate it. If she doesn't turn up by tomorrow, I'll organize a search."

I wasn't sure if I was trying to convince myself I was doing enough, or just laying out the next step. The phone system might be down, but we had emergency radios in the police station. They probably had more radios than I could get volunteers. The first few days after someone goes missing is the best time to gather volunteers. The longer she spent missing, the fewer people would help search.

"You'll see her tonight," Eric said. "If she don't show, I'll help search in the morning."

"Thanks." I clapped Eric on the shoulder, careful to avoid the exposed skin of his neck. After last night with Teresa, I wasn't touching anyone until I understood more of the rules we lived under.

Teresa. I had hardly thought about her all day. Guilt flashed through me. If she wasn't here for dinner, tomorrow's search could hunt for two.

Twenty or thirty people sat around at dark polished wood tables, drinking beer and talking loudly enough to drown out the whispers probably simmering in the back of every head. The bar's back door stood open, letting sunlight brighten the dark interior. I saw the edge of a trailer-mounted stainless steel smoker through the back door.

I looked around the bar, searching for familiar faces. Most of the people I didn't recognize. Teenagers had again claimed the space by the dart board. A paunchy middle-aged man with two days of beard played checkers with a stunning twenty-something woman. She seemed put out that he kept his attention on the board rather than her skintight dark blue dress. Two older couples sat at a table for four, heads together, talking. Fred Pearson, half of Frayville's firefighting team, sat in a booth with a younger couple. He raised a hand at me and nodded when my eyes met his.

Rose Friedman sat at her stool at the bar, in exactly last night's pose, face concealed by a different black veil draped over her head. If I hadn't come through there this morning and seen her empty stool, I would have suspected that she'd stayed straight through from last night.

She wore loose black slacks and a black blouse rather than yesterday's pantsuit, however. I felt a wave of affection for the retired kindergarten teacher. Kevin hadn't known her that well, but I wasn't Kevin and I understood Rose on a deep level. The only difference between her mourning and mine was that I mourned on the move. Sitting still and letting the world come to her made more sense than anything I'd done.

The stools on either side of Rose were empty.

"Don't go far," I said to Ceren, and claimed one. "Rose."

"Detective."

The word grated in my ears. Kevin had been a detective. I didn't seem capable of finding anything. "How've you been."

"Sober." She raised the veil to drain her beer—a Pabst Red, White, and Blue—and lowered it before I saw her face. Pabst. Jack must be scraping the bottom of the storeroom, but Rose seemed okay with it. "This is my sixth can in thirty minutes, and the only thing I feel is a distinct need to pee."

Drunkenness hit people differently. Last night I'd seen more than one person a little unsteady after an extra beer. Absolute hadn't taken drunkenness from us. But I'd expect to see her wobble on her stool, or overcompensate by sitting extra straight. Rose looked unchanged. Then again, I hardly knew her. Maybe her genetics let her drink me under the table. If we still had genetics. "Don't overdo it," I said.

"Why not?" She turned to stare at me, her wide white eyes glimmering behind her lace veil. "You're still thinking there's things worth doing. Running around. Looking for trouble."

"It's what I do," I said.

"It's what you *did*. Now? Now we're done. It's over." She pushed the empty can away, leaned over the bar, and grabbed another. Not even a cheap Pabst this time, but some bottom-of-the-barrel generic. The can hissed when she popped it. "Do yourself a favor. Do *me* a favor, a huge favor. Give it up."

"If we give up, we die."

Rose drained half the can in a single convulsive swallow. She didn't even belch.

"Die? We should be so lucky. Ask Acceptance about dying."

Rose needed help. A month ago I would have contacted a social worker or Adult Protective Services, or called her family. I had vague memories of her being a mother. Did she still have sons? Would they be enough to lift her spirits? I knew I wouldn't. You can't argue someone out of depression, especially when there's such a solid reason for it.

Rose would get through this. Or she wouldn't.

Like the rest of us.

Chapter 42

A TAP on my back rescued me.

Jesse leaned close, forcing me to lean back. Her face was flushed, her breath coming quickly. "You seen Teresa?" She had thankfully lost the furry sparkly sweater she'd worn this morning, replacing it with jeans and a gleaming white oval-neck T-shirt.

"She hasn't turned up?" I said.

"We were supposed to meet here at noon. I drove out to the Orchards and checked her apartment. She wasn't there. No one was there."

"Shit. Alice is missing, too." I didn't like this.

"What do we do?"

"I'm organizing a search for Alice early tomorrow. I'll include Teresa." Which meant more work to do if we would be ready tomorrow morning. I needed radios. First-aid supplies. It was either tonight, or bright and early tomorrow. "Here, tomorrow, nine AM. Put the word out."

Jack came in the back door, lumbering under a rectangular steel banquet tureen with a high lid. "Thank Deckard for tonight's chow," he announced, setting the tray on a long table at the back of the room beneath the neon Coors sign. When he pulled the lid off, the smell of grilled meat flooded the room. An industrial tray of mashed potatoes and another of mixed vegetables sat beside it, plugged into electric warmers.

The line formed quickly but with a surprising lack of fuss. Ceren took her plate and joined the teenagers at the back. I filled a plate and sat back down at the bar. The venison chop was a little rarer than I usually liked, but it sliced tenderly and went down smoothly.

Jesse sat down next to me and ate silently. I savored the moment while it lasted. "She hates cooking. She should be here."

Immortal Clay

I nodded. "We divide the volunteers into teams. Give each one a radio. Go house to house. We'll find them."

"Detective," said a voice behind me.

I made myself not flinch at the word, and turned around.

Ian Reamer stood behind me, wearing a clean mechanic's jumpsuit.

I tried to not show the surprise on my face. "Reamer." This morning, I'd chased him through the mall and made him confess to crimes he hadn't committed. Tension rippled down my spine, and I got ready to throw a punch.

"I'm in," Reamer said.

"Excuse me?"

"Tomorrow. Missing people search. I'm in."

I raised my eyebrows. "Okay."

"I don't want you to get the wrong idea," he said.

"Oh?"

"You're still an asshole. But I'm not gonna stand around while two women are lost."

I bit back my anger at his words, and nodded instead. "We can use you. Help put the word out, if you would."

"I will."

I didn't realize that Jack was behind the bar again until he said "I've heard that from four folk so far."

This seemed to be the night for people talking to my back. "What, that I'm an asshole?"

"No, that a couple'a women're missing." Jack frowned. "And you're throwin' a party tomorrow morning in my bar."

I shrugged. "Everyone knows where it is. We'll meet outside."

He shook his head. "No, you'll meet here. And I'll have coffee. See if I can scrounge up something for lunches, so you don' have to stop."

"Thanks."

"Yeah," said Jesse. "Thanks."

Rose, a few stools down the bar, snorted and popped another can. Her black dress and veil still completely cloaked her from sight. I'd lost count of how many she'd drank, but she had to have a cast-iron bladder.

"I heard you had some excitement today," Jack said.

"Searching for Alice," I said, slicing a thin strip of chop off the bone. "And Teresa."

"No, not that," Jack said.

"Oh?"

Jack said "Somethin' about monsters. And flamethrowers."

"Yeah." I stabbed the sliver of meat with my fork. It had lost its flavor. "That."

"What happened?" Jesse said.

I shook my head slowly. "Alice's dad is dead."

"You said he was dead yesterday," Jack said.

"No, I said he had trouble," I said. "*Now* he's dead."

"That thing killed him?" Jack said.

"No, the flamethrower killed him," I said, "after he turned into that thing."

The space around me went quiet. I looked over my shoulder. Reamer stood near a crowded table behind me, eyes fixed on my back. Everyone at the table had stopped talking. Even Rose had stopped drinking to watch me.

I took a deep breath. What happened to Doug could happen to anyone. They deserved to know, needed to know. I turned to face the room and raised my voice.

"Folks! Listen up a second. Folks!"

The hubbub faded out.

"Doug Tander… He changed, transformed. Two nights ago, he changed into—into something not human. I'm not sure what happened. Either something changed him, or he changed himself, I don't know. But changing like that uses energy. And his body basically ate his brain to fuel it."

The bar grew both quieter and even more still. A sea of pale faces surrounded me.

"That was bad. It got worse because he got hungry. I went near him today. He was still hungry. He wasn't Doug anymore. He attacked me. He tried to eat me and Ceren."

I nodded at Ceren and paused to let the crowd absorb what I'd said.

"I don't know how he changed. I don't know what triggered the change. Maybe it was something in the environment. Maybe someone did it to him. Maybe he did it himself. But be careful. He chased me down the road. He would have killed and eaten…anyone."

Another pause. A deep breath.

"I had to... I burned him to keep him from downtown."

"Two nights ago, Doug ate dinner here. Yesterday morning, he was gone."

Every face in Jack's remained locked in my direction, eyes staring.

"Doug's dead and now his daughter Alice is missing. As is another local lady, Teresa—" I hung for a moment, then glanced at Jesse.

"Umber," Jesse reminded me.

"Teresa Umber. I don't think Doug got to either one, but if they don't turn up by tomorrow morning, I'm setting up a search. Just in case, we'll meet at 9 AM, here."

People still watched me.

"That's all," I said. "That's enough. Thank you."

One by one, the crowd turned back to their own conversations. But they seemed a little more animated. Doug's transformation had given them a new topic, one a little bit scary. I caught bits and pieces of conversation. What had caused it? Had he done it to himself? Could it happen to me?

"You really don't know what caused it?" Jesse asked.

I shook my head, resting my elbows on the glossy lacquered bar. "Not a clue. He ate here two nights ago. Nobody saw him talking to anyone, nobody saw him leave with anyone, nothing."

"The whole thing was a lot more exciting the way other folks tell it," Jack said.

"What?"

Jack shrugged. "You sound all matter-of-fact about it. Nothing about being chased down the street, or the girl holdin' him off with melons."

"It's only exciting if you weren't there," I said. "Ceren did well with the melons, though."

"I saw him," Reamer said from behind me.

I looked over my shoulder. "Excuse me?"

"Doug Tander, right?" Reamer said. "The sleazebag electrician?"

Who couldn't bear to get rid of his wife's belongings. "Yeah."

Reamer jerked a thumb at Jesse. "He was hanging with her young friend."

I glanced at Jesse.

Jesse shrugged. "Maybe. We're not attached at the hip, but I thought she had better taste than that."

I looked back at Reamer. "Did they seem to be arguing?"

Reamer smirked. "Not quite. She had her hand in his. Walked him out while dinner was still going."

My heart lurched to a halt. "Did either one come back in?"

"I saw the girl here the next day. Talking to you. Before I left."

I spun back to Jack. "I have a dumb question, Jack."

"I've got high standards for dumb," Jack said.

"Sex."

"With you? No, thanks."

"No, in general."

Jack's brow furrowed. "Y'see," he said slowly, "when a mommy and a daddy love each other—"

I waved a flat hand to cut him off. "No, I mean since Absolute let us go. You see lots around this place and hear even more. Have people had sex since?"

"Sure," he said. "I mean, I haven't taken a survey or anything, but yeah. Look over a' the booth right by the buffet. That couple? You can't tell me they haven't just hooked up."

I glanced at the pair, sitting side by side over half-eaten chops, heads bent together, hands intertwined. The middle-aged guy stabbed a piece of venison with his fork and raised it to the younger woman's mouth.

"Looks like it," I said. "But do you *know*? Or is that just a guess?"

Jack's face flushed. "Yeah," he said, "I know. I've checked. Personally."

"And it worked?" I said. "Nothing weird happened?"

"I don't think that's your business," Jack said.

"You didn't change shape? Or melt together? Or anything Absolute weird?"

"No, no," Jack said.

"Shit," I said.

Doug and I had a common element: Teresa. We'd suffered a similar change. The question was, malice or accident?

I'd found a broken bra in Doug's bathroom. Size 36D. That was about Teresa's size. It hadn't seemed important to check the tag when breaking her out of her bra last night.

"Jesse," I said.

"Yes?"

"You went looking for Teresa. How did you look?"

Immortal Clay

"I drove around," Jesse said. "Opened doors. Shouted."

"So if she'd been hiding, you wouldn't have found her."

"Why would she hide?"

"Because she didn't want me to find her."

Jesse looked at me, then at Jack, and back. "You saying—"

"I'm saying that last night when we hooked up, I started to change. The only reason I'm here now is because someone set me on fire instead."

A few stools down, Rose choked on her beer.

"She wouldn't try to hurt you," Jesse said.

"I don't know if she *was* trying to hurt me," I said. "But I've got to talk to her now, before she picks up someone for the night." I glanced at Reamer. "Thank you."

Rose grabbed a napkin and thrust it behind her veil. She coughed, but I felt her staring at me through the black lace.

Reamer gave a minuscule nod before turning towards the buffet.

"Excuse me," I said, slipping off the stool. The crowd was getting thicker and the noise louder, but I shouldered my way through to the table where Ceren sat with another ten kids. "Ceren."

She looked up, jaw working as she chewed and swallowed. "Wassup?"

"I introduced you to Teresa and Jesse last night."

"Sure." Ceren leaned to the side to peer past me. "Hi, Jesse."

"Hey, Ceren," Jesse said from behind me.

So intent on my thoughts, I hadn't noticed Jesse following me. Kevin wouldn't have let that happen—but Kevin hadn't lived through my last week. I had to get sharper. I turned my attention back to Ceren. "Did Teresa know where you live?"

Ceren shrugged. "I told her the street. She asked."

"And if she showed up by your house this morning, would you have talked to her?"

"Sure. Why not?"

Years as a detective had taught me that if I didn't want to think something bad about a person, it was probably the truth. My head throbbed as I imagined the scene. *Oh, you don't have clean clothes? Kevin says he'll take you? He's busy, why don't I take you?*

But why Alice? What would Teresa want with her? Would Teresa want anything from Alice? I didn't know, but I hoped not.

"Thanks." I glanced at Jesse, then at Jack. "Listen, Ceren, can you get a few of your friends to walk you home again tonight? Maybe even hang out with you, so you're not alone?"

Ceren looked puzzled. "Sure." She glanced around the table at the curious faces. "What gives?"

"Hopefully I'm paranoid and nothing will happen," I said. "But just in case I'm not, I want you to be near some people for safety, okay?"

Ceren nodded. "First time I've been told to throw a party for my own good." The bravery of the joke made me smile, but the expression behind her eyes flattened the humor.

I looked back at Jesse. "If Teresa didn't want to be found, where would she go?"

Jesse looked distant for a moment. "She'd probably go back home to The Orchards," she finally said. "Lots of apartments there to hide in, and she knows the place pretty well."

"Okay, then." I started to walk around her.

"Hey!" Jesse stuck an arm across my path.

I stopped.

"You asked Teresa about Doug," Jesse said. "She sat here and lied to us both about him."

"Maybe," I said.

"I don't know what she was thinking," Jesse said, "going with Doug like that, but I damn-sure plan to find out. I'm going with you."

"Is this about Alice?" Ceren said.

"Maybe," Jesse said.

"Then I'm coming too," Ceren announced.

"No," Jesse and I said together.

I glared at Jesse, then turned back to Ceren. "This could get ugly. You don't need to see it."

"Alice is like my little sister," Ceren said. "I've protected her for years and I'm not stopping now."

"She's taller than you," Jesse said.

"That's just height," Ceren said. "I've watched out for her. Decked guys for her. I'm going. I can either go with you, or grab another car and follow."

"I've seen you drive. You'd never make it and probably die trying."

"I practiced today."

I gritted my teeth. "You come along, you do as I say."

"Right," Ceren said.

"I mean it," I said. "I'm not having you set yourself on fire. Again."

Ceren's face turned bright red. "That was just one time."

The two boys sitting next to her glanced at each other.

"One time, today. You come along, you follow instructions. Or you might get shot. By me."

"Fine," Ceren said.

"Let's go," Jesse said.

"I'm not watching both of you," I said.

"How many apartments are in the Orchards?" Jesse said sweetly. "And how are you going to find Teresa's without me? I'm coming. She *lied* to me and I need to know why."

My teeth clenched even harder. Reamer might be the liar—he might have offered to help find Alice, but that didn't make him a trustworthy witness. Or Teresa might have left Doug in the night and been unaware of what had happened after. Someone had tried to burn her alive last night. A smart person would hide, and it seemed Teresa was smarter than me.

What I would have given for another couple of officers to sit on Ceren and Jesse. "Fine. But you follow instructions, too. I'd hate for you to get shot. I'd hate it, but I'd do it. Understand?"

Ceren stood. "Later, guys." She shoved her chair under the table. "Let's go."

Damn kid. Almost as much trouble as my own lost Julie.

The good ones are always trouble.

I set out after Ceren, Jesse right behind.

Chapter 43

THE ORCHARDS, Frayville's public housing project, lurked on the far west side of town, far away from the Sand River, downtown, the electrical plant, or anything else the poor people might have infringed on. Five three-story apartment buildings loomed over a circular park. The builders had meant well, putting in the skateboard ramp and the pebbled concrete picnic tables and the maple trees. But an accidentally imported Vietnamese beetle had eaten the trees, graffiti artists had claimed the skate park, and the apple tree planted in front of each building only produced small, sour fruit that went wormy before it even got green. Just like most of the inhabitants.

It's not fair to label everyone in subsidized housing that way. Some of them were perfectly nice folks. But as a police detective, I'd grown jaundiced to public housing years before I even came to Frayville. Really, Frayville's public housing wasn't like Detroit's, where I came up. Down south they had the unemployable, drug pushers, and the batshit, bug-eyed, stand-in-the-mall-and-howl-at-the-moon crazy. Frayville's only had minimum-wage workers, drug addicts, and the mildly mentally ill.

I pulled the cruiser into the sweeping parking lot, Ceren and Jesse stuffed into the seat beside me. The two flamethrowers crammed into the back flooded the interior with the stench of gasoline fumes despite the open windows.

Only a few cars remained—most people on public assistance hadn't been able to afford gasoline for the last few years before Absolute's final victory. The few I saw looked like they hadn't been driven in months, soft tires and dirty windshields mottled with old rain.

"Where to?" I asked Jesse.

"The Pear."

Wedged between us on the front seat, Ceren took turns leaning over my lap and then Jesse's to take in the scene. I doubted she'd ever seen the Orchards before.

I pulled to a stop in the handicapped space right before the blocky Pear Orchard apartment building, about ten feet from the carbonized, shattered shell of a burned-out four-door sedan. "Which apartment?" I said.

"I'll show you," Jesse opened her door.

"Hang on," I said. "I need to talk to her alone."

Jesse glared at me. "She's my friend."

"That's right." I nodded. "And she'll tell me things that she won't tell a friend. If she lied to us, I'll talk it out of her. Then you can yell at her."

"Not a chance." Jesse climbed out and slammed the door behind her.

"Dammit," I said.

Ceren scooted into Jesse's space and rolled her shoulders before grabbing the door handle.

"Ceren," I said. "I want you to stay in the car. Doors locked. Open the windows for air."

"But—"

"No buts. Get behind the steering wheel."

Ceren blinked.

"Pull the car around to point at the exit." I pointed my thumb. "Don't open the door for anyone but me. Keep the windows down, but don't let anyone get close. If we come running out like there's a horrible creature chasing us, start the motor and unlock the doors. Got it?"

Ceren nodded, her gold hoop earrings sparkling in the light. Her face lost a little of its color.

Giving her a job should help her stay, I thought. And who knew? We might come running out of the building with a horrible creature chasing us. What happened to Doug might happen to anyone.

Or maybe it couldn't. Who knew?

I slammed the door behind me and waited for Ceren to lock it. At the click, I patted the roof twice and trotted after Jesse.

Jesse stood just outside the door, shuffling impatiently from foot to foot. "Come on, Detective." I was still ten feet away when she swung the door open and walked into the gloom.

The main lobby was dark. Puzzled, I looked up to the lights and saw only dark fluorescent tubes dangling from a concrete ceiling. It was public housing, and it hadn't been retrofitted with solar shingles, so no power to run the lights. I shook my head and followed ancient muddy footprints across the dusty tile floor. The cinderblock walls were painted a pale puke green obviously meant to evoke pears. The elevator door stood open, but the gap between them showed only black. I couldn't tell if they opened onto an elevator car or an empty shaft.

Someone stood in the dim hallway, facing the door, legs slightly spread, arms behind her back.

Jesse and I both stopped.

"Hi." The woman took a few steps forward, emerging from the shadows into the faint light reflecting through the doorway behind us. Mid-thirties. Carrying a little extra weight, not much, just enough to kick her shirt up one or two sizes. Black hair draped over her shoulders.

I let out a long breath. "Veronica Boxer." Or: Acceptance.

She smiled and gave me a nod of recognition.

"What are *you* doing here?" Jesse said coldly.

"Waiting."

"For who?" I said. "Why?"

"I don't know," Veronica said. "I'm here because this is where I need to wait."

"I don't suppose you've seen Alice Tander?"

"If I had, I couldn't tell you," she said.

I thought back on Rick in the parking lot. "Helping me find missing people isn't creepy," I said.

Veronica laughed, waving a hand. The gaudy gemstone rings on each finger scattered rays of colored light around the dim hallway. "You don't know what creepy is until you're there. And then it's too late. But keep going. I have faith in you, Detective."

"Creepy?" Jesse said. "I'll give you creepy." She started towards the stairwell. "Come on, Kevin."

Chapter 44

A BROKEN brick propped the stairwell door open. An emergency light glowed above the stairs, but the battery had run down enough that the light barely illuminated the yellow reflective tape at the edge of each step. I followed Jesse, both annoyed by her presence and relieved I wouldn't have to check every apartment.

"Up," Jesse said. She muttered "creepy bitch" under her breath as we climbed away from Acceptance.

Three steps into the climb and sweat trickled down the small of my back, in the clammy, closed-in air of the stairwell. My eyes strained in the darkness, but the standpipes, handrails and landings stayed invisible until they loomed out of shadow. I wished I'd brought the shotgun, just in case. Or even the flamethrower. A small trickle of flame would light the stairs far better than the distant light.

"Third floor." Jesse climbed swiftly despite the gloom.

A broken cinderblock propped open the door at the third floor. Jesse's brief silhouette looked small and lonely in the doorway before vanishing into the hall.

The hallway wasn't bright, but at least the large windows at each end admitted some daylight. The floor still had pale puke green paint near the walls, but countless feet had worn the center of the floor down to naked neglected concrete.

Jesse checked the number on each door as she went, stopping at number 38. "This is hers." She stepped to the side.

I don't know if it was the old habit of politeness or the old habit of suspicion that made me rap on the door. "Teresa?"

"Come in," came a muffled voice through the door.

The knob turned easily in my hand. I opened the door.

The room gleamed with harsh white paint, illuminated by the sunlight pouring through the window. A Salvation Army reject couch sprawled beneath the window, opposite the kitchen alcove.

Alice sat up straight on the couch, her hands in her lap.

Teresa sat on a padded bar stool next to the couch. Her hand rested lightly on Alice's head.

"Alice!" I said.

"Kevin, you're okay?" Teresa hopped off the stool. "You had me worried."

"Sorry, Teresa, really." I took a couple steps into the apartment. "I got caught up in a bunch of things and—I'm glad you're all right." To my surprise, seeing her cheered me. I missed being close to someone, even if she might be responsible for Doug's transformation and my change.

Even if Teresa was responsible, she might not know it.

"Alice?" I said.

Alice stared at the plain white wall beside me. Her lips twitched with words too soft to hear.

I walked to the girl. "Alice!"

Jesse closed the door behind us.

Keeping my front to Teresa, I snapped my fingers in front of Alice's emotionless face.

She didn't respond.

Behind me, the deadbolt clicked into place.

I'd focused on Teresa possibly lying to me about Doug. I'd worried about Alice.

I hadn't even considered that Jesse might have lied about her worry for Teresa.

A lot of facts shuffled themselves around in my mental jigsaw puzzle.

One of the reasons police officers have partners is so that someone can always watch their backs. At that moment I desperately missed Kevin's partners, even the bad ones. I turned to split my front between Jesse and Teresa, putting my back to the apartment wall.

"So, ladies," I said. "What's going on? Alice, are you all right?"

Alice said nothing. Her normally pale face looked flushed, as if she'd been running, but her hands rested lightly in her lap. She didn't blink. Drugs?

I glanced back at Alice. "What did you do to her?"

"We've just been talking," Jesse said.

"About right and wrong," Teresa said.

"How the world is—" Jesse said.

"—and how it could be," Teresa said.

My eyes bounced between the two. I'd heard them do the back-and-forth banter that first night we'd met, but here, locked in an apartment with them, it sent a faint chill down my spine. I should have brought the shotgun. Or found another backup piece. Anything but a Springfield XD.

I leaned against the wall, trying to look casual. "How do you think it could be?"

"Safer," Teresa said.

Alice weaved just a little, as if buffeted by a breeze only she felt.

"You're a good guy," Jesse said.

"Thank you." I kept my tone encouraging.

"No, really. There's a lot of bastards out there," Teresa said. "Even now."

"Is that why you changed Doug?" I asked.

"That was an accident," Teresa said. "I just wanted to change his mind."

"About what?" I said.

"Cooling it off," Jesse said, taking half a step closer to me. "I wanted him to stop being such a jerk."

I nodded. "So you made him a full-on dick."

"I didn't understand how things work now," Jesse said.

"I thought we'd figured it out," Teresa said, shuffling a few inches closer. "I was wrong. At the moment, every man wants more. Faster. Deeper. He stops thinking. I pushed it too hard."

I glanced between the two. "And what did you figure out last night? With me?"

"You're stubborn," Teresa said.

The chill on my spine sank into my gut. "You're Acceptance."

"No!" Jesse said, recoiling.

"So tell me what you are," I said.

Silence.

Jesse blinked first. "I told you how we'd run into an…unpleasant man after waking up."

I nodded.

"Al trapped us here," Teresa said.

"Beat us," Jesse said.

"He would have raped us," Teresa said. "Chained us up, and raped us some more."

"I believe you." I could easily see one of Pear Orchard's residents, some thug more muscle than brains, deciding that the end of the world meant he could declare himself a warlord and enslave a harem.

Alice blinked. Her changeless face sparked fresh dread in me.

"He knocked a tooth out." Teresa grinned, exposing a missing incisor.

"What did you do?" I asked.

Jesse licked her lips. "He threw Teresa onto me. We were desperate."

"Alone," Teresa said. "Bloody."

"I grabbed her hand," Jesse said. "And we connected."

Teresa smiled at Jesse. "I got the strength to fight back."

"And I wouldn't let her fight alone," Jesse said.

"We beat him to a pulp." Teresa made a fist. "We stayed out of each other's way, and pounded him."

"He never believed it was happening," Jesse said. "Even when I hit him on the head with a chair, he was screaming that he'd rape us until we loved it."

Connected. Like Acceptance's merging of the suicidally guilty, Jesse and Teresa had merged into…what? Doubly angry women? No, they hadn't been angry yesterday.

"You don't accept anything," I said.

"We're decent," Jesse said. "Hardworking."

"And we wanted you with us," Teresa said.

"You could have asked," I said.

"And you would have run," Teresa and Jesse said simultaneously. "Screaming."

"Connecting with someone, like this," Jesse said, "it's deeper than marriage. Than sex. Than anything."

"To know how they feel. To know what they stand for," Teresa said. "What they'll put up with."

"And what they won't," Jesse said. "I know everything she thinks."

"Everything she feels," Teresa said. "We're closer than sisters."

"I like her more than I like myself," Jesse said.

Teresa gave a little smile, and Jesse followed a heartbeat later. Some communication had happened there, something that completely excluded me.

I made my breath slower and deeper. "So what did you do with the man who attacked you?"

"He never would have stopped," Teresa said.

"We couldn't call the cops," Jesse said.

"We would have tried," Teresa said. "But there's no cops. Not even you. You'd try. But what could you do? Lock Al up and sit in front of his cell with a flamethrower?"

"So what did you do?"

"I tied him up," Teresa said.

"With duck tape."

"Knocked him out."

"I cut his wrists. But they just healed shut."

"So I dragged him out to the parking lot."

"Shoved him in a car."

"Put a burning rag in the gas tank."

I'd seen a burned-out wreck right by the front door. "You burned him. Alive."

"We didn't have a choice," Teresa said. "What could we do?"

"Self-defense," Jesse said.

"It was him or me," Teresa said.

"You could have left," I said. "You could have run."

"They're everywhere," Jesse said. "You aren't a woman, you don't get it."

"I know there are assholes everywhere," I said. "But other people would have helped you."

"We didn't know who else there was," Teresa said.

"And we're sick of running," Jesse said. "Sick of hiding. Sick of putting up with some asshole in the grocery store telling me to suck him just because he can get away with it."

"We're going to make the world better," Teresa said. "Get good people."

"Bring them in."

"To hell with the rest of them. If they screw with us, we'll burn 'em."

I took a deep breath, let it out.

On the couch, Alice's jaw loosened. One of her hands twitched.

"And what did you do to Alice?" I said.

"We're bringing her in," Jesse said.

"She's a sweet girl. Someone needs to watch out for her. Ceren, too." Teresa looked me up and down. "And you."

"She looks like you've drugged her," I said.

"Joining needs intense common feeling," Teresa said. "We'll figure out a way for her. And for you."

"We're fine," I said.

Jesse laughed. "You're anything but fine. You're a wreck. You needed a mystery to worry at just to keep yourself from chewing on your own fingers. We're not Acceptance—"

"—but we have what you need," Teresa said. "We have the purpose you're looking for."

"The old world is gone," Jesse said. "You don't even have your own name. Not really. You've just stolen a dead man's name."

That stung. That was a private sore. Even if everybody knew it existed, even if everybody else had it, nobody else had the right to poke at mine.

"But you can be anything you want." Jesse took another half step towards me.

If I reached, I could touch her shoulder. I shuffled away, pressing my back to the wall.

"Anything at all." Jesse smiled.

I looked between them. "I'm a wreck? Fine. I am a wreck. I *should* be a wreck. Anyone who's sane right now is—is crazy."

Teresa and Jesse nodded in perfect synchronization.

"You're right. Everything you said—you're right. I don't know my name," I said. "I don't know where I belong. I don't have a family, or a home, or anything, really."

My shoulders shook, and I fought down the urge to punch the wall, to punch anything within reach.

"But you're also so *wrong*. Right here, right now, I'm deciding. *His* name was Kevin Holtzmann, but he's gone now. I'm here. I'm alive and— and my name is Kevin fucking Holtzmann, and I—I, am one of the good guys. And that's why I can never be part of what you two are becoming."

Teresa recoiled at my vehemence, letting her hand drop from Alice's head.

Jesse leaned her head back and her eyebrows rose, but her feet didn't move.

"You tried to force me into you," I snarled. "You're trying to drag Alice in. Swallowing someone's mind against their will? That *is* rape. Or worse. What happened to you should never happen to anyone, but it doesn't give you the right to go around and do the same to others. And I'm going to do everything I can to stop you."

They stood in silence for a moment.

Then Jesse said, "It's not like that."

"You just don't get it," Teresa said. "Yet."

"It's for peace," Jesse said.

"And love," Teresa said. "It's about caring for someone, all the way."

The both looked to me.

I balanced my weight onto the balls of my feet. Rolled my hands into fists. When they attacked, I'd be ready.

"You'll like this," Teresa walked towards me.

Jesse took a critical step, putting herself between me and the door. "Whether you like it or not."

My mouth went dry. I had to grab Alice and escape. Fast.

My mental balance shifted. When one person fights two or more, tactics change. Each strike must do as much damage as possible. Don't punch a nose when you can claw out an eye. Don't knee the groin when you can shatter a knee. It needs to be fast. Dirty. And totally without regard for the other person. And don't let them get you in the middle. The only way to survive is to crush each attacker as quickly as possible.

My hands curled into fists.

Jesse and Teresa stood at right angles just out of my reach.

I dashed to the side, one elbow swinging out to knock Teresa aside. I'd grab Alice and the stool she sat on. Anyone who got between me and the door would get a broken skull.

My elbow cracked into Teresa's jaw.

Teresa stumbled, seizing my bare arms as if to keep herself from falling.

At her touch, electricity flashed along my arm and into my spine. I staggered, surprised.

Jesse came up beside me, pushed my shoulder so I faced her, and grabbed my shoulders.

I twisted my head back, preparing to smash her nose with my forehead.

Jesse flung her face into my neck, mouth open—

—and kissed me.

The same burning desire I'd felt the night before scorched into my neck and tingled across my face. Then Teresa's hands tore at my shirt, fingers running over my abdomen.

"Two on one," Teresa whispered.

I grabbed at Jesse, meaning to push her away.

My fingers locked in her hair instead.

Jesse's lips found mine, and passion tingled through my skull.

An endless moment later, Jesse pulled back a fraction of an inch. "You," she breathed into my mouth, "are going to love how we fuck with your mind."

Chapter 45

MY BACK slammed against the apartment wall. Plaster crumbled against my shoulder blades. Jesse shoved her heated lips onto mine. I tasted mint on her tongue. Her legs squeezed my thigh, promising to squeeze more. I shivered in unwilling delight.

Teresa wedged my arm between her flat stomach and the wall, her hand deftly unbuttoning my shirt. "Intense emotion," she said. "That's the trick for this to work." Her fingers slid into the shirt and brushed my chest. Electricity flashed through my nerves. "And this will be—intense."

My hands shook in Jesse's spiky salt-and-pepper hair. Fresh sweat burst forth from my back. I'd like to say that I fought, but Teresa alone had almost overwhelmed me last night. No, that wasn't true—she *had* overwhelmed me. The only thing that saved me last night was getting set on fire, and that had barely sufficed. I knew I should fight. But at this moment, I needed nothing beyond dragging Teresa and Jesse to the carpet and taking them both. The only question was, which one first? And the answer—whichever one I wound up with.

My pulse thudded in my ears.

Something deep inside me screamed.

I didn't care.

From somewhere at the far end of a long dark tunnel, Alice said "Bitch."

Teresa crashed against me—not seductively, but as if she'd been struck. From behind. Hard.

The passion pouring into me surged with shock and pain. Cut off cold.

Jesse spasmed in my arms.

I stared into her blue-and-green eyes for a beat.

Lust burned my blood. My chin and arms shook with the fight against that desire.

Jesse's lips parted, her tongue lightly brushing her upper lip as she moved closer.

I brought my knee up. Hard.

Getting kicked in the groin isn't the same for men and women. Yes, men have nerves that run from the groin to the diaphragm. A solid knee to the balls can stop a man's breath. But Jesse was smaller than me. And I'd practiced the straight-up knee kick every week for twenty years as part of my training.

Jesse rose a few inches into the air. Her breath rushed out of her in surprise and her eyes bugged. She tumbled backwards and fell to the carpet, head bouncing against the overstuffed couch.

Teresa collapsed to the ground beside me.

Alice stood behind Teresa, holding a table lamp by its top. Teresa's blood stained the lamp's heavy base. Alice's chest heaved in and out with the fury burning on her face.

The imposed desire flared out, leaving me shaking, sweating, and with my heart jackhammering against my ribs.

"Kevin?" Alice said.

On her knees, Jesse scuttled to Teresa and clutched her friend's head. "Teresa!"

Countless lines of electricity ran through my body, sparks radiating down my spine and through my limbs into the tips of my fingers and toes. I jerked my head at Alice and stumbled to the door. Wrenched at the handle. Grabbed the deadbolt with slippery sweaty fingers. Lined up the fingers to exert pressure on the latch. Painstakingly turned it. Grabbed the handle again. Staggered into the hall.

Alice stumbled.

Instinctively, I grabbed her bare arm to hold her upright.

My forcibly exposed nerves annealed to hers. Suddenly, I felt Alice like I felt myself.

Alice squeezed her eyes tight, but her vision still jumped and quivered uncontrollably as her heart beat hummingbird-fast. Acid churned her stomach and bile burned her throat. Most of all I felt a fresh, deep anger welling up from some place she'd never known inside her. She'd trusted Teresa, and been violated in a way she'd never expected.

I *knew* that Alice had been hurt before. Her mother had died right when she'd teetered on the edge of puberty. Doug hadn't given her the support she needed—he'd barely been able to hold himself together. A million tiny cruelties from other children echoed in the back of her head.

But Teresa's treachery had sparked something inside her. Alice's anger billowed and blossomed like she'd pierced an unexpected well of passion.

I jerked my hand away from her.

Alice grabbed at the wall, but held herself upright. Her mouth fell open as she stared at me.

I wondered what she'd felt in me.

"No time," I said.

We tottered down the gloomy hall. My legs felt unscrewed at the knees. Bowling balls rolled loose inside my skull. After two steps, I grabbed the sticky concrete wall for balance. I used my other hand to steer Alice in front of me. "Go," I said. "Move."

"You—too."

"Coming."

Alice didn't walk much better. She wobbled. She weaved. Her head rolled on her neck like she'd blown the spring that attached her skull to her shoulders. But she moved.

I'd just touched the stairwell when someone behind us shrieked.

I couldn't spare the energy to figure out if it was Jesse or Teresa. They were pissed. That's all I needed to know.

Alice didn't need urging to plunge into the midnight stairwell.

My nerves began to recover in the dark as my body remembered who owned it. Muscles began to respond. We lurched down the stairs, clenching the filthy cold metal hand rail for balance, scuffing our feet on worn-out non-slip treads and the remnants of reflective tape.

"Almost," panted Alice. "There."

We exploded into the lobby, just inside the main door.

Veronica Boxer stood on the far side of the hall, hands at her side, eyes wide behind broad-lensed glasses. "Go," she said, more fire in her voice than I'd ever heard from anyone who'd bonded with Acceptance. "You can't take another hit like that."

I blinked.

Veronica snarled "*Run*, you idiot!"

I put a tingling, half-numb hand on Alice's shoulder and pointed the other at the front door. "Outside."

The evening June sunshine felt like a blast of tropical summer. The warmth soaked into my muscles, and suddenly my legs felt more responsive.

I pointed Alice at the police cruiser across the cracked parking lot. "Ceren!" I shouted. My tongue felt thick and heavy, my words weak and small. "Get the flamethrower!"

The taillights turned on. The starter ground, the engine roared.

She'd listened to me, dammit.

I'd just put my hand on the trunk when Jesse shouted from behind me. "Kevin!"

Ceren popped the driver's door open. "Jesse!" she shouted, voice warbling in terror. "Come on! You can make it!"

Alice pulled the passenger door open. I shoved her in, then fumbled with half-numb fingers for the shotgun racked in the floor.

Ceren shouted my name.

I turned back to the apartment building.

Jesse was halfway to me, tears running down her face. Teresa stumbled out of the apartment door, one hand pressed to her bloody hair.

I pumped the shotgun.

Ceren said, "The shotgun won't work on a monster!"

"Drive," I snarled. "Ceren, drive! You two get away!"

Jesse was only yards away, running full-out, arms outstretched.

"Drive!" I screamed.

The car lurched.

Alice shouted.

The police cruiser jolted towards the road.

Jesse was only a few feet away.

I couldn't let her touch me again.

Shotgun held stiffly at my waist, I pulled the trigger.

The report echoed across the empty parking lot. Recoil yanked my arms back for the second time today. My strained shoulder screamed obscenities at the further abuse.

Jesse stepped closer. Hesitated. Stopped. She looked puzzled. Her hands fumbled at the sudden mass of blood over her stomach.

Immortal Clay

I didn't want to hurt Jesse. The kindness she and Teresa had shown yesterday still felt real.

But if she touched me, she'd swallow my mind.

I raised the shotgun. Braced it against my shoulder. And fired. Straight at her heart.

Shot ate into Jesse's chest.

Yards back, Teresa screamed.

Jesse's rich brown eyes stared into mine.

I tried not to stare back.

She stumbled forward.

I worked the pump. Aimed the shotgun into her midsection. And fired again.

The stink of blood and bowels filled my nose.

Jesse folded in half at the waist. Twitched.

Fell.

Her face relaxed. A last breath sagged out of her lungs, and the lines of tension in her limbs dissolved. Her eyes stayed open, but the pupils lost focus and swelled until they swallowed the brown irises.

I stepped back. Nausea blossomed in my gut.

Teresa ran up, tears covering her face. She ignored me, sinking to her knees by the body. "How?" Teresa took one of Jesse's hands in hers, and pressed the other hand to the side of Jesse's face. "How?" She glared up at me. "How could you?"

I wanted to vomit everything I'd eaten since falling face-first on the carpet all those days ago. "It was you or me."

"But how?" Teresa bared her teeth. "We can't die. And you killed her. With a stupid shotgun."

I hadn't expected it to kill Jesse. Doug had taken more without stopping, I'd seen a chicken survive beheading, and Rick had filled a deer with shotgun rounds without slowing it. I'd hoped a few rounds would slow her down, make her back off, give me time to think. The sight of Jesse's unmoving, broken body left me stunned.

Veronica Boxer's friend had put a gun in his own mouth and blown off the back of his head—and recovered to become Acceptance.

Jesse should have lived.

Had Acceptance lied? Or did I just not understand something?

Teresa shook her head. "But she's… she's…"

I hated the shotgun in my hands. I hated standing here, watching one person cry over the body of another. I hated myself for causing it, even as I knew I'd lacked another choice. Either I let Jesse and Teresa swallow me, or I fought back.

I couldn't report myself for an officer-involved shooting. I couldn't go to my captain and tell him the story. All I could do was make myself stand, shotgun cradled in my limp arms, and watch.

Teresa held her friend's hand in hers, and cupped Jesse's chin with the other. "No," she whispered. "No…"

I knew what she felt: loss, and grief, and rage. But I couldn't imagine what it felt like to lose someone you'd had that kind of connection with. Losing Sheila had almost destroyed me, and I hadn't lived inside her head.

Jesse's eyes convulsed in their sockets.

Teresa laughed hoarsely, and choked.

Jesse's head rose. She blinked.

I swallowed. *We're like the deer. We're not dead until we think we're dead.*

Chapter 46

THE JUNE evening sunlight burned into my back and the freshly-fired shotgun steamed in my hands. My nervous system still twitched and spasmed with the lingering effects of Jesse and Teresa's assault. Every muscle screamed for a big dinner and a very long nap. The decrepit apartment buildings of the Orchards loomed over us, their lengthening shadows promising a black night.

Teresa crouched over Jesse's body. I'd put four shells of shot into Jesse's gut. Her blood pooled around her, flowing into the cracks in the asphalt and away from what should have been her body. She'd fallen dead, but now raised her head and looked in my direction, a bloody Lazarus angry at the world and furious with me.

"Come on, girl," Teresa said, squeezing Jesse's hand. "You can do it."

Gaping shotgun wounds revealed white ribs and a loop of torn bowel through a sheen of blood. Tissue crawled over the bones one filament at a time, weaving itself together.

"Come on!" Teresa shouted.

Jesse's skin rippled and shuddered beneath her blood-soaked blouse. The wet fecal smell from her horribly exposed bowels grew stronger. Jesse's back arched, then her head tipped back as she sucked air in through her gaping mouth.

I found the stretching skin and twining muscles both fascinating and horrifying. I didn't know if this would work, if Jesse could will herself back from the dead, but I desperately hoped that I hadn't killed her.

Jesse sagged.

Her chest sank as the spasm of breath left. Then she inhaled.

But her eyes still looked in different directions.

"No," Teresa said. "No, no, no."

Teresa glared up at me. "You bastard. All she wanted to do was love you and you shot her." She pulled Jesse's slack body against her own. "Her body's alive, but... she's gone."

Jesse's heart might have been beating. The skin might have closed over the sunken abdomen. But her slack face had nothing behind it.

I let my breath out. I'd hoped she would sit up and swear at me. Or tell me they'd decided to stop dragging people into their group. Or anything, really. Jesse's blank eyes sickened me just as much as watching her die. Teresa's mind must have pulled Jesse's body back, but Jesse's mind had already dissolved.

Teresa grabbed Jesse's other hand. "You're going to shoot people, are you?" she shouted. "You cut her in fucking *half*!"

Jesse ratcheted upright. Her shoulders hung askew, but her head sat straight on her neck.

Teresa climbed to her feet, still clutching Jesse's hand. "You don't want to join us? Fine!" Grief reddened her eyes.

I raised the shotgun crosswise before me, like a shield.

She spat the word like a bullet:

"Run."

Teresa and Jesse, hand in hand, charged me.

The shotgun still held four shells. I couldn't bring myself to shoot again. Instead, I bolted towards the complex's central park, one arm pumping, the other gripping the shotgun by the narrow part of the stock.

Jesse shouted, "We'll kill you, Holtzmann!"

The words chilled me. I knew how Jessie spoke, how she put words together, the lilt and fall of her voice. Those words came out wrong.

Whatever had spoken through Jesse's mouth wasn't Jesse. Teresa? Or something worse?

I hopped over the curb and the sidewalk. As my feet hit the grass, I glanced over my shoulder.

Jesse and Teresa trailed far behind me in a grotesque parody of a march, feet lurching in synchronization, barely maintaining a slow walk. Jesse's head, neck still straight, shifted from side to side with each step as if rolling on its axis. Teresa tugged on Jesse's limp hand and gritted her teeth, her eyes never leaving me.

I slowed to a stop and waited.

Teresa stopped a few feet from the sidewalk. Jesse stopped precisely with her.

"We don't have to do this," I said.

"You've already done it." Teresa's eyes seemed distant, as if she was concentrating hard on something apart from talking to me.

I made myself breathe deeply and let it out all the way. As a rookie cop, I'd lost more than one fight because I'd forgotten to breathe. I didn't have a partner here. I didn't hear the cruiser—had Ceren and Alice fled, or had Ceren stopped short? I didn't dare flick my eyes off of Teresa.

Teresa bared her teeth. She raised Jesse's hand, and released it.

Jesse's empty body took a slow step towards me, unassisted.

Then another.

Teresa snorted with bitter laughter. "Let's see you stop this, *detective*."

Jesse's foot caught on a crack in the pavement. Her weight shifted, and she fell. She dropped straight forward, not even trying to catch herself. Jesse smacked the pavement face-first and lay still. Fresh red blood trickled out from under her face.

Teresa shrieked and leaped at me, arms outstretched.

For a frozen second, I thought her fingernails were growing.

I barely raised the shotgun in time. Rather than pulling it into firing position, I leveled the black plastic butt of the stock at her face and thrust as she charged in.

The Mossberg's stock met Teresa's jaw with our combined momentum. Her teeth clanged together, drowning her scream in blood from where she'd chomped her tongue. The impact knocked me back a step.

Teresa stumbled backwards, clutching her face.

"Enough!" I couldn't bear hitting her again. "You asked what I'd do if I figured out what happened to Doug? Let's find a judge."

Teresa lowered her hands. Blood poured from her nose, covering her lips and chin.

"I didn't want to kill her," I said.

She grabbed her nose, flinched, and jerked her hand away, taking a couple lurching steps forward as pain overwhelmed her balance. "You shot her." Her breath heaved in and out.

"I know."

"How many people have you killed? Really?"

"Just her," I said quietly. Doug didn't exactly count.

Teresa wiped her mouth and stared at the blood on her hand. "And you just killed her in cold blood."

I readied the shotgun for another swing. "You were trying to—to eat my soul." It sounded melodramatic, but even as I said it I realized that Teresa and Jesse had tried exactly that.

"How'm I supposed to let you live?"

"That's why we find a judge," I said. "Let him get a jury."

"Say I agree."

She sounded too reasonable. I kept my attention on her. If I shifted my weight forward, I could plant the shotgun butt between her eyes. She was close enough for me to touch, but not close enough to strike me.

Teresa started forward.

I raised the Mossberg's stock.

She stopped, maybe an inch closer, and raised her hands. "Okay."

I nodded. "Okay." I don't know what was okay, except we weren't killing each other.

She lowered her hands.

I was alert for her to punch. Or kick. Or something. But I didn't realize she was too close until she touched my hand.

My nervous system exploded in icy fire.

Chapter 47

TERESA'S RAGE scorched into me.

I thought I'd known pain when I shot Sheila and then Julie. Teresa's pain etched me even sharper and stronger, a thousand million binding threads that I'd severed, each stump flaring magnesium bright. My skin felt abraded, the tissue beneath soaked in salt. I wanted to scream, but it happened too fast.

And through Teresa's touch, her voice. *That's what loss feels like.*

I did the only thing that came to mind. I bundled up my own loss and shoved it back. *I stood in the shower, hot water leaving tracks in the dirt covering me, sobbing over the wedding ring I'd just discovered on my finger.* The memory filled my eyes with tears.

Teresa recoiled, but her hand squeezed mine more tightly. *She sat on a cold tile floor, hands upraised, gut burning from a vicious punch, a blocky-faced man looming over her with a snarl and scarred fists. Sick terror at her own helplessness. Jesse tumbling into her, knocking Teresa to a full sprawl and pinning Teresa's hand beneath her. Skin touched skin, and their anguished terror flooded into one another.*

Bile filled my throat. I choked and coughed. Teresa's terror felt as vivid and real as if I'd been there, as if I'd been the one sprawled hopeless on the floor, determined to fight but knowing nothing would stop the thug from beating and raping me. I wanted to pull away, but her hand gripped mine so tightly that her fingernails gouged my wrist.

I dug into my few days of life: the pain and fury of Alice standing at my front door, when Julie was gone. Acceptance, and her horrific offer to take away what little was truly mine. Embarrassment at chasing Reamer only to learn I'd renewed his enmity and learned nothing. The horror of burning Doug to tar, making the hard choice to surrender all hope that he might recover, appalled that I'd had to do it.

Teresa hissed, "You don't know hard." *Teresa and Jesse dragging the thug's breathing body to the parking lot, pouring gasoline over him, knowing they didn't have much choice. Realizing that Doug wouldn't be anyone but Doug, their hope to alter his attitudes dissolving into a night of abandon, their horror at seeing how badly they'd screwed up. She'd tried to alter Doug's psyche for Jesse, it had gone wrong, and now Jesse was gone. Every thought, every emotion they'd shared, shriveled, burned and fell away. Their loss flamed across Teresa's mind, maiming the last few weeks of her life. All the weeks of her life.*

My knees buckled, my weight pulling Teresa down with me. Nothing I'd done equaled the horror and shame Teresa felt, what she'd done for what she'd lost.

My head hit the grass. The shotgun slipped out of my grasp.

Teresa knelt beside me, the bottomless chasm of her grief opening wide inside my mind. I felt small compared to her loss.

Even that loss couldn't compare to the staggering emptiness at the heart of the life I remembered.

Meeting Sheila after a call to the Renaissance Center, her chocolate hair catching the gallery lights, walking away and running back to ask her to coffee. Casual meetings on weekends, and then on the odd weeknights, then on more nights than not. Her persuading me to drop Detroit and move to Frayville to raise our family.

Teresa jumped. Her eyes grew bigger.

A wedding on an antique lightship tied up at dock in Port Huron, her parents and my mother the only witnesses. Painting a new home. Swearing when I smashed a finger putting the new bed together. Dinners burned. And Julie. My constantly changing daughter grew, and changed, and unfolded and blossomed, every day a new discovery, learning to see, to laugh, to walk, to giggle and run and read and climb and cry and hope. Stolen, by Collins and Absolute.

Maybe all this had originally belonged to Kevin. Didn't matter. He couldn't complain, and Kevin's family deserved to have someone remember them. Sheila. Julie. And even Kevin. That stiff-necked, stubborn bastard who had driven almost four straight days only for the illusion of safety to burn down with them inside.

Maybe I couldn't forgive the poor bastard for leaving me alone in this impossible world.

But he'd had good points too. He'd been loyal. He'd made Sheila laugh, and cry, and challenged her ideas and goals even as he supported them, even as she challenged and supported his. The complex stew of a marriage simmered down for decades until nothing remained but impossibly healthy flavor.

Tears and laughter and fear and joy and always the bright thread of hope.

I missed hope.

I missed being able to think that tomorrow could be better than today.

Everything—the entire burning freezing weeping tangle of Kevin's life and loss—spewed into Teresa.

Our touch burned.

It felt like eternity. But I hadn't had time to take a breath.

Teresa jerked, quivered, her gaze locked in mine.

Grass tickled my nose, my entire body shaking to the rhythms of my spasming legs. The emotional dead of Kevin's life marched through me.

Teresa's hand went limp. She tried to fall back, but as her fingers started to slip from mine I clamped onto her wrist.

Loss? You don't know true *loss.* A retirement fund and a pension, set aside for the day when Kevin and Sheila could spend every day together. A mortgage that they'd slaved to pay off in only twelve years, so they could enjoy time later. Vacations canceled for work. All the times Kevin had gotten called into the station to help with some emergency, or when Sheila had worked late balancing a customer's misbegotten ledgers. A million pleasures deferred for a better tomorrow that would never come.

That better tomorrow.

Growing old.

Helping Julie grow. Watching her have children of her own.

Laughter at twilight.

Dark. Dead. Cold. Gone.

Teresa's eyes reddened, broken capillaries spreading. Her hand struggled in my grip.

Teresa's pain floundered under the immense weight of my own howling loss. My loss, truly mine, not Kevin's. I'd claimed it. I owned it. Or it owned me.

My grip weakened.

Teresa's hand slipped away.

"Don't you dare talk to me about loss," I gasped through clenched teeth, grass cooling my cheek as I struggled to catch my breath. "My family…my world…my life is gone."

My vision had held only Teresa, but the outside leaked back. The courtyard reappeared. The buildings still loomed around us, the expanse of littered parking lot ringing everything, the sun just starting to touch the pine trees. Nothing had changed. Everything looked different.

Teresa's hands shuddered, the motion traveling up her arms and into her chin, her face. She bent at the waist, hands pressed into the grass.

"We can find a judge," I said. My gut complained as I sat up. My hand fumbled in the cool grass, then closed on the shotgun stock. "Or we finish this ourselves." I pulled the weapon closer with a palsied grip.

"Your choice."

Teresa raised her head to stare at me. Her face shook. One leg jerked backwards, then the other.

I rolled to my knees, ignoring the wailing of strained muscles. We might have fought in our minds, but the tension and struggle had leaked into our bodies. Watching Teresa, I used the shotgun to lever myself to my feet.

Teresa grabbed a poured concrete bench and pulled herself up.

We stared at each other.

She stepped back, paused, stepped back again. Then she whirled around and bolted away.

The Mossberg rose to my shoulder, seemingly on its own. I glared at Teresa through the weapon's sights. Shooting her in the back might have been the smart thing to do. The kind thing. Instead, I watched her run, her legs moving disjointedly but constantly. In moments, she turned the outside corner of the Pear building and disappeared.

I sagged against the back of the pebbled concrete bench, feeling exhausted and filthy, both physically and spiritually. Every joint ached. Jesse's empty shell lay on her face, only a few yards away. The evening sun felt like a lie. I knew now what had happened to Doug, but the knowledge didn't make me any happier, wouldn't do any good for anyone.

"Kevin?" said Alice.

I lurched in a circle, my legs almost giving out as I staggered around.

Ceren and Alice stood a few feet behind me. Doors open on both sides, the police cruiser sat maybe a hundred feet back, near the parking lot entrance. Dried tears streaked through the dirt smeared on Alice's face.

"Are you… are you all right?" Ceren asked, her chin raised and eyes clear. Earlier, in fear for her life, she'd fumbled with the flamethrower. I saw no trace of that confused, dismayed girl. Alice needed strength, and Ceren stood straight for her friend.

Nothing makes us strong like someone needing us to be strong.

Shame flushed hot and red through my face when I looked at Ceren. I had to get myself together.

"Yeah." I fumbled the shotgun's safety on. "I think we've seen the last of her." I lowered the butt to the ground, keeping one hand loosely around the barrel's heat guard. "I thought I told you two to run."

"We did run," Ceren said. "You didn't say how far."

"Huh." I fought back the smile that threatened to escape. "Since you're here, you want to give me a lift?"

Ceren eyed me up and down, then shook her head. "You're fine. You can drive."

"I gotta teach you two how to drive." I made myself take a step towards them. To my surprise, my leg didn't fall off. I shouldn't feel this sore, but battered muscles insisted I did.

Alice and Ceren fell in on either side of me. Not like they would catch me if I fell, or anything, but I appreciated the thought.

"So," I said a few steps later, "Alice. I leave you alone, and you get kidnapped."

"Teresa said we were going clothes shopping," Alice said. For the first time since I'd known her, she didn't sound even vaguely like she was asking a question.

I nodded. "You showed a good swing with that lamp. And Ceren, here, throws a mean melon. Maybe we need to invent a sport."

"I don't think you get rich off of sports anymore," Ceren said.

"Fine." I waved my free hand. "We'll come up with something. Point is, I leave you alone and you get in trouble. I think you'd both be safer living with me."

Ceren stopped. Alice glanced between us.

I stopped as well. "That is, if you want to. Three houses seems like a lot of upkeep. If it doesn't work, you can always vote me out."

Ceren looked around the parking lot. "Seems to me like you're the one who's gimping around."

"Fair enough. You got me." I raised a hand in surrender. "The old man needs someone to make sure he doesn't wake up dead. Think about it. I'm not gonna bug you, but the offer's there."

Ceren could be strong for Alice. Alice was being strong for me. Maybe I could be strong for them. Something stirred in me—not hope, but something like it.

That's when something huge and unbelievably fast punched into my chest, blowing me backwards and off my feet.

Everything flew very far away.

Cold heat shattered my sternum, burned through my flesh, and ripped out my back.

Air gushed into the hole in my chest.

The sound of the shot arrived before I hit the ground.

Chapter 48

BLUE SKY filled my vision. The sun stabbed the corner of one eye. Blood coated my mouth and the inside of my nose. The asphalt radiated end-of-day warmth against my arms, through my clothes, and against the back of my head. And a silence I'd never heard before.

A silence so total it didn't include my own heartbeat.

My chest burned. A hot wire ran from my breastbone, through my heart, between the ribs of my back. I tried to inspect my breastbone, but my hands only fluttered at the ends of my wrists.

"Kevin?" Alice shouted. Her voice echoed inside my skull.

I heard the shotgun pump. *Ceren*. I wanted to tell her that the safety was on, but my mouth barely stirred.

I'd been shot.

Teresa. Where had she hidden a gun? No, that wasn't important. The important thing was, she'd shot me through the chest. Probably through the heart. Right through the chest and out the back.

Billowing gray haze ringed my vision.

I hadn't been able to bring myself to kill her. Now she'd killed me.

Hope? Hope died and I got to go with it. I didn't feel much of anything, beyond lassitude and a gently surprising peace.

I'd lost. Too bad.

But I was done.

No longer my problem.

Another rifle crack. Ceren shouted, pain making her voice wobble.

Outrage ate into the back of my brain.

Shoot me? Kill *me*?

Fine.

But Ceren and Alice were just kids. They had nothing to do with any of this.

Alice shrieked.

The edges of my vision crept inward. I saw only a narrow ring of sky, the edge of a cloud.

My feet were gone. So were my hands.

Not fair. Not fair. This was *my* fight, not theirs. And I was just shuffling off the stage? Leaving them to fight for their lives?

No.

Anger. Useless anger roiled quietly in the darkness.

Voices grew more distorted. Unrecognizable. The blue sky edged towards black.

The deer.

Deckard, in the bar. After shooting the deer. *It knows you've killed it.*

The deer was an animal. It couldn't reason. It died.

But Jesse wasn't an animal. She died, too.

Jesse.

Maybe Jesse hadn't died because I shot her.

She'd seen her vision go. Felt her thoughts fading as her blood drained out.

She died because she thought that's what she was supposed to do when shot three times at point-blank range. Her mind told her she was dead.

Maybe you don't have to.

That's it.

I am *not* dead. Not yet. Maybe not ever. I've been shot. Fine. That's real. But that gaping hole through my chest had to be closing up. The tissue is knotting together. I'd seen it on Jesse. It happens. That's how it works for us now.

My chest felt cold.

No! I was healing. Cold, yes, there's blood loss, but your body can make blood. Have zero doubt.

Jesse died from a failure of imagination. She didn't realize she didn't have to die. Teresa had healed Jesse's wounds, but too late.

I'd been living in a past I created for myself, from another man's memories. I had imagination.

You're a kid, playing make-believe.

Maybe. But make-believing was the key.

You're dead if you know you're dead.

I don't know that I'm dead.

I'd burned. And healed. Without trying. Without thinking.

I couldn't feel my legs. My arms. I hadn't taken a breath in what felt like hours.

Doesn't matter. You're still here. You're on the right track.

My chest shivered weakly.

Close up the heart, I thought. Pull damaged tissue together, and *beat*.

My vision faded to sparkling gray, like the static on a dead video channel.

Silence.

Darkness.

Then, faintly: *lub-dub*.

Beat, damn you! Seal up. Pull the holes shut, stop the bleeding, and *beat*.

My chest heaved as I gasped for a breath, and then another, my body demanding oxygen so intensely that it wouldn't give me a chance to push out the old air, and behind it all a regular, glorious double thump swelling in my ears, pushing warmth back into my thrashing limbs, the gray clouded vision dissipating and the outside world, the beautiful outside world leaking in through my ears, hot asphalt and whispering wind and someone crying and someone else shouting and the stink of greasy hot metal smearing itself all over everything.

My teeth clanked against something hard in my mouth.

"You can't quit poking," the vague shape above me said.

My lungs relented, pushing out a breath and sucking in more around whatever was stuffed into my mouth.

"You've got this *need*," the voice said. Maybe a man. "To hold folks accountable. To be the law. It's sick. *Sick*."

My arms and legs thrummed against the ground in involuntary seizures as fresh, rich blood hit my extremities. Hot oxygen burned in my fingertips and toes.

"I asked you to stop. I *begged* you."

Something stabbed the roof of my mouth.

The taste of metal. Blood?

No. Not blood.

Steel. Smooth, scalding steel.

My heartbeat steadied. Cooling blood stuck my shirt to my chest and congealed under my back.

"You can't leave bad enough alone because you *need* to do something. You have needs, Mister Holtzmann?" the voice said. "A gun in your mouth. That's what you need."

Chapter 49

"STAY *BACK*, you two!"

Hunger howled in my gut. I still couldn't feel my legs or my arms. But the black halo around my vision receded and color started leaking into view.

I could make out some details through the hazy vision of resurrection. All black clothing stood out like a silhouette. A black shirt. Black pants. A hood—no, a... a veil?

Rose Friedman. Julie's retired kindergarten teacher. Still dressed for a funeral and veiling her face. Holding a deer rifle, the barrel jammed deep inside my mouth.

I'd been shot by my daughter's kindergarten teacher.

The rifle barrel jerked in my mouth.

I instinctively clamped down, jamming my teeth into the barrel. Not my best idea.

Rose jerked in surprise.

I hadn't been alive again for a minute, and already I had to move quickly to buy a second minute.

Hot metal scalded my palate and scorched my tongue. I swung my arms up while turning my head to the side and trying to pull away from the barrel. My hands slammed into the muzzle, pressing it into the side of my cheek.

She pulled back.

Metal clanged against my back teeth. The impact shocked my jaw, stinging the teeth at their roots. My mouth lurched open.

Rose tried to stagger back, but I had a hand on the rifle barrel. My fingers felt cold and clumsy, but I clamped them around the hot barrel and jerked it to the side, away from my gaping mouth.

Rose yanked on the rifle, pulling it back into line for a shot at my skull.

Pain ripped through the freshly torn muscles crossing my chest.

The barrel jumped an inch in my clenched hand, but I kept the grip.

I rolled towards her, pushing the rifle ahead of me so it pointed at the asphalt inches from my eyes. Normally I could have slapped Rose across the street, but exhaustion burned in every muscle. I felt like I'd just swum a mile, fully dressed, in a cold lake. With weights around my wrists and ankles.

Considering I'd had a massive hole through my chest a moment before, I was doing great.

I needed to get on my feet, no matter how many tons I weighed.

I needed to get the rifle away from Rose, no matter how clumsy I was and how much strength Rose's passion gave her.

Rose thrashed the rifle from side to side.

The rifle slipped in my grip, my hands sliding down the barrel and within an inch of the muzzle.

If I didn't end this, Rose would have the rifle, the space to aim, and the time to pull the trigger again and again.

No way could I will myself back from the dead a second time in two minutes. Especially if the next bullet went through my head. Could I think my way back from that? My corpse might make like the beheaded chicken or Doug's husk and kill her in a haze of barbed tentacles—but it wouldn't be *me*.

I grabbed the rifle barrel with both hands, twisting my body over and around the rifle. I didn't jerk. I didn't yank. I rolled, pulling the weapon smoothly after me.

Rose tottered with it, two, three quick steps.

One of my hands slipped free, slapping the asphalt beneath me.

Rose huffed in anticipation.

I grabbed her ankle with my free hand.

She ignored that weak grip and yanked on the rifle, expecting me to fight her.

I went with her motion, sliding my hand down the barrel and onto the opening, shoving the rifle straight into her arms, pushing her backwards.

She stumbled back to get her balance.

Her ankle jerked in my hand. I tensed that weak grip. Fortunately, a bony ankle is much easier to hold than a slick rifle barrel.

Rose's hands let go of the rifle and waved in the air. Through the veil I saw her mouth widen. She croaked something unintelligible, then she toppled backwards.

I rolled over on the rifle. The hard metal jabbed into the raw wound of my chest. Had my chest closed? Was I twaddling my exposed heart with hot metal?

That didn't matter. Up. I had to get up. I had to end—

Ceren and Alice slammed into my field of vision in a hurricane of motion and color. Alice, her feet losing traction, jumped over Rose's prone form, bleeding off enough momentum to stop only after she landed. Ceren threw herself crosswise over Rose's gut, the younger girl's knees slamming into Rose's ribs. Air gushed from the old lady.

I tugged the rifle, leaning to my side to free the horrible thing. It slid freely into my hands.

"Don't move!" Ceren shouted. "Do *not* move! I never liked you! Making us take fucking *naps*! Don't move, you hear me?"

Alice stumbled in a circle and came back to me. She never looked away from my exhausted body, but spoke to Ceren. "You got her?"

"Oh, yeah," Ceren said. "This bitch won't be taking anybody's graham crackers for a long time."

Alice knelt beside me. "Are you—" Her eyes traveled over the gore-covered ruin of my shirt. "I don't know what we can do. This isn't first aid?"

"I'm okay," I wheezed. Hot hunger screamed in me. I wanted a hamburger. Or a cow. I'd settle for Paul's last bag of spice drops.

Alice shook her head, stopped, and nodded. Her eyebrows lifted over widening eyes. "Sure. Sure you are But—I mean—no." Her face grew hard. "I gotta say it. You've been shot in the chest, Kevin. There's no hospital. Can I get you anything before—before you go?"

"Get the rifle," Ceren said. "Alice, get that fucking rifle over here."

"Later," I said. "I'm gonna die. But not today." I smiled at the look on her face.

I pulled deep breaths of fresh air into my lungs. The fatigue didn't fade, but air cleared my head. I heard my heartbeat loud and clear, a bass drum in both my temples. And I was ravenous, again. I'd filled the hole in my chest by opening a pit in my stomach.

I patted my chest, grimacing at the sticky blood soaking my shirt and the tender flesh beneath. My ribs burned at the touch—bruises? A spot in my breastbone felt like a white-hot nail driven into the sternum.

But I was alive. "Watch this," I said, because any day you drag yourself back from the dead entitles you to show off a little. I nodded at Alice, took one more deep breath, and tried to roll to my knees. It took two tries, and left my brain swimming freely around the inside of my skull, but I managed it.

Ceren looked up from her position squishing Rose.

"It's okay, Ceren," I said. "*I'm* okay."

Ceren glared at me. "She shot you through the heart! How the fuck are you still alive?"

"You're too young for that kind of language," I said.

Ceren stared at me, astonished into silence. It didn't last long.

Just long enough to hear Rose crying.

"Let her breathe," I said.

Ceren suddenly looked unsure of herself, but eased her weight onto her hands and knees.

Rose sobbed louder. After a moment, she choked out, "You think you have it bad?"

"Help her sit up," I said.

Rose sagged back like a bean bag doll, but Ceren and Alice each took an arm and coaxed her to a sitting position. She breathed deeply and shrugged out of their hands, putting one hand on the asphalt for support. Her veil drifted away from her face with the force of her sobs.

I licked my lips, uncertain. "Talk to me, Rose. It's okay."

"I can't," she said.

"You can, Rose. Talk to us. Help us understand."

Rose pulled off the veil to rub her eyes.

I blinked in surprise.

When I'd seen Rose at last year's block party, she'd had not just crow's feet but the loose skin of a seventy-year-old woman. Her eyes had been sharp but rheumy, her hair pale gray with streaks of pure white. Today, she looked twenty-five. Brilliant green eyes and short-cropped hair bright red on her shoulders. The stunning combination would have startled me if I'd seen them on anyone, let alone a tired, broken, seventy-year-old woman.

"You—none of you. You don't remember," Rose sobbed. "You can live for a week under Absolute's control, and it won't make you remember. Some do. Some have a bit. A bit. But not me. Not me."

"Absolute made us puppets," I said quietly. "We were just passengers. We didn't have a choice. None of us did."

"You don't understand," she said. "I killed us all. Killed the whole world."

"It's not your…" Ceren said. Her voice trailed off as she looked at us, then back at Rose.

"Absolute took me the day we bombed Brazil," Rose whispered. "And I remember *everything*."

Chapter 50

IN THE last moments, the sun had slipped behind the peaks of the pines, fracturing the light shining through the apartment complex. The asphalt parking lot radiated more heat than the sky.

I felt exhausted and brutalized and terribly, terribly hungry. But Rose's words chilled my blood.

Ceren, shocked, released Rose's shoulder, leaving an ill-looking Alice to quickly stabilize the seventy-year-old retired teacher who looked twenty.

"Was touring Rhode Island," Rose said. Her voice came out softly, the words grinding against each other like the inexorable motion of rocks in a glacier. "Got up early one day. Walked the beach. Nobody around. Didn't know anything about what was going on—we bombed South America that afternoon. The seaweed, seaweed…" She gulped air. "Seaweed on the beach. Attacked me. Took me. He gave me a mission. To spy. To learn. I went everywhere. Watched everything. Absolute learned everything about us from me."

My stomach rumbled, demanding food. I ignored it. I didn't want to eat.

"Absolute wanted hunters. To find people." Rose sobbed again. Now that she'd started talking, she couldn't stop. Words gushed from her broken heart. "That last week. *The* last week. He sent me up to the prison. Marquette. And when he said to—I took them, I took them all. And set them to hunting people."

I almost fell over, my legs barely stiffening in time to stop me from tumbling to the ground.

Marquette. Where Jared Collins had been imprisoned.

Rose Friedman had taken Collins for Absolute.

She'd set that vile copy free to kill my family.

What would we have done if someone else had presented Absolute's offer? What if one of Julie's friends had offered her escape as I slept? Or one of Sheila's assistants? Hell, what about one of Kevin's fellow officers? Or Rose? What if it had been... anyone... anyone other than a psychopathic killer I'd put away? Sheila and Julie, or people very much like them, might be here. Now. With me.

The rampaging hunger swelled into nausea that made my brain weave in my skull.

Ceren looked ill. Alice seemed to have transcended her nausea into something resembling serenity, but wouldn't look at Rose. Her face was pale, and she kept nervously licking her lips.

I studied Rose. Steadied myself.

"You want to know why Frayville is okay?" Rose's voice rose. "It's a present. From Absolute. To me. This city is intact because Absolute tried to take it intact. It's a reward. For my good work." She sat up straight, waving her arms around. "All those cities burned, all those people dead? Not here! Because Absolute wanted to *thank* me. This body? It's a gift! Every time I look in the mirror—it's all on me, every God-damned bit of it! On *me!*"

Rose collapsed in on herself, burying her face in her hands. Quiet sobs escaped around her spread fingers.

I tried to breathe and kept forgetting.

Kindly old schoolteacher Rose. She'd sent Collins after me. After my family.

She'd released a prison full of convicts to hunt stragglers. Like Kevin, and Sheila, and Julie.

I sat for a moment.

Then slowly, painfully, I shuffled forward. I gently nudged Ceren to the left. Knelt beside Rose.

And put my arms around her.

Rose stiffened. Her breathing stopped.

I lowered my head into the cleft of her neck and shoulder and pulled her tighter.

Rose fell against me, her arms desperately hanging on as sobs overwhelmed her.

I tried to stroke her hair. Tell her it was all right. I couldn't speak through the tears, through the pain rising up and out of my own body.

Ceren and Alice murmured together, then put their arms around both of us.

It felt like the most natural thing in an unnatural world

For the first time, I didn't cry for myself. I cried for Rose. For Alice. For Ceren, for Jack, for Teresa and Jesse, for Eric the DPW truck driver and crazy Paul and Deckard the deer hunter, Becky and Mick, for billions of other people, and for the billions more who never made it through. And for Doug, who'd survived but hadn't understood the rules.

I don't know how long we stayed like that, but eventually Rose stilled. She patted my back. I slowly relaxed my arms and leaned back to sit crosslegged. My aching knees, imprinted with the texture of the asphalt and stray fragments of pebbles, added to my blanket of aches.

Rose wouldn't meet my eyes.

"I get it," I said. "I can't imagine living it. But I get it. And I don't hold you responsible. Rose Friedman didn't do those things."

"I am Rose," she said. "And I did them."

I wanted to blame her. No—I wanted to blame *someone*. I wanted to point my finger at someone and say that *they* caused our misery. In the back of my mind, all my buried anger and frustration and hunger and pain coalesced.

"Absolute did them," I said. "And I hold him—*it* responsible. Completely responsible."

She shook her head.

Ceren squeezed her shoulder.

"I don't know what to tell you," I said. "I'd suggest counseling, but I don't know that we have a counselor anymore. Getting drunk doesn't seem to work for you. I don't blame *you*, though."

Rose still wouldn't look at me.

"If you're here, though," I said, "we need you. I don't know why, yet. But Acceptance said that everybody who's still around has a job, something only they can do. Something that we need. From what I've seen, he's—*they're*—right. And we're going to need every advantage if we're going to get through this—this—" I flapped my hand. "This whatever this is."

"I can help you," said a voice from behind me.

Chapter 51

VERONICA OF Acceptance stood several yards away, distant enough to give the illusion of politeness but close enough to have heard everything. Her somber face contrasted with the gems sparkling on her fingers, reflecting the last light of the day.

I didn't say anything. I should have.

"Rose," Veronica said. "I am so, so very sorry. You're in horrible pain. I wouldn't take your pain if I could. You have every right to it. But I can help you cope with the pain. I can give you the balance to bear it."

Rose looked at Veronica, then stared back at the ground, shaking her head.

"It's your choice," Veronica said.

"And she said no," I said. I made my voice firm and clear. I didn't know how anyone couldn't see through the flimsy disguise I'd thrown over my complete exhaustion, but it worked. It had to. I would not show weakness in front of Acceptance.

Ceren glanced at me, then at Rose. Very quietly, she shuffled to the side, out of the direct line between the two women.

"You need redemption," Veronica said. "I can see that. The need burns in you. To find a way. To make up for what you've done."

Rose took a shuddering breath, then jerked her head in a nod.

Veronica said, "I can give you the strength make amends."

Rose sat, shaking her head.

"Thanks," I said, "but no thanks."

Veronica shrugged. "I have to offer. We accept everyone. That's the whole point."

"You've offered," I said. I set one foot flat on the ground, put my hands on that knee, and levered myself upright. I weaved, I wobbled, my head felt weak and fuzzy for lack of breath, but I had two feet beneath me again. I planted myself firmly between Rose and Veronica, bluffing myself upright. "Now leave."

"We have space for you, too," Veronica said.

I shook my head. "It's my pain. I've earned it. And I'm keeping it."

"Your choice," she said. "Ceren? Alice? Interested in smiling again?"

I spoke quickly, before the girls could say anything. "We'll watch out for each other."

"We're fine," Alice said.

"Too fine," Ceren said.

Veronica smiled. "Everybody needs someone to watch them. To care for them."

With my attention on Acceptance, I didn't noticed Rose getting to her feet. She stumbled past me, towards Veronica.

"Rose!" I said. "We can help you."

"No. Nobody can help me," Rose said. "It's worth a try. If I'm really lucky, she's lying and I'll drown in Acceptance and never have to think again."

I tried to lunge for her, but couldn't move any faster than a rusty lurch.

Rose clasped Veronica's outstretched hand.

Veronica twitched. Her free hand flapped twice.

Rose sagged on her feet. Her chin sunk to her chest. She took a shuddering breath. Then a second, easier breath.

"Rose?"

"I'm all right," Rose said. Her voice sounded steadier than I'd heard it in the last couple of days. Her tone wasn't light, but lacked the blanket of despair she'd worn in the bar.

"There was no other choice," Veronica said. "Not for me. Not for Rose. Either then, or now."

"That's how you do it, isn't it?" I said. "You wait till someone is at a low moment. We can't kill ourselves, but instead of the razor or the gun there's you."

"You say that like it's a bad thing," Veronica said. "If you can't live with yourself, you can live with us."

Rose nodded.

"You take away some of what makes us human," I said.

Veronica smiled, the corners of her mouth barely moving up, her eyes filled with sorrow. "Isn't not being human part of the problem?"

"You—Acceptance—were waiting for her, weren't you?" I asked.

"Her?" Veronica shrugged. "No. We saw things coming together, and thought we should have someone here. Just in case. My money was on Teresa. A couple of us thought Jesse would join. But they had their own way."

I felt too tired, too ravenous, to fight. "You're not getting me." I felt Ceren and Alice moving closer. "You're not getting any of us."

"That's fine," Veronica said.

Rose looked at me. "Thank you," she said with a tiny quaver. Tears still streaked her cheeks, but she'd stopped crying. "Thank you for everything. I'm sorry I—this sounds awful, doesn't it? I'm sorry I shot you. Teresa and Jesse would have taken more people, by force. You had to stop them. It's better to think you have a choice. Even when you don't really."

I stared at Rose. Moments before she'd been a mass of grief. Now she seemed almost serene. It felt fake, like an electrode in the brain.

Rose and Veronica studied us for a moment. Finally Veronica said "Have a good night, Detective Holtzmann." Both women turned to walk away.

Veronica had barely turned away before I sagged. My chest hurt. My calves and thighs and feet and arms back and eyes ached. Hunger tore my guts. My head pounded. Alice grabbed my arm, but her eyes still focused on Veronica and Rose. Acceptance. I watched them walk towards one of the blocky apartment buildings and hoped they weren't our future.

Moving in sync, as if one mind controlled both bodies, Veronica and Rose stopped and turned to face us.

"Remember," Veronica called, "we're here if you need us."

"Like hell," I muttered. Alice squeezed my arm.

We stood in silence for a moment.

Ceren said, "I've got one rule."

"Oh?" I said.

"Yeah." Ceren pointed at my gore-streaked jacket and shirt. "I am totally *not* doing your laundry."

I laughed. Right then, anything would have been funny.

"And it's not your house," Alice said. "It's ours. All of us."

"Fine," I said. I'd figure out a way to help them grow up. Help them cope with whatever we were. "So. I'm starving."

"You're bleeding," Ceren said.

"I don't think so," I said. "I mean, it's blood. It's mine. But I'm not leaking anymore."

Alice wrinkled her nose. "Oh, that's just *gross*."

"There's a blanket in the trunk. Put it on the seat, it'll keep the car clean."

Acceptance might offer connections, an artificial bond between strangers. But I'd make mine the hard way. And now I had reasons. Reasons to live. Reasons to fight.

Maybe even reasons to hope.

I'm not Kevin Holtzmann. Maybe I won't ever feel like him. But I had a good idea of what I was.

I'm one of the good guys.

I couldn't be a human being. But I could be a good *person*, the best person I knew how to be.

It's hard to be a cop without law. I'd have to find a way to get some law around here. Maybe a city council or something. We needed a way to deal with anything from Teresa and Jesse to the kid driving the Corvette through the back streets.

But there's one law I don't think I need.

And I *know* who to blame.

There's one crime that doesn't need a law to make it wrong: genocide.

No, beyond genocide. Extinction. Global extinction. Killing every living thing on the Earth, and replacing it with a duplicate.

The action is beyond crime, beyond war. It's a new kind of offense.

It demands a new kind of punishment, and a new kind of enforcer.

We have abilities. Abilities Absolute gave us.

I will learn to use them.

I will help the people I live with build a new civilization. We will figure out how to live together again. How to connect to one another without swallowing each other.

And somehow… somewhere… somewhen… I will make Absolute pay.

Immortal Clay

Maybe just me and a flamethrower. Or a nuclear bomb. Or some specially-brewed chemical that poisons only Absolute's brain.

We will pry Absolute's secrets out of Legacy, and out of our own flesh.

I'm one of the good guys, but I'm not alone.

We will see Absolute burn.

About the Author

Michael Warren Lucas lives in Detroit, Michigan, with his wife and pet rats, practices martial arts, and is busy writing the next Immortal Clay novel.

Never miss his new releases! Join his mailing list at https://www.michaelwarrenlucas.com.

Printed in Poland
by Amazon Fulfillment
Poland Sp. z o.o., Wrocław